Praise for *Trace Elements of Random Tea Parties*

"Lemus is a truly talented storyteller. Highly rec...

—*Library Jou...*

"A spry debut from a writer who's got the skills."

—*Kirkus Reviews*

"An edgy, exuberant debut novel. The sex is fun, rollicking, and a little dangerous; the characters are young and guardedly optimistic . . . this is an intriguing novel sure to attract readers searching for something urban, lively, and a bit different."

—*Publishers Weekly*

"A warm tale of 'princess dyke' life in L.A., *Trace Elements of Random Tea Parties* is a well-crafted and very refreshing debut novel, a welcome contribution to Chicana letters from the new generation."

—Ana Castillo

"Lemus' debut, a gen-X coming-of-age story, has a breezy tone that keeps the pages turning. Engagingly told . . . this tale will charm and earn this first-time author a following."

—*Booklist*

"Lemus' language shifts as fluidly as her heroine's gender. Think Anaïs Nin translated by James Ellroy . . . Her sentences at their best are so condensed, so packed and hot, they're on the verge of exploding . . . Bursting at the seams with pizzazz and invention, Lemus shows enormous promise."

—*San Francisco Chronicle*

"Lemus' dynamic language and pacing . . . offer deep insights into *familia* and *cultura* without an ounce of heavy-handedness."

—*Latina Magazine*

"*Trace Elements of Random Tea Parties* is both outrageous and glorious . . . It's a wild ride that's worth every damn cent you spent for the ticket!"

—Helena Maria Viramontes

LIKE SON

a novel by

Felicia Luna Lemus

AKASHIC BOOKS
NEW YORK

Published by Akashic Books
©2007 Felicia Luna Lemus

ISBN-13: 978-1-933354-21-7
ISBN-10: 1-933354-21-6
Library of Congress Control Number: 2006936533

First printing

Front cover photograph, *Nahui Olin, 1924,* by Edward Weston; Collection Center for Creative Photography ©1981 Arizona Board of Regents.

Akashic Books
PO Box 1456
New York, NY 10009
info@akashicbooks.com
www.akashicbooks.com

For T

PROLOGUE

5 March 2003. Ash Wednesday.
New York City.

All things considered, the flight home was uneventful. I watched a dumb romantic comedy, and I ate soggy broccoli and a dinner roll from the crummy free meal when it came around. After the trays were cleared, I stood in line and brushed my teeth in one of the tiny metal bathrooms. My left arm swollen and throbbing in its plaster cast, I took some aspirin. Eventually, I crashed for a few hours and tried my damnedest to prepare for a time-pressed dash out of the airport.

Finally, three in the morning, careful of my broken arm and the scabbed skin on my chest, I hopped a locked gate and walked across Tompkins Square Park to the Temperance Fountain.

The Temperance Fountain—a Victorian stone structure of humble elegance, distant cousin to the crumbling WPA fountain my father courted my mother at before they totally hated each other. The Temperance Fountain—also not so entirely unlike like the Mexico City fountain where my father's mother sat when she broke Nahui Olin's heart. Family cycle come full circle, there I was, a man of thirty, standing at a fountain, taking my turn.

The wind picked up, and I smelled pine. No forests anywhere nearby, only patches of dead landscaping and dirty ice all around, the woodsy olfactory effect was merely a pleasant by-product of the Christmas trees Municipal Services collected all January and crushed into mulch. I reminded myself that the smell, crisp and refreshing as it may have seemed, was still one of decomposition. A sharp gust of cold air cut through my clothes. Chills shivering up my spine, I breathed into my hands for warmth and continued waiting.

I'd wait all night if that's what it took. Damn, I'd wait for the rest of my life if I had to. And why not? I had only nothing and everything to lose.

My father would have understood.

PART ONE

CHAPTER ONE

1 March 1995. Ash Wednesday.

Los Angeles.

T he doctors tell me I'm dying. Let's go for a nice lunch," he said.

What a fucking crappy way to wake up. Still in bed, I pressed the phone closer against my ear. "Dad?"

"I'm at the V.A. in Westwood," he said. "Main entrance."

And, before I could answer, protest, or even just ask a question—like *Where have you been for the past fifteen years?*—he hung up. My father, Francisco Cruz: the ultimate drama queen. Eventually, he would even die on Father's Day. At sunrise. With me at his side. Seriously. He was such a theatrical bastard. This being the case, it came as little surprise when, although we'd been estranged since I was a kid, he called out of the blue to announce both his impending death and his desire for a lunch date.

As if the fates would have allowed it any other way, I had the day off from my crap job stocking bins at Aron's Records. So, after I hung up the phone, I pushed myself out of bed and got ready to meet my dad. The prospect of seeing my father must have left me looking scared or just simply like shit because one of my roommates stopped me as I was about to walk out of the apartment.

"Frank, everything okay?" Jen asked.

And this may not seem like much, but it was. That's not to say Jen was some sort of bitch who didn't care, it's just that she and her boyfriend, Ted, ususally minded their own business. Really, they were perfect roommates. Both referred to themselves as "preppy punk," like it was their way of trying to impress me, like they were so transgressive and cool, but honestly they were pretty square. Comfortingly predictable, sweet, and dull, Jen and Ted were grad students at UCLA, older than me and way more mellow. We all liked each other enough, none of us flaked on our bills, we cleaned up our own messes, but, like I said, it wasn't typical that I'd get in their space or that they'd get in mine. So anyway, given Jen's sudden concern, I figure I must have looked like a total wreck when I was leaving to meet my father.

"Yeah, everything's fine," I replied and continued out the door. "Thanks, though."

Jen didn't seem convinced. There was no reason she should have been. She stood in the doorway of our Echo Park apartment and watched as I crossed the street, like she thought I might pass out or throw myself in traffic. I got in my rusty tin can little car, forced a smile, and waved to her as I drove away.

Forty minutes of crosstown side roads hell later, I pulled my car up to the hospital's main entrance red zone. A man sat on the concrete slab bench near the automatic sliding glass doors. My father. I hadn't seen him since I was eight, but I would have known him anywhere.

In fact, my father and I looked exactly alike. Rather, we shared nearly identical features. But whereas I was dressed in post-teen skater slop, he was dressed to the nines. Fedora cocked on his pomade sleek head, his brown wool three-piece suit slightly wrinkled from a night spent in the hospital, but no worse for the wear, he looked like a Hitchcock flick leading man. Polished wingtip shoes, pocket square, cashmere dress socks—this was the way he had always dressed.

Case in point:

When I was in kindergarten, there'd been a big weekend carnival at school. It was the most awesome event of the year. There were tons of rides and booths. My favorite booth was the one where kids threw ping-pong balls into fishbowls, and if a kid got enough balls in, the carnies would give them a little plastic bag filled with water and a goldfish. I didn't win a fish, but I did get the consolation prize—a fish-shaped cutout made of red plastic paper like a spotlight gel. You were supposed to hold the plastic-paper fish in the palm of your hand, and depending on how its tail and head curled, it predicted your fortune. There were instructions on decoding the curls printed on the little white and red envelope the fish came in. My fish's sides kept curling up. I don't remember what that meant. Really, the curling was just a matter of body heat affecting the onionskin-thin plastic, but to me it was pure magic.

Anyway, the carnival had been on one of my dad's weekends. And that event marked the first time I realized my dad was unlike everyone else's dads. All the other fathers were dressed in totally casual outfits—jeans and trainers, some with turtlenecks and denim jackets, others with V-neck sweaters over T-shirts. Almost all of them had shaggy hair and sideburns. They simply looked cool. When we got home from the carnival, I asked my dad why he didn't wear comfortable clothes like theirs, why he went to the barber shop every week and shaved twice a day.

"Don't ever let anyone call you a lazy wetback," he said.

I had no idea how that was an answer to my question. I tried asking my magic fish, but upon closer inspection, its envelope claimed it could tell me only if I was in love, lucky, or tired.

Fifteen years later, I'd been dealt enough jabs—including one incident in junior high when a group of kids threw handfuls of pennies at me, called me a "beaner queer whore," and were only reprimanded by the lunch supervisor to *Sit down and eat*—that I'd come to understand my father's reasons for wanting to present a polished front. His attire and grooming was passive resistance of a most dignified form.

And so, there he sat on the concrete hospital bench, his manicured hands primly folded on his knees, back straight, clean-shaven face tilting side to side slightly as he listened to the sounds around him. As I approached, his body turned static. I stood directly in front of him. And still he didn't stand. He only adjusted his glasses—as if there was a chance in hell this might help him recognize me any better.

His glasses:

Opaque dark brown lenses framed by bulky rectangular solid side panels, an expensive version of the throwaway pairs ophthalmologists give patients after dilation, a more serious version of those many an old man put over the top of regular glasses to filter out all the sun's light—my father was wearing what as a kid I'd so bluntly referred to as his blind-man glasses.

"Dad?"

"Francisca, baby girl."

I cringed. But didn't say anything.

He rose to greet me, facing slightly right of where I stood.

"Ready to go?" he asked, like *he* had come to pick *me* up.

I put my hand on his left elbow and, after a briefly awkward moment, led him to the car.

"Where should we eat?" he asked, as if this was a casual little lunch date we had every week.

"Wherever."

"Canter's?"

"Sure."

I drove east on Sunset and then onto Santa Monica Boulevard. We'd made it all the way to Fairfax and were heading south before I got up the nerve to ask what was going on.

"Let's talk while we eat," he said.

Fine. A supposedly dying man should be granted such requests, right?

We arrived at Canter's. I parked in the side lot, took a ticket from the attendant, and led my father into the restaurant. A comforting stink of sugar cookies, pastrami, and pickle juice greeted us, so did one of Canter's many venom-spitting charm-haggard waitresses. My father and I sat at a table for two in the main dining room, under the stained glass false ceiling that looked like a canopy of giant autumnal trees. Why the New England forest motif in a Los Angeles Jewish deli? Don't know, but the resulting effect was simultaneously unsettling and perfect.

The second we sat down I did what I always did when I got to Canter's. I picked up the telephone. Like every other booth, ours came outfitted with an old-fashioned black telephone mounted on the mottled glass that divided the booth into its own little cubicle. You could make local calls for free from your table. I wasn't actually going to call anyone, but the gimmick was too good not to be acknowledged each visit. So I picked up the phone. But there was no dial tone. I clicked the receiver hook. Nothing. The line was dead. My dad must have heard me futzing.

He said: "Your mother didn't say much when I called to get your number. How is she?"

"Don't know, really."

"That bad?"

"Yeah."

I couldn't see behind his glasses, but I was pretty certain two heavy-lidded eyes precisely the same shape as mine went sad in response. My father took off his fedora and placed it on the table next to the napkin dispenser. With hands as big and bony and slightly freckled as mine, he smoothed his hair into place and sighed.

It was such an uncanny thing to sit across from a person I resembled so exactly, but with whom I'd spent so little of my life. That said, I knew it hadn't been my father's fault we were near strangers. The custody battle that ensued after my mother left him had been extremely messy, to say the least. By the time I was eight, my mother had done all she could—and she did a lot—to end my relationship with my dad. Still, there was no doubt about it, I was his kid.

"Son," our waitress interrupted our silence, "you ready to order?"

Not that my father could see it, but his little girl had become a young man. Starting in junior high, I'd wound Ace bandages tight around my chest to flatten my thankfully negligible breasts. Hoping for the healing benefits of a cold compress, I'd initially stored the bandages in the freezer overnight. Over time, I'd acquired less chilling and more sophisticated means for smoothing things out. And by the time I sat across from my dad at Canter's, I'd mastered counterbalancing most physical evidence of ever having been born a girl.

The careful staging our waitress unknowingly tested with her impatient stare: a baggy long-sleeved black T-shirt over a tight Hanes undershirt over a wife-beater over an extra-small binder; boxer shorts peeking out from under low-slung oversized black Dickies cinched with an Army surplus canvas belt; a bulky dark gray hoody sweatshirt, hood down. I pulled the visor of my baseball cap further over my face, shuffled my skater-sneaker clumsy feet, and cleared my throat to deepen my voice for a response.

"Son?" she repeated.

"I'll just have a coffee," my father answered before I could, oblivious to the way I looked, flattered by what he'd taken to be a waitress's flirtation directed at him. He was totally clueless. But still, I'd passed in front of my father. I ordered a celery soda to mark the occasion. What other options were there? Sweet fizz celebration was the best I could do.

"So, Dad, can we talk now?"

I watched as my father responded by retrieving a black Sharpie from his jacket pocket. He took several napkins from our table's dispenser, unfolded the white squares, and spread them out on the table in front of him. As we waited for our food, he mapped out a diagram of what he was leaving me in death:

His blindness.

I would inherit my father's ticking time-bomb vision.

I'd always known my father had been dealt a particularly bad set of eyes, but now he told me the specifics of his deteriorating eyesight. By the time he was seven he'd needed Coke-bottle glasses. As a teenager, he'd required a magnifying glass to read the Bible as his mother insisted he do each Sunday morning . . .

These details didn't make sense. I'd just picked him up from the V.A. hospital. He'd fought in Vietnam.

"Wasn't there an eye exam when you got drafted?"

"Once Uncle Sam found me, nothing mattered except trying to get me killed."

And then he started in on a rant about how Vietnam had never been his war to fight, about how he'd grown up in Mexico with no clue he'd been born in the States, so why should he have had to go to war for this country? And, unbelievable as it may have seemed, it was true—he really hadn't known he was a U.S. citizen until he was drafted. He also hadn't known until he was eighteen that when his mother was pregnant with him, his family had gone north as *braceros* to build railroads. 1943. Chicago. And—yet another detail you'd figure most people would know about their own lives—he hadn't learned until he was a grown man that he'd once had a sister. Rosario Maria Guadalupe Cruz. My father's sister Rosario had been four years old when the family went north. And when the family came home less than a year later, she was no longer with them.

Rosario met tragedy while she and her newborn brother were living with their parents—along with thousands of other government-indentured Bracero Program laborers—in a Chicago railroad company's shantytown. Their makeshift home was constructed out of barely modified old train cars located on a dusty stretch of land adjacent to a strip of railroad. The living and working conditions were barely one step from slavery. My father's mother was a proud woman; she didn't like leaving her home country to be so shamed. Hard work didn't upset her, but a lack of dignity did. She had wanted to be treated with respect. And she longed to spend more time with her newborn son, she wished she didn't have to leave him every day with the old woman who came to the shantytown each morning before dawn and watched the workers' children for a hefty cut of their pay. My dad said that his mother once admitted that in Chicago, after a particularly trying day of breaking stone into gravel to be laid out under the tracks, she had cursed God for giving her such a trying life. She told my father she'd forever regret that moment of weakness because, a few days later, in what she interpreted as retribution for her ingratitude, the railroad—that angry and almighty steel-and-oil God of industry—threw thunderbolts at her.

Quick rumble flash, a supply train derailed. Heavy weight skipped thick tracks. Screech metal snapped. Rattle impact, the train crashed into the perimeter of the shantytown. In the bright-sunshine middle of the day. It was a pretty day. A very pretty day. The camp was near-empty. Most everyone was working far from there. Few were injured. Only one died.

Rosario had been playing by the side of the railroad.

My father's mother, devastated by her little girl's death, refused to speak a word of their time in Chicago. She forbade her husband or anyone else ever to mention it. As it turned out, the gods weren't done with the family yet.

One afternoon five years later, the trio settled back into their life in Mexico, my father, now a young boy, was helping his father tend to the family's small farm. His mother was inside their shack home, presumably preparing supper. My father felt shivers on his arm as a sudden thunderstorm filled the sky with electric air and heavy raindrops. When a thunderclap rattled the field, his mother must have thought of the shantytown in Chicago. She would have thought of her little girl. A lightening bolt outside, too close outside, too near the house, much too close, shook my father's mother to the core. And outside, in the field, my father watched as celestial brilliance reached down and anointed his father. Singed black to his toes, the man died instantly. One could conclude, and many did, that traces of the flash seared my father's vision, swam through the veins of his eyes, and, although it took many years, slowly turned him blind.

Unfortunately, my father was not yet blind the day his pueblo's grocer, who was also the post general, found him at Sunday service and told him of the letter waiting. "It looks important, Francisco. It's from up north."

With nothing more than a piece of paper translated by the grocer into Spanish, the U.S. government took the farm tools from my father's hands, forced him to report to San Diego for processing, taught him how to shoot a rifle, and shipped him to a jungle in Vietnam.

Thirteen months of hell later, my father returned to Mexico speaking English and with ever-worsening eyesight. Soon thereafter, he decided to move to the States—a country he had never seen with clear eyes—to embark on his newfound birthright: the American Dream.

"Mami, come with me," he said to his mother. "We'll get you papers."

"I won't go," she said.

"It'll be good."

"No."

His mother knew that the roads up north were not paved in gold. But even after two years of an American war, my father was still naïve enough to hope for the best. As he boarded a bus north, his mother took his hand and in his open palm she placed a small honey-colored pebble, a memento she'd picked up once long ago as she walked along a rural dirt road leading to church. "Remember your home."

My father kissed the pebble and tucked it in his pocket for safekeeping. He hugged his mother and told her he loved her. He promised to write often, to send money and visit as soon as he could. He followed through on most of his promises, but he never saw his mother alive again.

Slowly, my father built a life for himself. He found employment. Worked long hours. Tried to save money. Fell in love. But no matter what he did, his world still blurred and darkened with each passing year. When I was a child, he often held me close, not exactly out of intense affection, but more specifically—knowing one day he might wake without the ability to see anything at all—to memorize the features of my person. More years went by. More work. Less love. Less money saved. On and on.

All throughout my childhood, my mother had tried to make me hate my father. Her efforts were useless—I'd always respected my father, if for no other reason than his ability to strike out on his own, to leave home far behind and just go. Countless were the times I'd wanted to follow his example. But I'd always been too chickenshit. Sure, I'd moved to the big city thrill of Los Angeles the instant I graduated from high school, but please, my disaster of a childhood home and mother were barely forty-five minutes south, and—although we'd stayed out of touch and our paths never crossed amidst the sprawl of L.A.—my father and I did both live in the same county. Ultimately, my move toward independence was like that of a kid who said he was going to run away and then went and pitched a tent in the backyard instead.

So there I was, wishing I could be far, far away from everything I'd ever known, and yet I sat in a booth at Canter's with my father. Me: a twenty-two-year-old with the self-absorbed myopic vision of youth. And my father: a middle-aged blind man.

"It's called *retinitis pigmentosa*," he said. The condition, he explained, caused degenerative eyesight and eventual blindness. And it skipped generations.

"So I *don't* have it?" I asked, ashamed to be so hopeful.

"No, you do."

Our order arrived. I bit into my sandwich for distraction.

The blindness actively affected only males, my father said. But female offspring of the blind generation carried the gene and could pass the blindness to their male children.

"*You*," my father emphasized, "are a *carrier*."

I choked a little on a dry bit of rye bread—more at my father's loud insistence that I was female than at learning my hypothetical son might be blind. Throat cleared with a swig of soda, I asked: "And *retinitis pigmentosa* is a terminal illness?"

"What?"

"You said when you called . . . the doctors told you . . ."

"Oh, no, that's unrelated." He waved his hand as if to shoo away an irrelevant and bothersome topic. "The pain in my gut got so bad last week that I called my doctor. They ran tests at the hospital. The pathologist says he found cancer. They'll operate, but they think it might keep spreading."

The pain in his gut? What the fuck was he talking about?

He mentioned it like it was some long-standing topic we'd discussed endless times before. The elephant my father tried to ignore sat himself directly on my chest. I was stunned. Confused. And speechless.

"Anyhow, if you ever get pregnant," he said, almost cheerily, "there are options."

He uncapped his Sharpie and felt for the paper napkins he'd spread on the table between us. At the center of the napkins, he drew a circle that was supposed to represent me. The marker's ink bled out in a spindly spiderweb mess as he drew another line. He meant the line to start at the circle's perimeter and extend outward. Instead, the line intersected the circle, and I thought of that old magic trick where the magician saws his assistant in half. I'd always hated that trick. I knew it was all smoke and mirrors, but there was something inherently creepy about the illusion. What if something went wrong and the assistant really got sawed in two? What then?

"You could selectively abort," my father said, and wrote a jumble of overlapping letters I presumed would have read *abort* if he could have seen his own writing. "I know it sounds awful, but it's an option," he said.

A searing hot pain surged in my stomach. My pastrami on rye threatened to travel upward and out. I pressed on my wrists to stay grounded and try not to puke. My discomfort was not caused by the thought of an abortion, per se, but by having a conversation with my father—who'd just breezily revealed he'd been diagnosed with terminal cancer—about being pregnant and selectively aborting a baby boy who might be blind because of something I had apparently inherited.

The situation sucked.

"Dad . . ."

"By the time you'd want a baby," he marched on, "doctors might be able to manipulate an embryo's chromosomes. It'd be expensive, but be sure at least to ask."

He found the left edge of the napkins, dragged his index finger halfway across, and drew another line from where he imagined his circle daughter to be. He wrote a long tangled mess of totally illegible letters that he probably intended to read *artificial insemination* or *test tube baby*, but could have just as accurately read: *I'm a freak show and you're a freak show and any kid you have will be a freak show too.*

"Really, Paquita, it's amazing what science can control," he said.

There we were, living proof to the contrary. My chromosomes defined me as a daughter. And cancer was irreversibly sabotaging my father on the most essential of cellular levels. Our bodies were failing us in ways science could never entirely repair.

"Dad, are you scared?"

Such a stupid question. But I asked it.

He sighed. The skin on his face hung loose and pallid. He was going to die. Soon. Sooner than either of us realized. He sipped from his heavy ceramic mug of coffee. Black. Two sugars. Plastic brown stirring stick still in the mug.

"Dad?"

He reached his hand across the table and I met him halfway with mine. With a squeeze as warm as his sick flesh could afford, he said: "I don't want to die alone."

And then he cried. Openly. Loudly. Uncontrollably.

I silently vowed to be the perfect son.

CHAPTER TWO

I emptied the feces-filled plastic bag secured to my father's abdomen.

"I can't do this. I can't," he said.

"It's okay," I said, and tried not to let him hear as I gagged.

"You shouldn't have to do this either."

"It's okay," I said.

Of course, nothing about the situation was okay. My father would be in the hospital for another week. His surgery had been only a partial success. After minimal recovery time and a round of chemo, he'd be scheduled for more surgery. As it was, once the surgeons had finished removing much of his intestine, they'd sealed the lower end of his colon. Then they'd removed a small circle of skin at the original incision site, led the top half of his colon through the hole to the surface of his skin, and sewed the colon into place. That thick fleshy pink little nub fit into the opening of a plastic bag, which was adhesive-secured to his shaved-clean lower abdomen. Hence the colostomy bag which I cleaned for him. An enterostomal nurse stood by and watched to make sure I drained the bag into the bedpan properly.

"Mr. Cruz," she said to my father as she supervised, "when you're able to get out of bed, you will empty the bag directly into the toilet . . ."

I imagined my father straddling the toilet as the nurse said many patients prefer to do, his shirt pulled up, pants unbuckled but not pulled down, boxers lowered slightly.

"It'll become second nature," she said. "You won't need help."

Thank God.

I loved my father. Dearly. And I wanted to help. In any way possible. I'd take as many days off work as I could without getting fired. I'd fucking get fired if I had to. I'd really do anything.

But thank God.

I checked the clip sealing his plastic bag twice for good measure. If that clip slipped, the nurse warned, contents would leak. Weeks later, the first time the clip came undone unexpectedly, we tried to laugh away the humiliation of his shit-soiled shirt. This was our failed attempt at controlling a situation that allowed us virtually no control at all. Dying. There was nothing we could do about it. My father's body was less his every day.

As months of chemo and subsequent surgeries passed, my father slept more and more. He was so still at times that I checked to find signs of his rib cage rising and falling. It terrified me to realize his slowing body was practicing for final sleep. And then there were his funeral marches to the bathroom to heave vanilla Ensure. He vomited a disgusting sweet stench of white fluid. Even applesauce wouldn't stay down. His face was gaunt. His eyes, already virtually useless, seemed to shrink outright in sockets that were themselves hallowing at a frightening rate. One day he woke up the color of stale flan. Jaundiced. His liver joining colon. It was all going to pot. Strangely, the physical misery of this protracted death was contagious. Depletion burned deep in my core. My vision blurred. My bones ached.

★

7 May 1995, my twenty-third birthday: My father woke me by

singing "Happy Birthday." I'd slept over at his house the night before, and I was still wrapped in blankets on his couch, yawning, when he handed me a padded manila envelope. The envelope was outsized, eleven by fifteen inches at least. I couldn't discern what was inside, but whatever it was didn't weigh all that much. My father had written *Paquita, Birthday Girl* across the front in fat marker. Reading those words was like accidentally chewing on a piece of tinfoil, but I said nothing to him about it. We'd spent time together nearly every day for months, and I'd come close to broaching the topic with him countless times, but it always felt forced. I mean, he was dying, for God's sake. And we were in each other's lives again. Insisting we have some sort of big talk about my gender seemed to miss the point completely. So on my birthday, I tried to focus on his intention, on what was, girl reference or not, a birthday gift my father had carefully chosen for me.

"Should I open it now?" I asked.

"Of course." He reached forward, found the couch edge with his hands, and sat down next to me.

I carefully loosened the envelope's taped-shut flap, reached in, and pulled out a solid rectangle of dimensions not much longer or wider than my hand. My father had wrapped the object. And not only had he wrapped it, but he'd wrapped it beautifully. The small something was tucked inside starched gold linen fabric and tied with a white silk ribbon. I peeled off the wrapping paper only to find two more wrapped objects stacked one on top of the other.

The top gift turned out to be an old clothbound book with a blank cover. I opened it to the title page. *A dix ans sur mon pupitre. Nahui Olin. 1924.* I flipped through the pages and found that although the title was in French, the book was written in Spanish. From what I could tell, it seemed to be a self-published collection of prose poetry, almost like an antique 'zine, really. I wasn't sure why my father thought I'd want a collection of poems, but the book was appealing in a vintage-object sort of way.

"Cool book. Thanks, Dad."

"Open the rest."

I did and found a small rectangle of cardboard with something pasted on one side. Upon inspecting the pasted something, I instantly felt like I had one time as a kid. I'd been spinning all around my mom's house, dancing like a total spaz to the Sparks' *Angst in My Pants*, when I ran over to the couch, planted my hands on an armrest, did a somersault, and, klutz-extraordinaire, *slam*, hit my back against the wall. I got the wind knocked out of me something good for my dorky dance move. That was the first time I'd ever lost my breath. It was terrifying. And thrilling. It was so intense that I thought I had died; all my other emotions up to that point, even if combined together into one single emotional whammy, came nowhere close to equaling the way I suddenly felt.

So, what could make me feel that way again? It probably won't immediately impress you as something very extraordinary. But just hang with me for a minute.

Pasted to one side of the cardboard was a peeling and crumbling black-and-white photograph of a woman. A portrait. Very elegant. Posed. Artsy. And melancholy as all fuck. Strangely, I was pretty sure the photo had been mounted on the cardboard as a makeshift retablo to be used on someone's home altar. I was confused by this because I thought retablos were supposed to depict saints—and the woman in the portrait was, from all appearances, most certainly not a saint. Still, the small cardboard object did seem to be a retablo. But, honestly, those pragmatic logistics were neither here nor there. What really mattered was that the woman in the portrait was hot. Beyond hot. In fact, the subject of the portrait just might have been the human incarnation of sex itself.

I greedily ate up every detail.

Written in a small careful cursive on the cardboard under the photo was: *Nahui Olin. Fotografía de Edward Weston. 1924.* Of course I knew who Weston was, but I didn't recognize the woman's name or the handwriting.

The portrait:

It had been shot with such a tight frame that the outer edges of the woman's bare shoulders were cropped. Only a narrow halo of empty space surrounded her head. She was so nearby and right in front of me that I could see the pores of her skin on her cheeks and the tip of her nose. Every uneven strand of her jagged bangs and blunt bob was visible. I could count each deep crease on the dehydrated cupid-bow lips that formed an expression more snarl than smile. The woman's conventionally beautiful features—lovely clavicle, outsized and thick-lash-adorned almond eyes—were almost an aside. It was her stare that punctured me so hard.

Even though I'd never seen her before, and I had no clue who she was, her wicked lovely stare made me want to worship the ground she walked on. I would be her most devoted servant. Of course someone had made an altar for her, who wouldn't once they'd looked into her eyes? Those eyes, pure crystalline fire, could burn all barriers—the barriers between here and there, between what she had and what she wanted, between the past and present. Even though the photo was dated 1924, she was so goddamned rough and melt-down beautiful all at once that if someone had said to me, "Dude, check her out, her band's playing tonight at Spaceland," I would have so believed them and, I can guarantee, her thrasher riot girl band would have been my new favorite. She was timeless *jolie laide* perfection.

But, to my deep horror, she was disintegrating. Like a mirror unsilvering, specks of black—photographic paper and developing chemicals turning cannibalistic to devour their own image—showed through the left side of her face and on her shoulders. I resisted the intense urge to lick each and every one of those ashen freckles. Honestly, I wanted to taste past her skin. I wanted to find a way into her soul. I wanted to consume and claim forever as mine any part of her that might be slipping away.

I swear you would understand if you saw the portrait.

"Dad, where'd you get this?"

"The retablo?"

I was such an asshole. Of course he couldn't see which of the two gifts I was holding.

"Yeah, the retablo."

"Do you like it?"

"A lot."

"It was my mother's. I found it after she died."

I wish I'd known how to respectfully tell my father that I appreciated the layered importance of his gift, that I understood that he gave me the retablo both because he knew I'd love it, and also because soon he, like his mother, would be dead. I wanted him to know I was grateful that he recognized mourning was in my near future. If nothing else, he was making sure I'd have a retablo of a surrogate saint to turn to in my sadness. I comprehended all of this immediately, but I was at a loss when it came to the subtleties of communication in emotionally steeped situations.

I blurted out: "Is the photo really a Weston?"

I hoped the question sounded sophisticated. It was hard to tell if my dad was impressed. But I think he might have been.

"Yes, but that's only a reproduction."

"Why'd Grandma make the retablo?"

The word "Grandma" felt dumb leaving my mouth. Even though I'd never met her, she had been, indeed, my grandmother. Still, no disrespect, it was weird to call her "grandma." My father seemed to pick up on this.

"My mother knew Nahui Olin," he said. "Or at least I think she did. I mean, I *know* she did, but she never told me as much. Anyway, they were close."

"Close?"

"Very close," he said with an undecipherable tone.

"And Nahui wrote this book?"

"Yes. That copy belonged to my mother," he said.

I looked at the retablo again. My dad's mother had been *very* close to this person Edward Weston took a photo of, to this avant-garde chick who wrote a book of poems? I wanted to know more, I wanted all the dirty little details.

"So," I cautiously ventured further into the conversation, "Nahui was a poet?"

At this my father laughed.

"Nahui was a cautionary tale," he said.

Huh?

"And she's exactly the sort I fell for every time," he added.

Wait, was my dad trying to talk ladies with me? I wasn't sure if I should be happy or miserably uncomfortable. Regardless, my end of the conversation would be inherently limited. At that point in my life I'd messed around plenty, but I'd never really had a *girlfriend*—the entire prospect had simply seemed too complicated. But, considering what my dad had said, I had to wonder, if I ever fell hard for a girl, if it ever felt like something big and real and lasting, if that ever happened, would it be for a fire-eyed girl like Nahui? Would I follow in what seemed to be Cruz tradition? Honestly, the possibility of being with such a handful sounded enticing as all hell. In retrospect, I can't tell you how many times I later wished I could go back to warn my naïve self: *Yes, she will be complicated. And, yes, it'll be hot. But seriously, fool, brace yourself. Loving her will be the hardest thing you'll ever know.* Like they say, hindsight is twenty-twenty. Right then, all I had was my own limited per-spective and the nostalgic insight of a blind man.

The *every time* part of what my father had said echoed in my ears.

"Dad, you mean my mom, right?"

"And my ex-wife," he said.

"You and mom weren't married."

"Not to each other."

Okay, first he all but tells me that his mother had a secret lover. A woman. A totally hot woman who Edward Weston had photographed, for fuck's sake. And now he was telling me he'd been married? To whom? When? Before he was with my mom? During? After? My head swam. What else could there be to find out? Did I have half-siblings somewhere? Was I adopted? What? Taking full advantage of my idiot silence, he continued:

Yes, he'd been married. Before he met my mom. And, no, my mother hadn't ever known about it. "You know how she is," he only briefly explained. "I didn't want to lose her, so I never told her." Anyway, it seemed my father and his wife had traveled on a rickety motorcycle up the West Coast for post-nuptial festivities. I tried to picture it. They were both young, but considering how bad my father's eyes probably already were at that point, I was sure she had driven the bike. She must have been so *Easy Rider* foxy on their chopper. It was safe to assume my dad wore one of his suits, a fedora for a helmet. I was impressed.

"She and I loved each other entirely," he said. "It was beautiful."

But then when he smiled radiantly as he said his wife took the motorcycle and left with some other dude in Death Valley, I wasn't sure if it was the codeine talking.

"Wait, what?"

"Exactly what I said. We stayed a few nights in Death Valley in this little cabin, she met someone else, and she left me." His voice turned syrupy, "I'll never forget that day . . ."

I scrunched up my face. Made no difference, he couldn't see it anyway.

"She had long cinnamon-colored hair like thick flames that reached down her back to her hips," he said and smiled even more, to himself, to the memory of her. "All morning we'd stayed in bed and made love."

Sour spit filled my mouth.

"Dad, please."

"There's nothing disgraceful about love."

"I just don't want to hear any more, okay?"

"We were hungry," he continued, "and we planned to buy some lunch at the nearby town store, something simple, some cheese and apples, maybe some honey and bread. We were going to picnic at the Devil's Golf Course, everyone had been telling us we absolutely had to go there, they said it was surreal—sparkling rocky fields of salt crystals for miles and miles. The crystals made popping sounds in the hot sun, it's simply one of the natural wonders of the world, so spectacular . . .

"So, we were going to take the motorcycle to get food and go there. But she wanted to take a bath first, just a quick bath to pretty up, she said. I told her there was no way she could be prettier than she already was. And she wasn't simply pretty, she was beautiful. She was the woman who taught me the difference between 'pretty' and 'beautiful.' She was beautiful, Francisca. Extremely beautiful."

He took off his blind man glasses. His white-fogged eyes started tearing up. I tried to be adult about it all. First hearing him talk about sex. Then him crying . . .

His voice quivered slightly and he said, "I guess I fell asleep while she was in the bath because all of a sudden I woke to a kiss on my temple. Just one soft little kiss. I opened my eyes. If I could have my eyes back for one single moment, I'd wish for her to be standing in front of me again like she was that day. Her blushed face, that fire hair licking at her shoulders, slick against her pale skin . . . She left that night, but for my entire life she was the most beautiful thing I ever saw." Staring toward me, his gaze aimed two degrees to the right of where I sat, my father added: "I knew she'd leave me. I figured we might as well go somewhere memorable to fall apart."

I sat there, not sure anymore who was sitting across from me. I began to realize I liked him a lot more than the person I'd always assumed my father was.

He wiped his face dry with the back of his hand and put his dark glasses back on.

"There's more," he said. "In the envelope, I mean."

I picked it up. My hands trembled. From frayed nerves. Overloaded brain. I sliced my wrist as I reached in. "Fuck," I yelped, and pulled my hand back.

"What?"

"Nothing. Paper cut," I mumbled. My dad was dying and tearing open his soul to share himself with me before it was too late, and I screamed about a tiny paper cut. I was pathetic.

I sucked a thin line of blood off my skin and shook the envelope gently. A key fell out and hit the coffee table with a clinking sound. Tied to the key by a small piece of string was one of those office supply silver dollar–sized circular paper tags with a flimsy tin border—the kind they write your car's license plate number on at the auto shop. And on that tag, written in my father's handwriting, albeit considerably smaller and neater than his writing on the envelope's exterior, presumably from many years before, was the following: *Wells Fargo Bank. City of Orange. Old Towne Circle.*

"What's this for?" I asked.

"Safe deposit box. Don't go until after I die."

I swear, he said that. It was so totally cryptic. Morbid. And narcissistic.

Given all the death and exhaustion floating around in the air, I was desperate for the safe deposit key to open a treasure box filled with uplifting fabulousness, a reserve of something extravagant and luxurious. In fact, I wanted to drive down to the safe deposit box in Orange right that instant to claim my prize.

"I'm serious, Francisca. Promise me."

"For real?"

"Just leave it for later, okay, Paca?"

"Fine, I promise."

"Put it on your keychain."

"I will."

"*Now*," he snapped.

"Shit, Dad, you don't have to yell."

"I'm sorry." He rubbed his temple with his hands. "I just don't want you to lose that key."

I reached into the overnight duffle bag at my side and found my keychain. I hooked the key on and dropped the metal jumble back in my bag.

"Done," I said.

My dad stood, reached down, found my shoulders, and pulled me up.

"Come on, I'll bake you a cake," he said, with his best attempt at a bright smile.

CHAPTER THREE

My birthday cake was a disaster. Ingredients dusted the kitchen counter and floor. I ended up doing most of the work. And then the batter wouldn't bake properly. It stayed raw in the middle. I blew out my candle with a wish that my dad, that we, wouldn't have to know more suffering.

Unintended consequence of my wish come true, the next day cancer sabotaged my father's brain. He stayed bed-bound for weeks. An IV drip in his arm was his only source of nutrients and hydration. In his hand he held the golden little pebble his mother had given him when he left Mexico. His fingers were white-knuckled for how tightly he gripped that worry stone. He giggled maniacally and rambled gibberish anytime he wasn't sleeping. A month into this ordeal, two days before Father's Day, I was sitting next to my father's bed, holding his hand, keeping vigil, when he stopped his manic nonsensical chatter and turned his head to fix his blind sight on me.

"I love you, kid," he said.

His succinct clarity startled the hell out of me.

Blind eyes locked onto me.

To memorize me.

To me more eyes.

Me.

"Love you, too," I said.

Father's Day Eve. I stayed up with him the entire night. I don't know how to describe it exactly, but I knew he was going to die before sunrise. His skin was clammy and without color, save the gray tinge of sustained illness, and he seemed very distant, already gone in a way. At times I could barely discern whether he was still breathing or if his body only quivered from the trembling clutch of my hand holding his. I shook my crossed leg to keep awake and bit my dry hangnail fingers as I watched over him.

"Dad," I whispered, "if you're ready, it's okay."

As if in response, the briefest choking sound escaped his lips. He was choking on air, not for a lack of it. No warmth exhaled on my fingertips when I checked his nostrils. The pulse was gone from his neck and wrists. The sun rose. 5:45 A.M. 18 June 1995. Father's Day. My father was dead.

I sat in the chair next to my dad's bed, hating myself for feeling relieved. I wanted to nudge him over to the metal rail edge of his rented hospital bed and climb in to join him. I wanted to sleep. Deeply. But I couldn't. Not yet. Details needed tending to. There were things to be done. I lay down on the floor.

Prone on the carpet, I closed my eyes. A bedpan over my shoulder, the acrid stench of dried urine at my nose, my legs under my father's bed, there, right there, I lay. I pulled a cord and dragged the phone off the nightstand. It fell with a thud on the carpet next to me. I made calls. And when the funeral home guys rang the doorbell an hour later, I was still on the carpet. Eyes shut, I listened as two men with loud feet hesitantly entered the house.

"Hello?" a man's deep voice called out from the entryway.

"Upstairs," I shouted in my natural high octave, too tired to give a shit how my voice sounded.

"Ma'am?" the voice asked from the base of the stairs.

I didn't answer.

"Ma'am?" he asked again from the bedroom door. "Oh, sorry," he cleared his voice and apologized when he saw me sprawled miserably on the floor next to the bed.

He and his assistant entered the room with their supplies. They readied the stretcher they'd brought and rolled it over to the bed's side.

"Son, would you like to say goodbye?" the one with an empty body bag tucked under his arm looked down at me and asked.

Hadn't I been saying goodbye for months?

"Already did. Thanks," I whispered.

The brawnier of the two guys reached his thick meaty hand toward me.

"He was holding this," he said.

The worry stone. I took the pebble and squeezed it hard in my hand. Certain only the sensation of its polished worn-down surface was keeping me conscious, I focused on my oxygen intake—one breath in, one breath out, repeat—as I watched them wrap my father's body in a white sheet and put "him" in the body bag and then on the stretcher. I hated that those guys were seeing my father in his pajamas. He would have wanted to go in one of his suits, his brown three-piece linen, probably, and his fedora, the cocoa straw one. Instead he was bareheaded and wore flannel and cotton.

My thoughts looped dizzily.

He was dead when I got here. Officer, I swear, I didn't do it. It wasn't my fault . . .

The funeral home dudes took my father downstairs to the front door, to their hearse, and to a refrigerated morgue. A research lab that my father had contacted soon after his cancer diagnosis met them at the morgue and took my father's eyes. The rest of his body was no use to anyone all rotted like it was, so the funeral home stripped it down and burned it up and made bulky ashes. All of this happened as I barely managed to prop up the top half of my body's weight on shaking elbows, my legs nailed to the carpet on the floor next to the bed on which my father had died.

CHAPTER FOUR

Three days later, I woke at 5:45 in the morning—both the time my father had died and an absolutely ridiculously early hour for me, especially considering how fucking zapped I felt. But there I was, awake with the rising sun blasting through my bedroom window and directly into my eyes. Try as I did, I couldn't fall back asleep. I lay in bed for an hour, head cloudy and limbs aching to the bone, until there was no more delaying it—my father's ashes would be ready for pickup soon. "Come by any time after 8 A.M.," the man at the funeral home had said pleasantly when he'd called the day before, like it was a cake or business cards or something totally innocuous I was scheduled to take claim of. All I wanted was to go back to sleep. Instead, I got up, showered, and drove to Disneyland for the Dead.

Forest Lawn in Glendale, a place like no other:

A concrete cherub boy pissing fountain water greeted me at the entrance. As I pulled past him and into a parking spot, I looked up toward the cemetery's rolling and insidiously kelly-green landscaped hills. I knew that tucked up in those hills was a sculpture garden that included a scale-accurate replica of Michelangelo's *David*, sluglike uncircumcised dick and all. Michelangelo must have been rolling in his grave. And as for graves, I was grateful my father hadn't decided to be buried in one of the plots on those hills, thankful that I wouldn't have to attend some impersonal assembly-line memorial service in the Little Church of the Flowers, a place that encapsulated all that I hated about Southern Californian insincerity and its bullshit happy sunshine for everyone. It was bad enough my father wanted Forest Lawn to cremate him.

But to be fair, my dad had thought of Forest Lawn as some sort of modern American measuring stick of success, like having your dead body handled by them was equivalent to scoring the winning touchdown in some cracker All-American football fantasy where everyone suns themselves and laughs the day away as they picnic in the bleachers with Coca-Cola and Fritos, bologna on Wonder Bread with Miracle Whip sandwiches, and apple pie with processed American cheese desserts. Or maybe I underestimated my father (it wouldn't have been the first time); maybe he had realized how campy the place was, and he saw being incinerated there as the ultimate way to thumb his nose at death. Either way, Forest Lawn was indigestibly plastic.

I wish I could convey the nitty-gritty of that bizarre experience—of what exactly it was like to go to Disneyland to pick up my dead father—but I don't remember much. Honestly, I'm not sure if I cruised through all green lights as I drove there, or if school-bound kids and doughnut-munching crossing guards flooded the crosswalks. And how were Forest Lawn's office interiors decorated? Beats me. What did I do once I was inside? Who did I talk to? Well, I imagine I had to sign for my father's ashes. But I'm really not sure. There was probably someone who tried to comfort me in that stale-empathetic way professional death-tenders do, but that's just a guess. And as for paying, my dad had taken care of that before he died, so no money changed hands that day. What I do remember is being back in my car with a box of ashes on the passenger seat next to me.

I was instantly numb. Terrified. And about to explode. All at the same time.

Ashes, ashes, we all fall down . . .

Fucked up and clichéd as it was, that stupid kids' song surged forward from some deep vortex in my brain. And it wouldn't stop. Hardly an innocent children's rhyme, I remembered learning somewhere that the annoying little song was actually about the bubonic plague. *Ashes, ashes, we all fall down*... if infected bodies weren't cremated, the plague would spread. *Pocket full of posies* . . . people carried nosegays to ward off the stink of death that filled the streets. Fuck. I wanted the song to stop. Worst part was, the first line started looping over and over in my thoughts. *Ashes, ashes; Ashes, ashes; Ashes, ashes* . . . maybe we really would all fall down. So not cool. I felt so disrespectful. And I was going insane from the repetition.

Still parked and desperate for distraction, I opened the glove box and grabbed a birthday gift mixtape this skater Betty girl from work had given me. We'd worked some of the same shifts at Aron's and her name was Chloe and she was sexy and sweet in a scraggly your-best-buddy's-little-sister-hits-puberty sort of way. We'd kind of made out a few times in the back room, nothing serious, but she'd most definitely been crushing on me. Evidence: Not only did she make me a mixtape, but she'd gone so far as to cover said tape's plastic case in a thick layer of red (like Valentine's red, like I *love you* red) glitter. Embedded in the glitter were ugly little beads shaped like hearts and stars. She must have smeared a whole bottle of Elmer's glue on the case and then dumped an entire Michaels craft store on the damned thing. Small handfuls of the red stuff coated my lap and hands as I retrieved the tape. I popped the tape in the deck and tossed the case to the passenger floor mat, where it landed with a ruby *poof*.

Engine on. Music started up. Five melancholy guitar strings were plucked. Again. And again. Cymbal crashed. A steady somber drumbeat joined in. Five-string refrain. Low bass reverberated deep in my rib cage. I backed out of my

Forest Lawn parking space. And then, coasting past the pissing cherubs, past the ridiculously tall wrought iron and crested gates, turning left onto Glendale Avenue:

> *It's a long time coming, it's a long way down, it's long division, crack and divide.*
> *This is a parting, some separation, we lay in pieces, cracked to survive . . .*

Fugazi. One of my favorite bands. "Long Division." Not necessarily one of my favorite songs, but only because it always left me wanting more. I didn't like wanting more of anything from anyone. But I did. I wanted more of the song. And I wanted my dad to not be dead. It ended too soon.

There was a long gap of silence on the mixtape. A clicking sound. More silence. Too much damned silence. The box of ashes on the passenger seat was so criminally small. It just sat there, an inconspicuous little black cardboard box, not making a peep, but so totally filling me with noise. Even though he'd thought to take care of every other detail, my dad hadn't ever told me what I was actually supposed to *do* with his ashes once I had them. Maybe he figured he'd be lucid on his deathbed and planned to tell me then, not a minute sooner than he needed to. Maybe it was just his one strange form of denial, like if he didn't talk about the cremation he'd never actually die. Regardless, I had no clue what I was supposed to do with the ashes. Fuck, what was I supposed to do, period? Something heavy swelled in my chest. I could feel the pulse in my neck. I wanted to scream. My head ached like a demon. There was a steady hot unfamiliar pulse pushing from behind my eyes. Finally, another song started. The music was so loud it became distorted static and hurt my eardrums. I pulled onto the 5 Interstate southbound.

Entirely paranoid that my dad's ash-box lid might

somehow pop off, that the interior plastic bag would tear and particles of my father would fly away into the smog, I kept all the windows rolled up and didn't turn on the air. It was mid-June. In Southern California. Sweat stung my eyes. Head to foot I was a soggy uncomfortable mess. My hands kept slipping off the steering wheel. My entire body was tense, and I swear I could feel the individual molecules of my body buzz. Anxiety? Frustration? Anger? Pain? Whatever it was, it was too much. I clenched my jaw and tapped beats with my left foot. My right knee hit the keychain hanging down from the ignition each time I shifted. Keys rattled. My apartment keys. Deadbolt and lower lock. Car keys. Door and ignition. Keys to my dad's house. Front and back door. And the one strange saw-tooth key with the paper label. That key was extra long and kept jabbing my leg.

Morning rush-hour traffic was at its worst. At one point on the 405 south, where the stinking asparagus fields fill the air with noxious fumes, each lane came to a near-complete stop for almost half an hour. Ready to jump out of my skin, tempted to open my door and run into the fields in search of sprinklers—I swear, if I'd gone in the fields and found a source of cold water, I would have stripped down to my Skivvies and lay in the cold mud and just given up and died— I read the label attached to the safe deposit key my dad had given me for my birthday.

Wells Fargo Bank. City of Orange. Old Towne Circle.

The paper label turned limp from my humid touch, and the ink smeared. Just looking at my dad's shaky handwriting on that label, I knew there was no chance in hell the safe deposit box would contain a storybook happy ending.

An hour later, entirely unfamiliar with protocol, I stood in line at Wells Fargo and waited for a teller. When I was finally called to a window, I said, "I have a safe deposit box."

Shit, I sounded slow.

"And do you have a key?" the teller asked.

I pried it off my keychain and handed it to him.

"I'll also need photo identification," he said.

Great. There was nothing more fun than some O.C. conservative dude in a cheap tie and Dockers asking to see my driver's license. Trying to play it cool, like nothing out of the ordinary was about to hit, I reached for my wallet and handed him my license.

As he stared at it, his thick face pinched into a confused mess of wrinkles. He looked up at me. Then back at my license. The photo had been taken when I was sixteen and far less of a man. The name on that little laminated plastic card read: *Francisca Guerrero. Sex: F.*

"Excuse me a minute," the teller said.

He came back with, guessing from the stuffy polyester suit, a manager.

"Social security, please."

I gave the numbers. Boss man checked it against something in a manila file folder. He shrugged his shoulders and handed me my license, but not the key.

"Meet me over there," he said, and pointed to a smoked-glass door at the other end of the room.

I did as told, and he led me past the locked door and to a row of closetlike rooms. He opened the door closest to us and waved his hand into the small room like some sort of valet.

"Have a seat," he said.

It felt like 1910 in there. Everything—the walls, the heavy desk chair, the low narrow shelf, the square cups filled with pencils and rubber bands—was carpentered out of expensive and antique-looking dark wood. The size of the space was somewhere between a phone booth and a handicap-accessible public bathroom stall. You'd think with all the nice wood furnishings that it would have been a pleasant place to chill. But it wasn't. In fact, I think the air in there had been preserved from the same early-twentieth century period when the room was constructed. Unable to sit there any longer than I had to, I stood in the doorway and waited for the manager to come back.

Several minutes later, he returned with a small metal safe deposit box. He handed me the box, sniffed toward the shelf inside the room to indicate that—although who knew what I might want to do—that's where normal people put such things. Then he gave me my key.

"Close the door for privacy," he said and left.

I stepped back into the room and pulled the door shut behind me. That part was easy enough. Metal box on the wood shelf in front of me, I tried to take a deep breath. I felt like I might start hyperventilating. I hadn't ever really considered myself claustrophobic, but I was starting to think maybe I was. Sitting in that dimly lit and narrow space—the air stiff and totally silent, heavy wood surrounding me in close proximity at every angle—was truly like being entombed. Happy Belated Birthday to me. Thanks, Dad.

I unlocked the metal box. Hinged lid lifted, there it was, my birthday gift.

A bundle of letters.

Fading ink and yellowed paper, some of the letters were accompanied by stamped envelopes postmarked *Orange, California* or *New Haven, Connecticut.* Others, scratched out on scrap pieces of paper, appeared never to have been mailed. The handwriting was familiar (my father's, my mother's); the words and sentiments were not. *Francisco, sweet love, meet me at the plaza fountain tonight, please.* And: *Darling Paco, you are my everything.* Then: *You have made me the happiest woman in the world.* Another, this one from my father: *It's true what you say—Paquita does have my eyes. But she has her mother's brilliance . . .* Letter after letter offered up blissfully-in-love compliments and hopes for a long life together from two people I'd known to share only sadness, resentment, and anger.

Numb, I decided to approach the letters as artifacts of a sort. I played archivist and examined primary-document evidence of the long-extinct society I'd stumbled upon:

A coffee stain here and there. Lipstick kiss signatures. One letter smelled of sandalwood and was marked with a large perfumed oil spot that bled out and blurred its accompanying ink message. Many were signed with hearts and curlycue-headed squiggle happy faces like the ones my kindergarten teacher used to draw on handouts I'd completed with particular excellence. One envelope contained a clipping of long black hair braided and tied with green ribbon at either end. Blue ink. Black ink. Some written in red fountain pen. Near the middle of the stack I found two movie stubs for *Five Easy Pieces*—7:30 P.M., November 2, 1970, Orange Theatre (the plaza theater that had been converted into an evangelical church for as long as I could remember)—paper clipped to the top corner of an envelope addressed to a plump pink heart and the letter F.

None of the letters were dated past 1974. This was little surprise—my parents officially split in 1975. By 1974, I imagined only threats and legal documents were exchanged. I half-wished my dad had included those papers in the time capsule. Without them I felt like I was floating in some alternate universe. I'm not sure how many hours passed in that room, but a security guard knocked at one point.

"Everything all right in there?"

Bastard. No, everything was not all right. The foundation of everything I knew was crumbling. Air particles were separating and falling heavy all around me.

"Everything's fine. Thank you."

I listened to the security guard's heavy shoes retreat down the long linoleum hallway. And instantly I wondered why I'd sent him away. I didn't want to be alone with the letters. What was I supposed to do now that I'd seen them? What had my father intended? Why had he left them to me? I wished the box had been full of money instead. Or jewelry. Diamonds. Something I could pawn. Not only did this daydream fill me with greedy shame, it was also just plain unrealistic. Because even though my father had worked his way up to a supervisor position at the medical research lab before he got sick, he'd never had any extra dough to stash. There were living expenses, a mortgage on his house, and, until I was eighteen, my mother had sucked him dry of any remaining money by demanding he pay child support. It was so fucking ridiculous—she was beyond rich, she'd never needed his money, she wouldn't let him see me, but she made sure he paid child support. "It's the principle of the matter," she'd said. Bullshit. It was vendetta.

My darling Francisco, I will love you forever.

How was it that my mother had written these words? My whole life she'd been cold and distant at best, outright vicious most of the time. Had I somehow misunderstood? Was that what my dad wanted me to know?

I gently stacked the letters in the order I'd found them and put them back in the box. They'd be safe there. I didn't trust myself with them. And I didn't want their weight in my possession—but, of course, it already was.

I found the security guard. He called the manager. The manager took the box from me and situated it back in its place. Jagged long key looped back on my keychain, I was released. I got in my car. Turned on the ignition. Music blasted. Bikini Kill. Tobi Vail's atonal loveliness:

> . . . *take out a piece of paper, write everything down. Then you can read it back to me and maybe you can hurt me, you can read it back to me, maybe you could know something—about me. About me . . .*

In search of the woman I'd met in the safe deposit letters, hoping she still existed somehow, I drove. To my mother's.

CHAPTER FIVE

W ho are you?"
These were my mother's very words as I stood at
her doorstep holding the box of my father's ashes.
I hadn't called to see if she'd be home. In fact, my mother
and I hadn't talked in nearly five years. But—from the bank,
through miles of flatland tract housing, up curving Laguna
Hills roads, past increasingly wealthier homes—I'd driven to
her house with absolute certainty it was the right thing to do.
When I'd reached her property, I'd worried my car would
have trouble making it up her absurdly steep, long, private
driveway. So I'd parked my car on the street, brought the box
of ashes with me, and walked up. Relieved to see her vehicle
parked in the carport, I'd rung the doorbell. A long wait later,
my mother finally came to the door.

"Who are you?" she asked.

Classic. This was vintage insane behavior for her. Five
years apart or not, of course she knew damn well who I was.
I had wanted to tell her about the letters I'd read at the bank,
to tell her they'd been so special to my father that he'd kept
them all these years, to ask if maybe she wanted to keep the
ones she'd written, but then she said what she said, and I
decided she didn't deserve such generosity. Fuck her. She
probably wouldn't want the letters anyway. Instead of sentimental niceties, I stuck to the obvious.

"My dad died." I sort of tapped the box of ashes.

She just stared at me through the still-closed screen door,
mounting frustration only slightly visible under the unnatu-

rally smooth façade of her face. Seduced by even the less prestigious perks of being an Ivy League–educated doctor, my mother wore, as she did whenever she was home, one of the endless oversized and tacky T-shirts pharmaceutical companies sent her as promotional gifts. That day's poly/cotton knee-grazing T-shirt housedress was emblazoned with a prescription anti-inflammatory pill's logo. Knowing my mother as I did, she most likely wore a threadbare pair of old cotton granny-style panties under the T-shirt, and, although I couldn't see them through the screen door, I was certain she had on one of her pairs of tan vinyl Velcro-flapped acupressure sandals, plastic insole peeling up from rubber heel.

A word of caution:

Anything and everything I say about my mother will most likely seem unbelievable. You might think I'm exaggerating or lying outright. I'm used to this. I've spent an entire life not being believed when I talk about my mother. But I swear to you, each and every word I say is true.

My mother. Even in her freebie T-shirt, she imagined herself a glorious phoenix risen to elite hills out of barrio chaos. As stoically elegant an image as it was, she'd never considered that being a firebird inevitably meant you'd singe both your nest and baby chick along the way. Still, as much as she'd done me wrong over the years, and damn how she'd done me wrong, I knew that from a public view—not as I saw her—she did seem quite the Wonder Woman. Presumed blue-collar girl from the 'hood, my mother was the first Mexican-American woman ever to graduate from Yale Medical School. Class of '75. And she didn't just graduate, she graduated with honors and acceptance to one of the most prestigious surgery residencies in the country. My mother was an academic and medical genius. She even had impeccable bedside manner. Eventually, she found her true calling and became a sought-after plastic surgeon. And through it all, she was beautiful with big dark brown eyes, a thick mane of shining black hair, and a quick smile. She was the perfect poster girl for a model minority against-all-odds success story.

Granted, it was truly remarkable that she made it to Yale in an era when civil rights and feminism were considered new-fangled nuisances by much of the country. And yes, it was equally impressive that patients traveled from places as far as Portugal to receive her care. But thing was, the poor-little-brown-girl-made-adoring-career-mother role she played in public was a complicated mess of half-truths and dysfunction.

There's no good way to begin explaining. So let's just start with this:

Even though I hadn't stepped foot in her house for five years, I could assure you with absolute certainty that the kitchen cabinets and drawers of her multimillion-dollar home burst forth with a combination of the finest china, crystal, and silver . . . alongside precariously tall stacks of Taco Bell giveaway plastic cups, rubber-banded bundles of broken ballpoint pens, piles of junk-mail envelopes saved to be used as note paper, at least five American Society of Plastic Surgeons coffee mugs, a Botox Cosmetic wine opener, and a seemingly endless supply of Pfizer Post-it notes.

And:

Although my mother's closets were filled with a couture wardrobe, designer jewelry and shoes, it'd been years since she could fully open the door to the master bedroom without knocking over the leaning piles of trash that literally filled the room wall-to-wall. Her queen-sized bed was covered ceiling-high with unopened mail, old medical journals, and drab complimentary magazines sent for her office's waiting room. She slept on a La-Z-Boy recliner in the living room. And she bathed with a washcloth in the front hall bathroom. Why? Because raw sewage seeped up through all the showers in my mother's house.

"It's the septic system. I can't do anything about it," she'd said on countless occasions.

I rather doubted that the other richies in the neighborhood put up with shit flooding their homes. To be fair, I also doubted they'd grown up in as damaged a family as had my mother. But trust me, that knowledge didn't make it any easier to be her kid. Considering how much my mother's screwed-up-ness had interfered with my life, it was really tough to empathize. So, while I wished I could have just loved my mother pure and simple, at least I understood that, even though she shone angelically in public, deep down and in the safety of her home, she was a sad mess in exactly all the ways she was raised to be.

See, my mom came from a long line of sick twisted wealth and seriously perverse notions of love. She grew up in a tight extended family that lived very simply but provided total financial support for life to those who deferred their personal sanity and needs to unfair family rules and expectations. With multiple bank accounts in various names and a net worth reaching into seven digits, the family had more money than they would ever use. Where did all that immigrant barrio dough come from? Mexican Mafia? Drugs? Black market jumping beans?

Official story held that my mother's family had pinched hard-scraped pennies until the copper screamed. But please. You don't get that much money from collecting pennies. Besides, my maternal great-grandparents were Mexicans who had come to the States during the Depression. There weren't any pennies to pinch back then even if you'd wanted to, especially if you were Mexican, doubly if your marriage was the equivalent of that between an American black boy and a Southern white girl, which my great-grandparents' was. My great-grandfather, often mistaken for Japanese in the States, was full-blooded Chichimecca Mexican Indian, and my great-grandmother was green-eyed Michoacán Spanish-ancestry pale. Forget how they had money to burn, it was a wonder they didn't get lynched—either in Mexico or in the States. Years of piecing clues together, eventually I learned that the true source of all the family money came from a blue-collar twist on white-collar crime.

It seems my great-grandfather was an Uncle Tomás. Perfecting what must have been a humiliating role as compliant darkie, he had worked as a scab for Sunkist during their most devastating Depression-era union strikes. As all the company's other immigrant laborers—Mexican, German, and Irish—picketed in the fields and factories, lost the small savings they had, went without food and housing and were forced to return to their home countries, my great-grandfather had worked for the Man. And for his loyalty, the bosses paid him pretty under the table and later gave him breaks on buying up orange groves, company housing, and undeveloped lots when the company was ready to unload them. By the time my mother was born, her family owned acres of orange groves, entire city blocks of houses in their barrio, and clusters of homes all the way north to Sacramento.

In 1955, the family opened a little neighborhood grocery and sundries store. Remember, this was back in the era when signs reading *No Dogs, Niggers, or Wetbacks* were still a common sight in many Southern California store windows. Mexicans had few places to buy necessary goods. My mother's family saw a market need, and so they met it. Plus, confirmed rumor around town was that if you needed a fake green card or papers, that store was the place to go. Located in the heart of the city's barrio, it was a cash business. Hand over fist and into various shoebox stashes and accounts, my mother's family played creative with their taxes and made bags of dough they then invested for even more profit.

Through it all, the family played like they were still as poor as their neighbors. They wore thrift store clothes, drove old rusted cars, and stood in line for government food. They could have eaten out at nice restaurants every meal, but they stocked their pantries with government grub instead. Completely strange and twisted, right? Even more bizarre and contradictory, as they did all these things to blend into their neighborhood, my grandmother insisted my mother lose her inherited accent, attend services at the local United Church of Christ, win 4-H blue-ribbon prizes, and assimilate as best she could. Given this mess of circumstances, no one was too shocked that my grandmother didn't approve when my twenty-year-old mother met my father.

"Don't marry a Mexican," she told my mother.

I don't care if that Francisco boy is fair-skinned and tall. And it makes no difference that he was born in Chicago—he grew up in Mexico, on a farm no less, he has no formal education, and he's poor. Don't you dare love him, she'd meant to say.

"I won't marry Francisco. I promise, Mother," my mother said to hers.

Technically, she kept her word. She and my father never did marry. But they did fall in love. She, an undergrad honors student working long hours in the university research lab, was earning gold stars for med school applications. And he, the lab's minimum-wage assistant (really a glorified guinea pig cage cleaner and toxic chemical janitor), was courting my mother by retrieving coffees for her late at night from the coin-operated vending machine located on the other side of campus. Their flirtation started out so innocently. But the lovey-dovey stars in their eyes brightened and brightened until there was no recourse save for universal expansion.

And so, when my mother received early acceptance to med school across the country, my father asked if she would allow him to come with her. She radiated an excited yes. Boxes were packed, my father got a job in the lab at her new school. Within a year, they were living together. And then they had me.

When I was born, my mother sent my grandmother a photograph. My grandmother—mind you, she took after her father in her dark brown, stocky Mexican Indian appearance—said: "At least she looks white."

It was true; the only trace of Mexican Indian visible in my features was the flatness of my cheekbones. In every other way I'd taken after my father, a man who was living evidence of old Mexico's European colonialization. Like him, I was fair-skinned, hazel-eyed, big-footed, taller-than-short, long-limbed, strong-nosed, and vaguely French-looking. Ironically, it was exactly because I didn't look "Mexican"—because I so entirely resembled my father, the man my grandmother had forbidden my mother to love—that my grandmother resented me.

For the first two years of my life, whenever my grandmother's friends asked if her daughter was enjoying living in Connecticut and how her little granddaughter was doing, she replied that she didn't know, that she didn't have any family living in New England. For real. She said that.

My mother's mother was a grand liar.

Somehow, I don't remember how exactly, my grandmother mentioned to me once that she'd voted for Nixon. Both in 1968 and in 1972. I couldn't understand how she—a woman who read the entire newspaper from front to back each day, a registered Democrat, a Mexican-American living in a working-class neighborhood—could have supported such a conservative prick. It just made no sense to me. So, precocious teenager that I'd been, I tried to discuss the topic with her. Much to her annoyance.

At first I thought maybe she had voted for Nixon because he was a local boy. He'd grown up just a few towns away. Nixon's Yorba Linda birthplace and my grandma's City of

Orange were both old citrus towns. They were sister cities. But I was pretty sure that alone didn't explain her allegiance.

I asked. She didn't answer.

Then I proposed that maybe she had voted for Nixon because of the whole visit to China thing in early 1972. I said I could sort of get that being the reason she liked him because publicly reinitiating relations with a Communist country back then was a seemingly radical thing for a Republican to have done. But, I prodded, even though that may have contributed to her decision to vote for his second term, it still didn't explain why she'd voted for him in 1968.

No reply from my resistant debate partner.

When I learned Nixon was supported through each campaign by evangelical church leaders, things began to make a little more sense, especially considering all the speaking-in-tongues and no-dancing rules of my grandma's strange whitey church. Still, something about the intensity of her loyalty just didn't add up.

It wasn't until 1994 when Nixon died and I saw old press footage on the evening news that it all clicked in my brain. There was a familiar essence to Nixon's face—the flat gleam of his eyes, the drooping jowls, stiff smiles, and that unquantifiable something I recognized from the faces of my mother's family . . . and then I knew. My grandma had Nixon's back because they played the same game—the lying game.

Maybe accomplished liars can pick up the scent of deceitfulness on each other, because I'm pretty sure that even before the Watergate fiasco, my mother's mother had looked at Nixon, and she had known that together they had plenty in common. Both of their families started out working class and scratched upward. Both told pretty lies all the way. Just like Nixon, my mother's family was the Great American Dream come true via the untrue.

By the time I graduated from high school and moved out

of my mother's house, I'd long been unwilling to play along quietly in my maternal family's collective psychosis. But then, five long years later, there I was at my mother's doorstep. Of course, finding those letters at the bank had been the immediate and obvious push for me to go to her house, but my standing in front of my mom that day was something bigger than just that. It was as if my father's death had abruptly reconfigured my existence within a larger genetic framework. The disintegration of my chromosomal matrix had triggered a need for reunion. Finding myself at my mother's house only a handful of days after my father died, with the dead man's ashes actually tucked under my arm no less, was primal chemistry asserting itself involuntarily.

It was like those freak instances when you stretch your back years and years after you did a particularly strong tab of acid, only to suddenly have the traces of illegal chemical stored dormant in your spinal fluid burst active into full-blown glory all over again. Like one of those glowsticks they sell at carnivals, *snap*, all you meant to do was adjust your alignment, but too bad because now you've got hallucinogens rushing your brain and you better just chill and enjoy the ride because you're tripping and seriously spun.

My dad was dead and I missed my mom. I also missed the house I grew up in. I knew the actual fibers of that place by heart. I could walk from cluttered room to room close-eyed without crashing into a single object. Forget unrealistic regressed expectations of some saccharine Hallmark moment, that day I just wanted to be with my mother in her house.

But she was insane. My mother. Truly, she was insane.

"Who are you?" she asked.

Fucking bizarre question. But it got me thinking. Really, who was I? Where to begin? Let's see, for starters . . .

Well, I'd been the human my mother gave birth to in a doomed love affair when she should have been focusing on her med school texts and clinics. And I'd been the toddler she said used to huddle under the kitchen table with an upset stomach in a graduate housing apartment when insults and pots and pans flew through the air. I'd also been the three-year-old whom she, one day when my father was at work, snuck onto a plane and took back with her to Southern California.

And three years later—when she, by then the star member of the acclaimed UCLA surgery residency program, fell in love with a young hotshot anesthesiologist she met on rounds while extracting the compressed shit out of an old man—I'd been the six-year-old she brought along into marriage. My mother's husband was the only child of a wealthy political family—his revered mother, a lawyer like her husband, had been a member of President Carter's cabinet. Add to it all, my stepfather was towheaded and as Waspy as could be. My mother's mother finally approved. We existed in her world again. Our future seemed golden.

I remember thinking I was some sort of royalty when my Prince Charm new stepfather told me I could call him "Chip" as he drove us, his perfect little insta-family, in his cherry-red 1978 Porsche 911 SC Targa to his fancy Laguna Hills home. I'd gone from living in my grandmother's barrio home to living in a multimillion-dollar estate with my own swimming pool and Jacuzzi and private hilltop view.

My father, who had relocated back to Southern California to be close to me and to fight for custody, was a burdensome reminder to my mother of her old life. For a year, each time I returned to the fancy house from my father's court-mandated every-other-weekend and Wednesday night visitation privileges, I was required to strip down to my underwear in the foyer. My mother took my clothes and sleepover bag and placed them in a sealed trash bag in the garage for a day before "disinfecting" them twice in the washing machine with bleach at the hottest setting. She said she did this to kill cockroach eggs on my clothes. I had made the mistake of telling my mother once that I'd seen a giant cockroach outside my father's apartment. So, yes, technically, there were probably cockroaches at his place, but still, she might as well have hosed me down naked in the carport every other weekend and Wednesday night. I was thus filled with deep shame. Not to mention self-loathing.

When I was eight, Chip's parents helped my mother file papers to terminate legally my father's visitation rights. They had no true legal right to do what they did. But they had the pull. They were that powerful. My dad still had to pay child support, but he couldn't see me anymore.

And, presumably because I had become, for all intents and purposes, as Chip said, "his girl," Chip hired a design team to glitz-up my bedroom. Looking back at it, the miniature pied-à-terre that resulted should have been a red flag that he thought of me in ways other than purely parental—which it turned out he definitely did—but no one seemed to think anything strange of it then. All I knew was that I was totally stoked when an interior decorator came over to consult with me, still only eight years old, on possible themes for the renovation. With my approval, we settled on new rattan furniture à la *Three's Company*, what I thought were awesome Hawaiian-print linens, a custom paint job that included an OP-surfer-style sunset on one wall, and adhesive glow-in-the-dark stars on the ceiling in a perfect recreation of the Milky Way. Construction workers installed a bar sink and dorm-sized refrigerator (blended into my bedroom with tiki bar rattan accents and forever stocked with those cool squat eight-ounce cans of Coke and vacuum-sealed glass jars of macadamia nuts). One corner of my room held an entertainment system that consisted of not only a turntable and speakers but also a remote control color television with stereo sound. I even got my own phone line and answering machine.

I felt so damned grown-up. A third-grader missing two front teeth, I was crowned an American princess.

On most weekends, Chip, my mother, and I drove up to a super snooty section of hilly suburban Los Angeles to visit Chip's parents. They held dinners and introduced us to congressmen, senators, and a hodgepodge of renowned musicians, artists, and other famed people. Two quirky examples I loved to brag about when I was a kid: my step-grandma knew astronauts, and she'd met Andy Warhol once (she'd been bombed on wine—as she often was—the night they met, according to an entry in Warhol's later published diaries). Sir Edmund Hillary, drunk and sans the Sherpa who really reached the summit first, posed for a Polaroid with me by my stepgrandparents' fireplace for my Famous World Figure social sciences report in fourth grade. Official NASA satellite photographs illustrated my planet report in sixth grade.

I glowed in limelight. I traveled. I sat front row at rock concerts. I wore cashmere sweaters and drank from a crystal glass filled with Martinelli's Sparkling Apple Cider at the fancy yuppie wine-tasting parties we hosted in our home. Chip liked to play Frisbee golf on the weekends. He also had a thing for secretly snorting pharmaceutical coke lifted from hospital holdings. Hippocratic Oath and all human ethics out the window, by the time I was nine, Chip had taken to drugging and fucking his prepubescent stepdaughter in the middle of the night.

And my mother dared ask who I was?

Well, I'd been the little girl who woke inexplicably groggy and aching and sad in the mornings, who still managed to always keep her braids combed tidy, to tuck her shirt in, to say thank you and generally sit politely when told to. I'd been the one who worked like a dog in school to get high marks so my mother would be proud of me. I'd been the strange kid who cried at her desk before elementary school exams from the anxiety of trying to be perfect.

I'd also been the child Chip came home to once after a shift in the ER and told about a little boy he'd worked on the night before.

"It was like he melted, Francisca," he said.

Chip told me that the little boy's father had taken his only son to a motel room, poured gasoline on him, thrown a lit match, and left him to burn to death. Firefighters found the boy and put out the flames before he died, but not before his entire body was covered in third-degree burns. He would live. The father would go to prison for sure.

"Monster," Chip said, presumably in reference to the boy's father.

And then he sat across from me at the kitchen table and cried. I continued eating my Tony the Tiger cereal afternoon snack. And I know this is sick, but I wished I had third-degree burns from head to toe like the little boy. I fantasized about being in the hospital, about being covered in gauze and icepacks, about IV tubes sticking out of me and machines keeping me alive. I wanted nurses and doctors frantically flitting about treating me. I fantasized about suffering unearthly brutal but easily diagnosed pain. I daydreamed about Chip being arrested and spending the rest of his life in prison.

So, who was I?

I'd been the person who knew best how full of shit my mother's airs of impeccability were. She, entirely invested in surface—sculpting, plump-injecting, and laser-beam smoothing other people's aging bodies, perfecting the false flawless mask she herself put on each day—probably would have stayed married to Chip forever if it had been an option. Given the opportunity, she would have stuck by his side and taken endless holiday card portraits smiling with him in matching sweaters next to the Christmas tree. But, in a glaringly public addition to his early midlife crisis, he'd had an affair with a nurse coworker and then served my mother with divorce papers. It was so pathetically *Seven Year Itch*.

My mother refused to sign the divorce papers. Shut down and totally depressed, she diagnosed herself with Epstein Barr Virus. Desperate for company, I guess, she told me that I too was seriously ill with the virus. After months of her insistent, persistent diagnosis, I gave in.

January 1986:

Bedridden and covered in severe hives that I'd somehow manifested as medical proof of what an obedient kid I was, I watched hours and hours of live news coverage leading up to the Challenger shuttle launch. I was completely fascinated with NASA stuff, with knowing every little detail about the preparations and equipment and crew. I liked the science teacher guest astronaut who gave thumbs-up and big smiles at press conferences. She looked like she'd be a cool teacher, unlike the ones who threatened to fail me for the countless days of eighth grade curriculum I'd missed that year. I woke so damned excited the day of the launch. I sat right in front of my bedroom television, volume all the way up, glued to the set, counting down with Ground Control. And then . . . well, you know what happened.

I watched the explosion and all the instant replays. And I sobbed. Uncontrollably. Hives in my throat swelled from the stress. I couldn't breathe. My mom wasn't home. She was meeting with her lawyer that day. I was alone. My windpipe constricting, I gasped for air. Several seconds passed. Blue specks and white streamers filled my line of vision. My ears felt heavy. I heard buzzing. The sound in my left ear went out entirely. I was unable to inhale a full breath. I gasped. I was going to pass out. Panicked, I reached for the EpiPen my mother had left in my room in anticipation of such an event.

She had explained how to use the clunky penlike contraption when she first diagnosed me with hives.

"The EpiPen is filled with 0.3 milligrams of epinephrine, a dose sufficient to halt a grown man's anaphylaxic reaction. The syringe is spring-loaded and automatic. Just press the tip of the pen to your outer thigh until you hear it click. Count to thirty. It'll inject on its own," she'd lectured with a slight glimmer in her eye.

The hives were visibly worsening. Dizzy, my hands tingling and losing sensation, I yanked up my pajama boxer shorts and jabbed the pen against my thigh. The pain was immediate. Stinging medicine flowed hot up my leg toward my heart. I massaged the spot of injection to sooth what I was sure would become a bruise.

Within seconds, my hives subsided. I could breathe again.

But I couldn't stay awake. I fell asleep. I slept and slept. And slept some more. Lurid images of explosions filled my dreamless brain. Everything was too much. Everything. I simply didn't want to be awake anymore.

"What in God's name is wrong with you?" my mother asked when she got home.

"I used the pen. I'm sleepy," I said.

After a few more days of my endless sleep, my mother— my sole physician and guardian—reached into her bag of tricks, diagnosed me with mononucleosis, told me to stay in bed, wrote a letter withdrawing me from school indefinitely for medical reasons, disconnected my phone line, told my friends who stopped by that I couldn't come to the door, and said I'd enroll at a private middle school once I was better.

And I was the sick one?

I was thirteen and I was angry, and being angry made me brave. Memories came back to me from the deep haze they'd hidden in. Simultaneously numb and scared, I told my mother what Chip had done to me. She listened, looked at me with blank eyes, and forbade me to tell anyone else.

"Don't complicate the situation, Francisca," she said. "We risk losing too much, especially now."

Central to my required "proactive cooperation," as she called it, was maintaining all appearances of loyalty to Chip as my father.

"The court needs to know you miss him, that you think of him as your father. Your *only* father," she said.

I was forbidden from reinitiating contact with Francisco.

"When you turn eighteen, you can make your own decisions on this matter. But honestly, I don't know why you would want to associate with such trash," she said.

And so, just like that, I became the kid she wished she'd never taught to speak. She said this often, as an aside, as if I was a mouthy brat, which I wasn't. She said it with a smile and slight laugh—to her colleagues, to her patients, to the gas attendant dude, to whomever would listen to her supposedly innocent maternal teasing. They'd laugh with her, charmed by her as they always were.

During the divorce proceedings my mother fought for the house—the house I'd been repeatedly raped in. I told her I wanted to move. "Don't *you* want to move?" I asked. I pleaded. Blind fury, she fought tooth and nail for her society-marriage-expensive-house-wronged-wife martyrdom.

"I absolutely refused to let him have the house, for Francisca's sake," she later liked to say. "I wasn't going to let him rob our baby of her home."

Years and years of bullshit and lies, but still, when my father died, some part of me wanted nothing more than to sit on my mother's living room couch and rub elbows with her—of course, even that fantasy wasn't untainted by reality. Even if she had let me inside her house to sit down, I hated the couch in her living room. When I was fifteen, two of her rich patients had delivered that particular hand-me-down from their garage.

Why? Because we had no furniture.

Two years post-divorce, Prince Charm had come to the house with a court order permitting him to select and claim possession of items he'd left behind in his frenzied departure when insufficient blood was reaching his brain. He strolled through the house with his young-nurse-fake-tits-trophy-wife and pointed to things for moving guys to carry out to trucks parked in the carport. Total asshole, Chip didn't even need any of the stuff he took. He'd been gone for two years, he already had a new house with all new things. That day was pure power trip.

A man who wouldn't know how to prepare a meal to save his life, Chip took the ice-cube-dispensing refrigerator from the kitchen, the Cuisinart, the Krups coffee grinder, and most of our pots and pans. He pointed to our cool kidney-shaped couch and it disappeared from the house along with a few matching modernist chairs. He took throw pillows and several lamps. And when he ordered the movers to pack the living room's custom-length curtains, sun glared in and revealed dented spots on the carpet where furniture should have been, scuffs where framed photographs had decorated walls, cobwebs exposed in what had been, just minutes before, dark hidden corners. He took all the master bedroom furniture. He even pushed past me to retrieve the headboard, nightstand, vanity, stereo, and television from *my* bedroom.

As I watched Chip move through my room and pile up my things for the movers to carry away, scenes from old *Waltons* episodes played in my brain. Back then, I watched reruns of that show religiously, and my favorite episode was the one where the young redheaded freckle-faced Walton girl turns thirteen and gets all these spooky witchy powers and shutters slam when she's mad and chairs skitter across the floor when she doesn't get her way. It was like, *whoa*, a girl starts to bleed and watch out, she's dangerous and devil-possessed. I think it was a Halloween special. Scared the shit out of me. I loved it.

My stupid ex-stepfather was in my bedroom, stealing all my things. I figured it was worth a shot to try to conjure spirits and demons and whatever else might come to the aid of a pissed-off fifteen-year-old kid. I hated Chip so fucking much. I focused hard and willed any supernatural power I might possess to strike him down. Gilded golden boy, he drove away that day without a scratch.

And then, about a week after Chip emptied out our house, two of my mother's fancy patients, a husband and wife, brought their old furniture, including a crap-brown couch, to our house. My mother had learned the faux-poverty grovel bullshit family game from her mother perfectly. She thanked her patients profusely and nudged me to do the same, to play like we were humble inferiors dependent on the kindness of strangers. It was fucking humiliating. I recognized the looks on their faces from early in my childhood.

Once when I was young my grandmother took me on her weekly trip to get government food at the barrio community service building, the Friendly Center. As we stood in line, my grandmother's neighbors, usually so chatty, didn't talk to us or even look at us. But the do-gooders who volunteered at the Friendly Center and distributed the cardboard boxes of cheese and giant tubs of peanut butter, they looked at us— like they were examining us for defects. I remember watching the wheels in their heads turn as they tried to figure out why I, seemingly a little white girl, was there with an old Mexican woman.

I could almost hear them processing: *Oh, she must be the girl's nanny.*

And then: *So help me God, if our nanny took my baby with her to get handouts, I'd have the woman deported.*

When my grandmother told me to help her carry some heavy cans of white-labeled government applesauce, the volunteers watched with what could only be described as disgusted disapproval. But it was their initial expressions of pity and superiority that came back to haunt me on my mother's patients' faces.

They looked at us like we were pathetic. And my mother thanked them in return.

My mother confounded me.

Apparently, the sentiment was mutual.

"Who are you?" she had the nerve to ask.

I was the child she probably wished she'd never had. I was a person who wanted out of the life I was born into. But there was one thing I most definitely wasn't . . .

I was *not* my mother's daughter.

Time had come that even she, queen of false reality, couldn't help but see the man—granted, awkward and still somewhat gawky—I'd become. All through my adolescence she had tried to convince herself that my ever-more-confident boyness was only some sort of *unfortunate phase*. For years, she picked apart my layers of oversized boy clothes, my short haircuts, my ever-failing attempts to deepen my voice, the way I hunched my shoulders to hide any visible curve of my small breasts—she scrutinized all of this as if she were making a diagnosis. She showered me with mean criticisms veiled as motherly advice about my supposed lack of grace and untapped beauty. I rarely managed to articulate any sort of response in my own defense. All I knew was that I was a boy and that being a boy felt safe and true and right.

As a teenager, I desperately wanted to leave my mother. I dreamed about running away or filing for emancipation, but she would have never allowed it. She'd have sent me away to juvie on trumped-up charges before she would let me embarrass her by showing the world I wanted to get away. I knew I'd have to wait until I was eighteen to leave. My friends told me I should apply for early admission to universities on the East Coast and have her foot the bill for my freedom. They so didn't get it. I mean, sure I wanted to go to college, I'd busted my ass getting perfect marks all through school, but I knew my mother would continue somehow to control me for as long as I was doing things her way. And going to college like a good kid was most definitely doing things her way. Stupid and self-defeating as it may have ultimately been, I wrote off college. I wish I'd known a way to take her money, go to university, and flip her off all the same time, but I didn't. So, starting in my junior year, I worked after school and on weekends and all summer long. I saved money. Neurotic over-achiever, I still earned all A's and even graduated high school "Most Likely to Succeed." But the second I graduated, I used my savings to move to L.A., where I got a new job and worked more and saved less money, but finally slept well at night.

Being away from my mother for five years was one of the best gifts anyone could have ever given me. But then my dad died and I had his ashes and I was exhausted and I'd read those letters at the bank, and damnit, there I was at my mother's house. Part of me had hoped she might show at least a little kindness. I needed that from her. I really did.

Instead, I got: "What do you want? Money?"

"No, Mom . . ."

"Wait," she said and disappeared into the house, the screen door still locked.

She returned, cracked the screen door open, and pushed her manicured hand through, a thick roll of cash in her fingers. The top bill was a hundred. It was safe to assume the rest were too. Strange knowledge I'd gained from my mother's family, I could eyeball a wad of cash and accurately estimate how much was there without even needing to hold it, let alone count it out. My mother was pushing approximately five thousand dollars at me. Same as her family, she was desperate for control and more than willing to buy it.

"Here," she said.

"I don't want it, Mom."

"Take it."

Fuck, what would you do? Honestly. If someone was shoving thousands of dollars at you and you could just waltz away that much richer with nothing required of you, no debt incurred (of course, the situation would never be so simple as that)—what would you do?

"Thank you," I said. Perfunctorily. And took the money.

And then she said: "Do you realize what people say about you?" Her eyes scanned me up and down.

Forget apron strings attached, the money I'd already tucked in my jeans pocket—like any other support my mother had ever given me—came with a noose. Payment for abuse, past and present. Hush money. Blood money. Retribution funds.

I had my money. And I should have done the walking-away part. I should have held my head high and left. But I didn't. Instead, I dug in my heels and refused to budge. I was hungry for kind words, one warm hug of reassurance, a single atom of unconditional maternal approval and kindness. Clearly the woman was incapable of giving me these things, but I argued my case one last time. I spoke quietly and calmly at first, then, mounting frustration, my hand trying to open the screen that blocked my entry into her home, into her heart, I begged please to be let in. My voice loud and strained, I cried and pleaded with my mother to please, please, please let me in.

My screen-door-pixilated mother edged away and paused to signal that the end, the absolute not-another-word finale was about to hit. And then, almost whispering, the ultimate of insults from her, she said: "You have your father's blood in you."

I half expected her to cross her nonpracticing Protestant self for protection before she closed the front door with a purposeful push. She didn't slam the door. Uptight repressed tragedy, even then, even as she essentially orphaned her child, her only child, even then my mother didn't let her emotions rage. Strangely, her lack of emotional display was itself just for show. She didn't want any neighbors who might be looking down from their own hilly views to catch sight of her slamming the door on the miserable horned creature standing on her *Welcome* mat.

Horns. Yes, I'm certain I had horns emerging from my temples. My father did too. God-fearing woman that she was raised to be, my mother had always insisted she hated my devil father from the day they met.

"Actually," she once said, "at first I pitied him."

What a romance love story: First comes pity, then comes marriage, then comes little me all pink blanket and bouncing baby carriage. Perfect. Take a snapshot and put it in each and every tacky gold picture frame sold in dime stores across the country. Buy the frame and get the dream.

She said, "You have your father's blood in you," and I saw in her eyes all the times my father had grabbed her tiny wrists and forced her to listen, the times he had screamed and thrown things against walls. I was not violent, but, unforgivable as it was, I did understand why my father had snapped with anger at her. The way she refused to speak when she disagreed and didn't think you worth her time—it drove me mad, the holier-than-thou air she doused herself with in the way some people wear perfume. Not just a spritz behind the ears or the backs of the knees, or a polite little cloud walked into. No, my mother poured herself big tubs of righteousness and soaked ritualistically. She was rigid and bloated from such long baths of stoic false humility.

And still, I had wanted her to let me in.

A thick wad of money in my pocket, my father's ashes tucked under my arm, I walked back down my mother's tortuous driveway to my car. There was nothing to stay around for.

CHAPTER SIX

From my mother's house, I got on the I-5 north and drove directly to the lawyer's office.

"Something's come up," I told him. "Can you sell my dad's house and whatever?"

"That's why he retained me, Ms. Cruz."

I stood at his desk, holding the compact box the funeral home had given me.

"My dad wanted his ashes in the Pacific," I said, knowing full well my dad had never said any such thing.

"Would you like me to arrange those details also?"

"Yes. Please."

One final tap of my fingers on the box of ashes (how does one show affection to a box of ashes?), I handed over my father's remains.

By the time I got back in my car it was nearly five, but still the sun was relentless. Bright light blasted through the windshield and forced me to squint the entire way to my father's house. Irony was that by the time I arrived, my pupils were so constricted that I felt particularly worthy of the first item I retrieved:

A red-tipped white walking stick. From the hallway coatrack. I tucked the folded-up cane in my hand and continued to my father's bedroom. Blind man dark glasses from his bureau, golden little worry stone from the nightstand—I placed these on the rented hospital bed and sat to rest for a second.

My suits would fit you nicely, I swear I heard my father say.

His presence shivered me.

"I don't wear suits," I said aloud. As if he could hear me. I think he could.

Take them. Think about it later.

Considering I was filled with guilt over leaving his ashes at the lawyer's, I felt inclined to obey. I had no idea when I'd ever wear his fancy clothes, but I went to his closet, gathered his suits, a few dress shirts, and lay them next to the small pile of his things on the bed.

A gentleman needs proper accoutrements.

Gentleman? Me? Hardly. More like skater rat, but still, I wondered, had he understood more than I'd given him credit for? If he had, then why the birthday gift with *Paquita, Birthday Girl* . . .

The fedoras and pocket squares. Take them too. And my briefcase.

Again, I did as told.

My father's suits draped over the hook of my left arm, and his cane, glasses, and the worry stone safely packed in the serious-looking Secret Agent Man black leather briefcase in my right hand, I walked downstairs. At the second to final step, the atmospheric pressure was suddenly wrong. Bright blue sparkles filled my eyes. Pins and needles flowed through my veins. I started to hyperventilate. Try as I did, I couldn't get a proper breath in. The suits and briefcase fell from my grip to the floor. I stumbled to the couch and sat. No, that wasn't good enough. I lay on the couch, my feet stuck on the carpeted floor, my torso and legs forming a twisted right angle. I closed my eyes. Fuck, I was going to black out and choke on my own tongue and froth at the mouth and die and nobody would find me until the lawyer sent people to clear out my dad's house. I was so going to die. That was it. I was dead. I was totally dead.

Minutes later, still very much alive, no longer woozy, with no audience to applaud my maudlin misery, yet able to breathe properly once again, I opened my eyes. And that's when I saw the large manila padded envelope. *Paquita, Birthday Girl*. Hot tears filled my eyes. Practically the second he'd died, I'd remembered the safe deposit key on my keychain and gone to the bank, but I'd all but forgotten about the envelope with the retablo and book my father had given me. I was such an asshole.

Still lying in an uncomfortable right-angle position—it was the least I could do to suffer a little as punishment for my prickish oversight—I leaned over and picked up the envelope. As I opened it, the book slid onto my chest. I reached into the envelope and pulled out the retablo.

Sweet mercy. Those eyes again. They were truly hypnotic. Staring into the blissfully brutal assault of Nahui Olin's eyes, I managed to think clearly through the noise of blood pounding in my head.

I understood what my father's mother must have felt when looking into those eyes. And why my father couldn't help but follow in his mother's footsteps. It hit me then— without question, my mother had been for my father what Nahui had been for his mother. And as much as it grossed me out to think of my mother in this way, I had to admit that, indeed, she did have the stare. Her entire life she'd used it to seduce, charm, and control. It occurred to me that my mother might hate me most simply for refusing to fall under her spell.

I opened Nahui's book. I wanted to read her poems, but my Spanish was rocky at best, and her pseudo-scientific poetic diatribe was more effort than my brain could afford. About to put the book down, I stumbled upon the peeling art deco bookplate pasted on the inside back cover. Written in Spanish was:

> My love,
>   *"She went through me like a pavement saw."*
>   *Yours as ever for the revolution,*
>   *Nahui*

My eyes lingered over the inscription written so long ago—to my father's mother?

Had my father even known about the inscription? He must have.

Fuck.

I put the book down and picked up the retablo again.

"He's dead," I said.

As I admitted this fact aloud for the first time, I was certain Nahui Olin reached out to me, to my exhausted and totally senseless body. She held me. I cried. And cried some more.

When no more tears came, I knew it was time. I'd take what my father had given me and go further than he'd ever known possible.

CHAPTER SEVEN

Back at my apartment a couple hours later, I tore through my closet and dresser, threw stuff on the floor next to my father's suits and hats, and packed whatever would fit in the two large maroon Sergio Valente suitcases I'd taken from my dad's garage. Everything zipped up and ready to go, I placed the birthday envelope containing Nahui Olin's retablo and book, along with the cash my mother had given me, in my father's . . . in *my* briefcase next to the cane, blind man glasses, and little stone.

Now came the pain-in-the-ass part.

Phone in hand, I dialed the number I'd called far too many times in the past several months. My boss . . .

"'ello," he answered.

I'd always hated how he acted like it was a private line, not the store's office number.

"Joe?"

"Yeah?"

"This is Frank."

"Yeah?"

"I'm really sorry for the short notice, but I won't be working any more shifts."

"You haven't been around much anyway. It's all good," he said and yawned.

I felt a swell of both hatred and gratitude in response. What a prick for acting like I'd been flaking on shifts for kicks. I'd been taking care of my father, my dying father, for fuck's sake. Still, I was glad Joe couldn't care less. When it came down to it, I was happy to avoid another confrontation.

"Okay, well, thanks," I said.

"Later," he said. And hung up.

I only hoped the next necessary task would end up going as smoothly.

"Guys?"

My roomies were sitting on our living room's crappy IKEA couch, studying in unison.

"What's up?" Ted asked.

In one exhale, I blurted: "I'm moving out."

"Why?" Jen said, confusion and maybe a hint of hurt in her voice.

"Well, it's that . . . I just need to is all."

"Alright," she said with a gentle nod, "do what you need to do."

Although our relationship had always been mostly surface and pragmatic niceties, Jen was a momma bear by nature. She was the person all her friends came to when they needed a shoulder to soak in tears and snot. She'd been the head cheerleader in high school—not only because she was the prettiest girl in her town, and not only because she wanted to hang with the jocks and popular kids, but because she truly loved cheering people on. She was just like that, pure benevolence. Even though I'm sure it sucked to receive essentially no notice about losing my share of rent, she genuinely wanted me to be happy. Besides—I tried to soothe myself as I prepared to leave the lovebirds high and dry—Ted and Jen would dig having to the apartment to themselves. At least for a while. Until they found another roommate or had a baby or did whatever it was they had scheduled for the next segment of their five-year plan.

"Any chance you two still want to buy my car?" I asked, hoping my luck would hold.

In the few years I'd lived with them, any time I'd complained about my piece-of-shit car, they'd joked that they'd gladly buy it off me. Ted and Jen were a bicycle-and-two-bus-passes couple. In Los Angeles. And they went to school full-time crosstown. A set of wheels would absolutely come in handy. But only if the clunker came at a bargain rate. "We're starving students, after all," Ted always added before punching me in the arm and offering one of his guffaw laughs. Total dork, but sweet.

"For cheap?" Ted asked and laughed his laugh.

Jen looked at me all bright-eyed hopeful.

Their babies would be so damned jovial.

"If you drive me to the airport," I said, "it's yours for three hundred dollars."

I figured the low asking price was the least I could do by way of peace offering.

"Seriously?"

"Totally."

"Sounds good to me. Thanks, man."

"Cool. Give me ten minutes."

"Whoa . . . you want to go to the airport *now*?"

"Can you take a break from studying?"

"Wait, you're moving *today*?" Jennifer asked, more than a little concerned.

"Yeah. I hope that's okay . . ."

"Well, whatever you need," Momma Bear replied. "But what about your furniture?"

Somehow I hadn't thought past two suitcases and a briefcase. There was my futon. Linens. A garage sale dresser and the mirror I'd installed on the back of the bedroom door. A lamp. Minor stuff.

"Do you want it?"

"You'll need it, Frank."

"I'd rather leave it."

They could chop up my furniture and use my blankets for kindling and host living room campfire sing-alongs with S'mores if it made them happy. I just wanted to go. With as little baggage as negotiable. As soon as possible.

"When's your flight?" Ted asked.

"Don't know. I'll get a ticket at the airport."

"Do you know *where* you're going?"

To the place furthest from where I was. Antarctica? Or maybe Mexico? No, silly. Manhattan, of course.

"New York," I said.

"Do you have a place to stay?"

As kind as they were being, the parental unit act was beginning to annoy me.

I sort of snapped: "Why?"

"An old college buddy of mine lives in the East Village and wants to sublet," Ted said with a shrug of his shoulders.

Nice guy that he was, Ted called his friend. And it was settled. I'd have a place to look at when I arrived.

Half an hour later, just after eight, the sun barely starting to set, the three of us piled into what would be my car for only a very short while still. We stopped at an ATM en route to the freeway. Ted withdrew three hundred bucks. I slipped the car keys off my key chain, handed them to Ted, signed over the title, and took a seat in the back. Ted hopped on the freeway and drove us to the airport. When we got to LAX, he offered to park and said that he and Jen would be more than happy to go with me to the ticket counter and hang out until my flight. I thanked him, but asked if he could just stop at an unloading curb instead.

"If you insist. Which airline?"

"Any one, I guess."

My hands started to sweat and I felt panic swelling up. Shit, what was I doing?

Just in time, right before I could freak and change my mind, Ted pulled up in front of American and helped me haul my monster-huge suitcases to the curb. Hugs all around. Jen made me promise to call if I needed anything, then started crying. Why hadn't we been good friends before? If I was going to go, I realized I better do it quick. And so I did.

Inside I bought a discounted standby ticket, a red-eye direct to JFK. The whole fucking thing was kismet.

At 11:25 P.M., I boarded the plane.

It wasn't until after I'd settled into my seat that I looked at my boarding pass and noticed the date. June 21. Summer solstice. The longest day of the year. No fucking shit.

CHAPTER EIGHT

The second I'd claimed my luggage at JFK, I found a pay phone and called Ted's friend. He gave me an address—150 East 7th Street, between avenues A and B (as if I knew what that meant)—and said, with total sincerity, that he was so sorry but he wouldn't be able to meet me until nine.

"Tonight?" I asked, hoping he meant in half an hour instead.

"Yeah, really I'm sorry, *tonight*."

I had twelve long hours to kill. With two huge suitcases. And this was in the prehistoric era so very long ago when dinosaurs roamed the earth and not all suitcases came outfitted with wheels. But what was I going to do? It wasn't as if I could tell this friend of Ted's who was doing me a huge favor, *Fuck you, get there NOW because I'm ready to put my bags down already* . . . No, of course I couldn't say that. So, I thanked him profusely and said I was looking forward to meeting him. Then, the awkwardly distributed bulk of my briefcase and two suitcases nearly pulling my arms out of their sockets, I proceeded to bumble around like an idiot tourist lost in the big city amidst what was, at barely 9 A.M., already an insanely hot and humid summer day.

First thing first, I had to get out of JFK. No way was I going to waste money on a cab, but all my Los Angeles "I'm not some country bumpkin" ego and posturing aside, I knew shit about the subways. Somehow I figured out how to catch the airport shuttle bus to the Howard Beach station. There I paid for tokens, got on the A train, missed my stop at Jay Street, got off the train, got on another train headed back to Jay Street, went two stops too far, got off the fucking train again, got back on a Manhattan-bound train, disembarked at Jay Street like I was supposed to the first time, transferred to an F, exited at Second Avenue, and, hallelujah, finally made it up the stairs to a steaming high noon Houston Street. The air was thick with exhaust and the stench of sewers, I was soaked in sweat, my shoulders were cramped, and my hands throbbed from the weight of my suitcases. But I was ecstatic.

Hoping to find an air-conditioned booth I could rent for a handful of hours by purchasing a coffee with refills, I quickly learned that Manhattan waitress stink-eye came free of charge with slowly sipped beverages. So I trekked from one air-conditioned diner to the next, buying mug after mug of coffee, staying at each booth no more than an hour. I was drenched with sweat all over again each short journey between diners, and I turned clammy cold every time I settled into a new batch of cold processed air. But I was nonetheless loving my first New York day. Still, I have to admit, I did look forward to the sun setting—both because then I'd get to see the apartment and because I figured it would blessedly cool down outside like it always did on summer nights back home.

The sun did eventually set, but the temperature and humidity didn't budge. And, as I finally walked to the apartment to meet Ted's buddy, it struck me that I really had no clue about the foreign world I'd landed in. I didn't know the climate, the layout, nothing.

Some things, I learned, were universal—the type of apartment one could get for the amount of money I was willing to spend, for instance. Ted's friend's microscopic studio was, generously speaking, total crap—as was all the stuff he said he needed to leave in the place for at least the time being. As shitty as the furniture was, I didn't have any of my own, so it was a positive in some twisted way.

But, he warned: "The super doesn't know I'm subletting. So you'd have to be quiet about it, okay?"

"No problem."

I stood at the curtainless apartment windows. The Empire State Building was visible to the north and all lit up glowing white electric brilliance like a postcard come to life. Added bonus, the southern edge of Tompkins Square Park was practically right under the windows. The trees, there were so many gorgeous trees in that park. I don't know what I'd expected exactly, but I know I didn't think I'd find an apartment where I could practically reach out a window and touch the leaves and branches of huge, hundred-year-old elms and oaks. Earlier, I'd even seen hawks circling overhead. And then, still taking in the view, I caught sight of an ethereal, almost spooky, fuzzy patch of flickering lights in the park.

"Trippy," I said. I was immediately embarrassed to have said it out loud.

"What?"

"That," I said, and nodded toward the low-to-the-ground on-and-off sparkles.

"Fireflies," he said, very matter-of-fact.

I wasn't sure I believed him. Yeah, I guess the lights could have been fireflies. But I would have been equally convinced they were fairies, or even Nahui Olin maybe, dancing in my magic forest, welcoming me to a dream come true.

"They renovated a few years ago," Ted's buddy continued, in response to my speechless fixated stare into the park. "With the band shell torn down, you can see the Temperance Fountain from here."

He pointed to a barely visible stone gazebo structure just northwest of the park's center.

"This used to be Little Germany," he said. "Back in 1891,

some dude built the Temperance Fountain so people would drink ice water instead of booze. Racist crap, but the fountain is sort of cool. Too many junkies there at night, but check it out sometime."

Okay, so maybe the park wasn't exactly the Garden of Eden, but the lit-up city was still completely ethereal and stunning to my L.A. eyes.

"So, you interested?" Ted's buddy asked.

"Totally," I said.

"Awesome."

We talked money. I handed over the cash. He gave me keys. We shook hands.

"The sheets are clean," he said. "Use the dishes, towels, whatever you want. Push stuff out of the way if you need to, no worries."

"Cool, thanks."

He left. And I had a New York apartment.

No matter how fantastic a view is, it's inevitably a good idea to take a little break from admiring it after a few hours. So eventually I left the window. With how exhausted I was from the flight and everything else, I had zero desire to unpack. But I felt I should at least make an attempt. I opened my briefcase and took out the padded envelope. I leaned the retablo of Nahui Olin against the windowsill. I didn't get much further—in fact, I barely grabbed Nahui's book from the briefcase and kicked off my shoes before flopping down on the bed.

A dix ans sur mon pupitre. Nahui Olin. 1924.

It was so strange. I still wasn't sure why my father had given me the book. The retablo, I totally understood. But the book was like a puzzle. And the fucking inscription on the back cover:

My love,
    "She went through me like a pavement saw."
                    Yours as ever for the revolution,
                            Nahui

Talk about cryptic. And the *revolution*? What revolution? Questions flooding my brain, my eyelids turned heavy. Fuck, I was tired. I wanted someone to tuck me in and give me a kiss on the forehead and praise me and tell me how brave I was being. Just under the layers of exhaustion from travel and the thrill at having arrived in New York, there was very tangible uncertainty. I could feel it on my tongue. It tasted metallic like a zinc tablet. It made me salivate and gag a little. Maybe I'd made the wrong decision. Maybe it was more chickenshit of me to leave California than it would have been for me to stay. I wished I could have called my dad because then he could have told me if this was how it felt when he left Mexico. There was something soothing in knowing that even though I'd left Los Angeles with crap for a plan and only a vague notion of destination, my father would have understood why I felt compelled to go and never look back. Of course, inevitably, exactly because I was trying to run forward with blinders firmly in place, I was completely preoccupied with all that existed just beyond the peripheries of what I knew. I wanted to sleep and get rested so I could wake up early in the morning and start in on my new future, but— winding, repetitive, stumbling thoughts—I found myself trying to piece together an unknown past instead.

Exactly how did my father's mother know Nahui Olin? It made absolutely no sense to me. Just from looking at her, it was obvious Nahui had been a fancy-pants boho artist from a rich family. And from what I knew, my dad's mom had been a simple working woman to her dying day. Day in, day out, she had worked alongside my father on their small farm until he left for Vietnam and then the States. He said she'd go into town for church on Sundays, but that was about it. And any time she wasn't in church or the fields, she was in her little house, cooking or washing or sleeping too few hours. So where'd she meet Nahui? I found it highly unlikely that Nahui was a church friend. My father told me once that his mother had cleaned houses in town before he was born. And she did again after he headed north. Maybe that was how they knew each other? Had my father's mother cleaned Nahui Olin's house?

I'll *send more money*, my father told me he'd written his mother when he found out she was cleaning houses in the city. *You shouldn't have to do that kind of work.*

I've done it before. It's honest work, she had written back and refused more of his money.

He said he'd hated thinking about her knees bruised and hands shriveled from long hours of scrubbing other people's floors and windows. Each day she must have left exhausted and with still more work to do in her own home and neglected fields. She must have looked dead in her eyes those days, he'd said. But maybe she didn't. Maybe everything my father thought he'd known about his mother had been wrong. Maybe, yes, she had cleaned the houses of rich people when she was young, but maybe, just maybe—my eyelids fell shut, my breathing slowed—maybe just maybe . . .

★

"Consuela, I wrote this for you," Nahui Olin said. And startled my father's mother out of her daze.

The year was 1943. Very pregnant and prone to such moments of being caught in daydream, my father's mother was at the zócolo to give a final prayer at the church she'd attended each Sunday of her life. She would start for Chicago the next morning. The thought of leaving behind everything she knew filled her with dread. But there was nothing she could do. "We are going," her husband had said. And she knew they needed to. Forty-six cents an hour for legal work up north—it was the sort of opportunity they couldn't let slip by.

Easily tired with my father inside her, she was nonetheless still strong. And determined, same as her husband. Tall, muscular, and broad-shouldered, he'd been an obvious hire for the railroad company, but the recruiter had looked at his young wife's protruding belly and had wanted to hire only him. Disgusted to have to play such games, she batted her eyelashes and, a convincing smile lighting up her pretty face, flexed the muscles of her right arm for show: "I promise, I am a good worker."

She signed the paperwork along with her husband.

And cried herself to sleep that night.

Something tragic was waiting for them. There had been signs. Only hours after she'd been hired, she had seen warning in the pueblo curandera's eyes.

"Will you please bless my babies?" she had asked when she arrived at the curandera's home with her toddler daughter in tow.

"Of course," the curandera had said, and invited them in. "Sit, please." She motioned to her one chair and then to the clean-swept dirt floor beside it for the girl.

The curandera kneeled in front my father's mother. One hand on her pregnant round stomach, the other hand on the little girl's head, the old woman closed her eyes and breathed slowly, the deep wrinkles of her face smoothing as she concentrated. This quiet stillness continued for minutes.

And then: "No!" The curandera yanked her hands away as if she'd felt fire.

"The baby?" my father's mother asked nervously, her hands moving in an instinctive, protective gesture to her middle.

"It is a boy," the curandera said. And then she stared at the little girl and refused to say more.

The next morning, the curandera visited my father's mother.

"This is for the girl," she said, and handed over three slices of candied sweet yam. "Give her some each night before she sleeps."

"Is she sick?" my father's mother asked.

"And this is for you, Consuela," the curandera continued without answering. She handed my father's mother a powder of crushed chamomile flowers and roasted chili peppers. "Mix it with hot water. Drink one cup each morning at sunrise until the baby is born."

"Thank you."

"Go to church before you leave. Pray," the curandera said.

And so, the final day before her departure, my father's mother woke before sunrise for her visit to the church and, as was her new habit, she prepared the sour tea she'd been prescribed. Nose pinched to get the mixture down into her empty stomach without retching, she drank the tea. Cup cleaned and left to dry, she kissed her still-sleeping daughter and husband and set out on the five miles of dirt road to church.

May we all reach our destination in good health. May my son know his home even though he will be born so far from it, she planned her prayer as she walked in the foggy morning air. Tired after only a mile, she stopped to pick up a honey-colored pebble from the dirt road. When her son was born, she thought, she would put the rock in the palm of his hand. She would tell him to reach for it whenever life brought anxiety. Over the years, the small, rough stone would turn smooth-comfort and dark-oiled from his fingertip caresses.

This pebble is your home, my love, she could hear herself telling him, and she bristled against the sentimentality of her thoughts. She missed her usual unwavering sensibility—life was so much easier without strong emotions—but she'd come to accept that her old ways simply weren't possible when she could feel a child squirming and kicking just below her heart. She felt possessed, this creature inside literally moving her, making her as sensitive and emotional as the original gods. Frustrated, she continued toward the church.

Once there, my father's mother lit candles and prayed to have her overwhelming fears lifted away. Usually God warmed her to let her know she'd been heard. That day the church remained damp and chilled. She wandered out to the plaza to stand in the late-morning sun, to collect herself for her final walk home. As she sat at the plaza fountain's edge, Nahui Olin appeared and stood directly in front of her, much too close for a simple friendly hello.

My father's mother, the young woman who had cleaned Nahui's dilapidated family manor for years, knew personally about Nahui's intense flirtations, the sort that back then could only be politely referred to as *eccentricities*. Countless were the times Nahui—a woman of fifty who painted her face brightly, dressed in the manner of teenaged harlots, and who sometimes spoke as only sailors did—had made her blush and forget the task at hand. There was the day Nahui serenaded her with the mariachi song "Por un Amor" as she tried to sweep and mop and dust. *For a love/I've cried droplets of blood from my heart/You've left my soul wounded* . . . And then there was the afternoon Nahui insisted she choose which she thought was the prettiest dress in a fancy Parisian magazine. The next week, my father's mother arrived to clean Nahui's house and was presented with the dress, custom-made for her. *Please, mi amor, try it on. The color suits you so.* But my father's mother knew instinctively—from her upbringing, from all she'd been taught at church—that such behavior was scandalous, that it was devil's play. And so, although she was flattered and she sometimes smiled in return without intending to, she tried not to encourage Nahui. Really, all she could do when Nahui suddenly appeared with her insistent interruptions was pray that she would walk away just as abruptly. The day at the fountain, my father's mother hoped for the mercy of such convenience. But it was not meant to be.

"Consuela, I wrote this for you," Nahui said, tapping the book she held in her hand.

Everyone knew of course about Nahui's artist friends and that she herself wrote poems, that she was one of the uncommon women whose name could be found printed on the front page of a book. But, like everyone else in town, my father's mother also knew Nahui had written the particular book she held, *A dix ans sur mon pupitre*, as a ten-year-old, decades before my father's mother had even been born. Clearly, there was no way Nahui had written the book with her in mind.

Did she really know about me before I was born? my father's mother wondered silently. *No*, she pushed the thought from her mind, *that simply couldn't be*.

The explanation to Nahui's outlandish claims had to be simple: She was surely insane. But my father's mother, too polite, too poor, and too cautious, didn't argue. She just sat there, blushing furiously, as Nahui, the grown daughter of wealthy and powerful parents long dead or moved to Paris or wherever it was such money and comfort settled, stared her down. And when Nahui thrust the book at her, my father's mother took it.

"Thank you, Miss Nahui," she said, and nearly dropped the book for how much her hands trembled.

"You'll kill me if you go," Nahui said then.

Sitting low on the fountain's edge, eyes averted, desperately hoping Nahui would decide to leave and not create more of a scene, my father's mother felt upon her chin a hand that had never done a day's labor, a hand pale from silk gloves, a hand soft from the thick honeysuckle-scented creams she herself had dusted on vanity table silver trays. That smooth hand cupped her chin. Head tilted back gently, my father's mother looked directly into green eyes she felt certain were owned by God himself and the devil too. In fact, though she was shocked by her own boldness, she looked into Nahui's eyes the entire time.

The entire time Nahui kissed her.

And Nahui did kiss her. For all to see. Seriously, *everyone* saw. The whole city and all the surrounding pueblos. Those who weren't there when it happened saw it later through busybodies' recounted tales. Everyone saw. And talked about it. But right then there was silence. Not a single person said a word. Not even Nahui as she turned and walked away.

Her heart stopped. My father's mother's heart stopped outright, though not literally, of course. It hurt. The kiss had truly hurt. But she wanted another. And another. And another still. The pain of that kiss was delicious. The pain was a life she could understand. The pain was one she'd carry with her for the rest of her days.

The book Nahui had given her held tight to her chest, my father's mother felt her son kick with particular force. She sat at the fountain for hours and read the book's intricate words until the hot sky blushed her cheeks. That blush never went away.

Eventually, she walked home, carrying a little honey-colored worry stone and the book inscribed to her by the most elegant of hands.

. . . and then, in Chicago, after the train crash . . .

My father's needy infant mouth still hungry at her breast every night, his mother worried for his safety. She feared she had caused her baby girl's death. *An innocent love,* any God-fearing soul would concur, *was taken away as punishment for wicked love*. After all, hadn't she longed for more of Nahui's kisses, for more of her touch? Hadn't she thought of Nahui when her husband sought her affections? Wouldn't she run back to Nahui if she could? Didn't she think of Nahui still? The possibility that God had more punishment arranged terrified her.

And so, soon after the railroad company took what remained of her little girl's body and buried it, she made her decision. Barely twenty years of age but not so young anymore, she cautiously prepared her four worldly possessions for travel.

Twelve-inch iron skillet. Threadbare sock filled with earned green bills. The tiny pebble she had collected from the dirt road back home. And Nahui's book. The skillet was oiled and wrapped in old newspaper. The sock sewn shut. Those two items she handed to her husband for the journey. The worry stone she placed carefully into her pocket. And in the warm snug space between the small of her back and the stiff denim of the American bluejean workpants she'd taken to wearing, she tucked Nahui's book.

The book. Her husband knew about the note Nahui had written on the inside of the back cover. He knew, same as everyone else. With a heavy heart, he'd heard gossip about the day Nahui gave his love the book. He knew the details of the fountain kiss almost as clearly as he knew the small of his wife's back—her skin there pale and untouched by sun, soft with a dusting of fine hair as innocent as he liked to think they'd once been together. A private spot. One of *his* spots. To see her let the book touch her there was more than he could bear.

"Please, leave the book, Consuela," he said.

"Take the boy," she said and handed my father to him.

. . . and in Mexico, five years later . . .

As my father helped his father tend to the crops, storm clouds gathered overhead and turned the sky dark.

"We'll go in soon, just a little more work," his father said.

Meanwhile, my father's mother sat inside their simple shack home, stealing time with thoughts of Nahui.

Sweet love, how I've missed you, Nahui had said when she returned from Chicago.

Nahui, why do you do this to me?

Be mine.

I can't.

Thunder and lightning struck the field.

★

That same thunderclap woke me from my lucid dreams. I opened my eyes to see it had started pouring outside. For a moment, as I lay in the bed of my new apartment, the lights off, all the smells and sounds unfamiliar, I wasn't sure where I was, let alone how long I'd been asleep. It was like waking up into yet another strange dream. I'd never experienced a thunderstorm in the middle of summer before. The thunder-claps were so loud, car alarms wailed in beeping mechanical choruses on the street below. I heard people scream and laugh in the sudden downpour. The air was thick with the over-powering scent of city rain, the mix of damp asphalt and diluted motor oil. There was the occasional splashing sound of tires driving by on the wet street. In all that earthly dampness, my mouth felt unbelievably dry. And my gut was in knots for how hungry I was. My stomach was empty. Literally. I wasn't sure how it had happened exactly, but only coffee had passed my lips for two days. No wonder I was so goddamned loopy.

The wind shifted outside, and rain started coming through the open windows in horizontal sheets. I couldn't see much in the dark room, but I realized the retablo of Nahui would be soaked shortly if it wasn't already. As I stood, my vision blurred, I saw blue sparks, and I had to sit back down quick to avoid falling outright. An embarrassing thought filled me: I was a young brave on a vision quest, I had fasted and I was in the woods, the deer were talking to me now, everything would soon be clear, I would know my spirit name, and I would learn my mission in life. Told you it was embarrassing. At least I can admit to shit like that. Of course, all that was really going on was that I needed something to eat. And some more sleep. I was just a dumb kid alone in a big city with a big scary thunderstorm outside. I took some deep breaths, stood up slower this time, and managed to close the windows. Somehow, miraculously, Nahui was untouched by the rain.

Fireflies still sparkling in the park like microcosmic parallels of the lightning filling the sky above and Nahui watching me from the windowsill, I fell asleep again before the rain subsided. Until early the next afternoon, I slept the most refreshing sleep.

I woke the next day with Nahui's book pressed between my face and the pillow. Not only had I kept it in bed the night before, I'd slobbered on it in my sleep. Hoping to not injure the book further, I slipped it back in its padded envelope, returned the envelope to my father's briefcase with the rest of his things, and tucked the briefcase up on the top shelf in the closet.

By week's end, I had a job with a courier service in the financial district. Starting at 4 A.M., eight hours each day, Monday through Friday, I manned dispatches. The hours seriously sucked and the work was beyond dull, but it paid decently, and I was able to leave it behind when I clocked out. My life was simple. And it was mine entirely. Sure, I met some people—work buddies and random people at coffee shops, a few parties here and there—but mostly I kept to myself. On the average day I'd work my hours, grab a couple slices and a soda on the way home, watch television until I was tired, sleep, wake, and do the same all over again. Heck, sometimes on my day off I'd throw a movie (or two, if I could sneak a second showing) into the mix. Very exciting . . . Not really, but I was happy this way. Don't get me wrong, living in New York was totally cool, but mostly I was stoked just to be far from what I'd left behind.

Two months into my subletting, Ted's buddy's lease ran out. When he came to move all his junk, he asked me if I wanted to buy some stuff dirt-cheap. Sure, I said. Why not? He sold me the bed, kitchen table, a couple chairs, the ancient television, and the stereo with its two foam-covered speakers for fifty bucks total. He even threw in two pillows, sheets, and some towels for another dollar. It was like stumbling on my own personal bargain stoop sale. He must have left a good luck horseshoe tucked somewhere amidst the things I bought, because for some reason the realtor knocked on my door that same day and asked if I wanted to take the place—with a huge rent increase, of course. No big deal, I just picked up more hours at work. For three months I coasted along and nothing major or notable happened in any way, shape, or form. Then, without any warning whatsoever, *wham*, everything, absolutely fucking everything, changed.

CHAPTER NINE

Okay, please don't laugh, but I swear meeting Nathalie was like being hit by a force of nature. It was as if all the challenges and ups and downs in my life had existed only to strengthen and improve me, to try and make me worthy of the moment I'd meet her. I know, it sounds so fucking corny. Total gag reflex material, right? But I swear on my father's ashes, I swear to you it's true.

Nathalie. Gorgeous, addictively engaging, ballsy, and, devil help us all, she had the stare. Those eyes. Those golden brown spark eyes. The sort of eyes my father had tried to warn me about. Sweet mercy. Nathalie had Nahui's stare.

So: *as if*. As if I could have done anything but be floored when our lives collided. Cautious for one brief second the night we first met at a bizarre and otherwise terrible post-Thanksgiving you-survived-dinner-with-your-family-of-origin or celebrate-with-your-family-of-choice bullshit cocktail party, there *was* a moment when I thought Nathalie might be crazy. Like, seriously, clinically demented.

At said party, I stood in a small cluster of people listening to Mr. Party Host, a fashion photographer, talk about how he'd just been hired to art direct the next ad campaign for Diesel Jeans and how, blah blah blah, he wanted to do something high concept about the bullshit of domesticity and family, something with an ironic country kitchen twist. His inspiration, he said, was his mother.

"She's a chronic liar. Covered in gingham. Entirely pathological."

Naïve me, I felt a sudden bond with him.

"I totally know what you mean," I said. "My mother's a Pilgrim."

"You mean she's a *Puritan*," he corrected me with a snooty sneer.

My neck and face burned.

"No, I mean she's a *Pilgrim*," I said. "Square white starched collar, clunky buckle shoes . . . the whole Plymouth Rock gig."

Of course I hadn't been speaking literally.

And then, the most incredible scratchy-voiced creature standing next to me said: "What a coincidence, my mother's a Pilgrim too. Jewish, but she's a Pilgrim."

I turned to face this saving grace girl. And, damn, one look and I knew. It was her. She was the One. As I stood there staring and wondering how I could get her to be mine forever and ever and then some, she laughed the most wonderfully insane laugh and socked Mr. Party Host in the arm—hard, too hard—as if he were in on the joke. I smelled her breath as she laughed. Bergamot and peppermint and just a hint of expensive vodka. She had on this wrinkled vintage Ginger Rogers copper-orange ballroom gown, teetering faux–leopard fur open-toe platform heels, and a rust-colored rabbit fur jacket—an outfit that would have looked like costumed ridiculousness on anybody else, but on her was just right. Her flyaway auburn hair was a tangled mess of a Vargas girl updo. Her perfume was incredibly sweet, almost too sweet, like rice milk about to turn. Sorry for the hokey factor, but seriously, that was it; I was done for.

And from that moment forward, everyone else at the party hated us because it was obvious that we were so goddamned perfect—at least together. So they despised us. But they stayed near us. To watch. And listen.

Once her laugh eventually wound down, my wicked little angel retrieved one of the hand-rolled cigarettes she kept tucked behind her powdered ears like some glammed-up rockabilly moll. Her ears were small and perfectly shaped, but for some reason they reminded me of mothers scolding their kids to put a washcloth and a bar of Ivory to work.

"Cigarette?" she asked me.

That glimmer in her eye. Her boldness. God she was hot. At absolute worst, I figured a quick fuck in some dark corner outside wouldn't hurt any. No strings attached, easy exit if things turned slack, just two kids getting off in an alley. Who could argue with that? She took a small box of wooden matches from her dirty fur jacket.

"Cigarette?" she asked again. I thought I'd already answered.

"No. Thank you."

"Because you don't smoke, because you don't like unfiltered, or because you don't want to be obliged?"

Everyone stood silently and listened like we were some radio play performing for their benefit.

"I don't smoke," I said.

"What a good boy you are." She tapped the tip of my nose with a bitten-down crimson-polished fingertip.

I didn't want the conversation to end.

"But . . ." I stalled, and prayed the gods would have mercy on my stunned brain, "given the right occasion, I might smoke."

Didn't matter if it was true or not. The game was on.

Eyebrow raised, cigarette hanging from her lips, Nathalie stopped mid-strike of a match.

"What exactly would the *right occasion* entail?"

I shrugged.

She pressed the match against her cigarette, thinking, staring at me. And then she tucked the cigarette, still unlit, back behind her ear.

"Don't want one after all?" I asked.

"Just waiting for the right occasion," she said with a devious smile.

Heart be still. Dear motherfucking Jesus Christ, please just kill me now.

"My name is Nathalie," she said.

"Frank."

Thank God succinctness could pass as tough and cool. I no longer seemed to possess the ability to speak more than a single syllable without gasping outright.

"It's a pleasure to make your acquaintance, Frank."

"Same."

"Goodnight, darlings," she said to everyone still watching us, and wiggled her fingers at them in the most perfect sexy evil-bitch wave. "Come on," she pulled me out the door. Once we were downstairs and outside the building, she said: "Take me to your place, handsome."

For real? Yes, for real. I half-expected the director to call, "Cut!" But nobody did. So I continued on. And we were off on our thrilling madcap adventure! Well, sort of. It wasn't like the soundtrack's tempo pumped loud and everything turned quick camera shifts and accelerated speed. In fact, Nathalie was slow. I thought she was trying to torture me with expectation. She walked the entire way to my apartment like an old man on a Sunday drive—long full stops at intersections, deliberately looking both ways before crossing. Granted, I imagine walking fast in her stiltlike shoes wouldn't be the easiest trick in the world, but I later learned she always walked slowly. No matter the situation. Even when barefoot. Still, that night she was extra slow and careful. She was thinking things through. As it turned out, she was map planning, deciding our entire future. I knew this because once we finally made it to my apartment, she claimed the right side of my bed as her own. For keeps.

Look, we were young. Things happen fast. Without hesitation. Or too much foresight.

So, yes, *duh*, it made little sense that she basically moved in the night we met, but logic to hell, being together felt more right than anything either of us had ever known. And so, happy brick by brick, we built a fantasy fort to live in together. Our fort had invisible walls. We were absolutely everything in our fort. We needed nothing else.

A week after she'd moved in, Nathalie woke up one morning and walked over to the windowsill. She picked up the retablo of Nahui, still the only photo in the apartment.

"I've been meaning to ask, where'd you get this?"

"It belonged to my father's mother."

I went to the closet and retrieved the briefcase from the top shelf. I got Nahui's book and handed it to Nathalie.

"That portrait is from the same year this was published."

"Cool," she said, carefully turning a few of the book's pages before handing it back to me. She watched as I returned the book to the briefcase. "What's all that other stuff?" she asked, pointing toward the briefcase.

"Just some things I took from my dad's house when he died."

"Oh."

And that was that. I put the closed briefcase up on the shelf and joined Nathalie back in bed for a lazy morning.

CHAPTER TEN

21 February 1996.

Nathalie came home from what I thought was just another day of work and declared: "Tonight, we repent."

"Excuse me?"

"It's Ash Wednesday. We're going to play a game," she said.

"Gin rummy? Scrabble?"

Mischievous smile, she replied: "I get to be Nahui."

Did she say . . . And repent? . . . What . . . ?

"Wait, I don't get it."

"I know every fact about Nahui Olin. I've seen every photograph of her. I've studied her paintings, her poems, everything."

I'd never even heard her say Nahui's name before, and now she was an expert?

"*Nahui Olin?* Her?" Incredulous, I pointed to the cardboard retablo still propped up on what had become its dusty and permanent spot on the windowsill. Best I could figure, Nathalie had convinced herself that she somehow *knew* Nahui just by looking at her portrait. I couldn't blame her, I mean the eyes and—

"Frank, I unequivocally know everything about her that there is to know. *Everything.*"

Damn, the implications. Was this about my father's mother? What? And then it occurred to me to ask: "Nat, *how* do you know about her?"

"*A dix ans sur mon pupitre* and interlibrary loan. Duh."

Duh was right. Why hadn't I thought of that?

"Frank, did you realize she wrote *four* books?"

No, I hadn't realized.

"Anyway," she continued, "the library had only this one biography someone published in Mexico a few years ago. But I swear, some of the stories about her are so totally scandalous—"

Wait . . .

"Was the biography in Spanish?" I interrupted, preoccupied by my confusion.

"Yeah, so?"

"And you read Spanish?"

"Spanish, French, German, and a smidgen of Portuguese."

"You never told me that."

"Darling, you never asked."

Nathalie could have told me she was a secret operative for the CIA, and I would have believed her. I mean, I could tell she wasn't bullshitting. She was being absolutely serious and honest. I'll be the first to admit how totally turned on I was by the sudden disclosures. I mean, really, here was the woman I'd adored for months, drop-dead gorgeous in her vintage dress with her foxy little pin-up girl face, but, and I'm embarrassed to admit this, I'd never really thought of her as a brain. (Not that I thought of myself as one either, mind you.) I mean, from day one when we met, Nathalie was witty as all hell; she had a sharp and quick tongue, we could blather on and on about movies and music and random stuff, but I'd never seen her read anything other than glossy magazines and maybe the Fashion and Style section of the Sunday paper. And now to learn suddenly the true range of her nerd abilities? Holy crap. She was perfect. I just sat there with this stupid puppy-got-a-squirrel grin.

"Go get ready," she said very sternly.

Get ready? To melt outright from the thrill of her proximity? What? How exactly could I prepare for that?

"Shower. Dress extra nice. Go. Now," she commanded.

And I obeyed.

I went to the closet and, sending a silent thanks to my father for his classy taste in clothes, carefully gathered a few choice items. Behind a closed and locked bathroom door, I undressed and showered. Hot water turned the room a soapy fog. Once I was thoroughly scrubbed clean, I dried off, wrapped a towel around my waist, and stood at the sink. Way more toothpaste on the brush than usual, I brushed my teeth. Twice. I wiped mist off the sink mirror and combed my hair as tidily as my scraggly cut allowed. And then I dressed in the clothes I'd let steam in the bathroom with me—my father's best suit: natty dark brown fine wool tweed slacks and jacket, matching silk tie and pocket square, a brown straw fedora, the one with the black band. The suit was sort of slouchy around the ankles and a little short on the arms, but it mostly fit okay. As I put on the fedora, I noticed the inside shone from years of oily pomade rubbed in. A little of my dad's warm skin clean scent could be detected in the damp air around me.

I tipped the fedora just so, straightened my tie, and refolded the pocket square. But, try as I did, my true self showed through. The good-luck Pogues T-shirt I'd put on as an undershirt—the *Peace and Love* tour shirt, the one with the crumbling silkscreen of a boxer dude on it—remained slightly visible under my father's best white dress shirt. And even though I was wearing my least thrashed pair of shoes, they were still Vans (granted, the super-sweet charcoal suede slip-ons). I couldn't pull the look together totally perfectly, but when I checked myself out in the full-length mirror on the bathroom door, I was passably dandy, in a punk sort of way. Finally, ready as best I knew how to be, I opened the bathroom door to join Nathalie again.

Burnt-sienna organza silk cocktail dress gracing fishnet calves, gold platform heels cleaned of their usual mud, hair pinned in a twist—Nathalie sat at the kitchen table. She'd lit a tall glass cheapie Virgin Mary candle from the corner bodega. The Holy One looked superhero on that votive label, laser beams shooting out from her downward-turned palms. And Nathalie, for her part, had laser beams too. Fully aware that anticipation is half the fun, she ignored me and continued to stare through the candle flame at the kitchen wall, intently burning pinholes through bricks, drywall, and studs. I sat next to her. And even then she didn't look at me. I waited.

The kitchen chair's back was too short and it angled too far backward. Its seat edge hit my leg mid-thigh and cut off circulation. My lower back cramped. Five minutes, maybe seven minutes passed, my entire spine ached, and I couldn't wait any longer.

On your marks. Get set. We had our roles. Go.

"Nahui?"

"*Buenas noches, amor*," Nathalie said, and turned to look me square in the eye. Her voice turned extra gravel deep. And those eyes. Nahui's stare was looking directly at me.

She told her life to me:

Nahui Olin. Poet. Artist. Genius thinker. Wonder star of the Mexican 1920s avant-garde. Favorite muse of boys and girls alike.

(No wonder my father's mother had blushed as she did.)

Nahui Olin. Name meaning: Earthquake Sun—the final epoch on the Aztec calendar wheel, the destroyer of all human existence. Four Suns—Jaguar, Wind, Rain, and Floods—preceded Nahui Olin. We live in Nahui Olin. But according to ancient wisdom, nothing, absolutely nothing, will remain in her wake.

Earthquake. Sun. Nahui. Olin.

Born Carmen Mondragón on 8 July 1893, the daughter of a famous general, her daddy invented a cannon that won the revolution. And when Huerta made her father Secretary of War, her already good life turned golden Mexico City and Paris extravagance. Private school nuns taught her to paint, to write, to think big thoughts. Star young student, under the proud supervision of the sisters, she wrote what would eventually become *A dix ans sur mon pupitre.*

Ten years later, at twenty years of age, she fell hard for a cadet. Manuel Rodríguez Lozano, a handsome boy of good upbringing. Daddy approved. Her nuptial ceremonies were the event of the year. The wedding portrait showed her serious-eyed and Manuel so pretty. It wasn't long until she learned that Manuel admired the male form as passionately as she did herself. They continued on together, but Manuel soon found opportunity to escape. Nahui's parents wouldn't allow a divorce, but she proceeded as if one had been granted.

She took lovers. Many lovers. One, an artist big shot, Dr. Atl—"Doctor Water," his slumming-it-bohemian Aztec chosen name—was the grandfather of modern Mexican muralism. It was he who suggested she take the Aztec name of Nahui Olin. Proud blasphemous creatures, Nahui and Atl lived together out of wedlock . . . in *el ex Convento de la Merced*— Dr. Atl had converted the capital city's former Mercy Convent, located just blocks from the central zócolo, into their sprawling home. Nuns covered their eyes and gripped their rosaries when they passed by on the street. The ungodly feuds of their household were legendary.

Once Nahui was reading on the rooftop patio when she caught sight of Dr. Atl talking to a pretty blonde on the sidewalk below.

"Beware, the sky is falling!" Nahui screamed, as she threw well-aimed roof tiles at the flirting pair.

The blonde ran for cover, but Dr. Atl only laughed in response.

"You are making a fool of yourself, Carmen Mondragón!" he called up to the rooftop. And then, smiling, the play on words occurred to him. He said quietly to himself: "Mondragón—*mon dragon*, indeed."

The pun-turned-lover-pet-name stuck.

Devoted admirer of Nahui's spitfire tantrums, it was Dr. Atl who convinced her to make public the precocious poetic musings she had written as an adolescent. At age thirty-one, the year 1924, Nahui assembled and published *A dix ans sur mon pupitre (From My Desk, at Age Ten)* to the delight of her artist friends. Soon thereafter, she published two collections of poems, *Óptica cerebral, poemas dinámicos (Cerebral Perspective, Dynamic Poems)* and *Calinement je suis dedans (I Am Tender Inside)*.

And the parties Dr. Atl and Nahui gave in honor of those books . . . damn, the parties they threw. Sweet mercy, the winks and smiles and kisses and big talk about politics and art and grand strikes and leftist global overthrow, clusters of costumed revelers wandering off to tangle tongues and fists and opinions in the halls, everyone drinking one cognac sidecar after another. No matter how many cocktails they drank, there wasn't ever sugar rim enough in the world to snuff the Molotov burn of those parties. Blue haze smoke air and mariachis kept them alive to well past sunrise as they brought the world to its pretty little knees and made it their begging love. Comrades to the end, they promised upon their lives to disavow wealth and privilege for the cause. But pledges the flimsy contracts they were, it was always Nahui who owned the party.

Nahui Olin. The Earthquake Sun.

Yes, those were crazy glorious earthquake days.

"Nahui, forgive me," I said to Nathalie/Nahui, "but if all of this is true, how come nobody knows about you anymore?"

She explained:

Unlike that peasant-faker Frida Kahlo with her hair in braids—that poor little injured bird, that martyr mild wild girl—unlike her, Nahui was the real thing. She was serious dynamite. Frida's husband Diego told Nahui as much himself. As did Edward Weston when he took her portrait. Pained eyes. Lips turned downward. She was so beautiful it hurt to look at her. It was too dangerous to take something so explosive, to try to bottle it as iconography. Far easier and safer was to try and pretend Nahui never existed at all.

But she did. Did she ever.

Nahui Olin:

Communist. Radical feminist. Fucked whomever she wanted to. Here, there, and everywhere. Scandalized her barrio. And then slipped into obscurity by middle age. Few people even realized she published a fourth book, *Energía cósmica (Cosmic Energy)*, at age forty-three. By that point she could often be found in the zócolo, packed in one of her tight vixen curve dresses, staring at the sun. Outsize green eyes bloodshot and dilated from the heat and lack of blink, passerby sophisticates—those who didn't heed the local rumors that cast Nahui as a witch who could turn herself into a bat and others into dust—would call out "*Fuego, fuego*" in admiration. *Sizzle, sizzle*, she remained hot as fire. As response, Nahui would only adjust her gaze eastward in unison with the shifting sun. Years and years of this and then, 23 January 1978, eighty-five years of age, Nahui died. In her own bed. While sleeping. Her last breath was peaceful. And, although ancient Aztecs had prophesied that the end of Nahui Olin the Earthquake Sun would be the death of all humanity, the universe continued on in her wake.

Those were the facts.

Her poems crumbled to dust.

She was dead.

Take it with a dose of salt.

Salt was what Nathalie and I tasted as her tears fell.

Nahui was alive.

She was every masked soldier who ever bore arms for their land. She was the little girls in their white communion dresses, playing dress-up as virgin angels. She was a punk whore, eyebrows shaved and lips rubied in homage to professional sluts who turned tricks out of Mexican street booths. She was revolution itself.

Nathalie as Nahui said to me: "*Querido*, you and I, we are revolutionaries."

"Nahui," I asked, "do you know that the dictionary defines revolution as what happens when a body goes around an orbit and returns to its original position?" I continued: "Makes no difference if that body belongs to a planet, some holy whatever, or me. The same rule even applies to you."

Silence.

"Think of it this way," I said, "we're really just tacky little papier-mâché marionettes. We can do only what the puppeteer allows. Life is a controlled performance. Pennies thrown at you. Gravity keeps you in line. And it always pulls you right back to the same place that made you want to revolt to begin with." I ended with words I hoped Nathalie would hear again that night in her dreams: "There is absolutely nothing revolutionary about your revolution."

I said this as much to Nathalie as to Nahui.

And it was true.

Because for all of Nathalie's wanting and needing everything to be so fantastically hyperbolic and transgressive all the time, for all her perpetual 1920s party attire and zany observations and bizarre take on etiquette, no matter how much she wanted to think she and I and her life entire were some sort of brilliant freak show, I'd come to learn exactly what Nathalie was. She was normal. Just plain ol'

potentially boring N-O-R-M-A-L. Seriously, strip away all
the pyrotechnics and you'd find nothing truly revolutionary
about Nathalie's revolution. She wanted a happy home. She
wanted a man to love. And she wanted her man to love her.
Passionately. Devotedly. She wanted that day in and day
out. But, I also knew with absolute certainty, nothing
scared Nathalie more than how thoroughly normal she
really was.

Consequently, when I think back on our Nahui play-date
in my old age, it'll be Nathalie administering a slap to my face
that I'll remember most. The slap wasn't hard and it didn't
sting much, but I'll never forget it. Hot damn and then some,
Nahui could be such a bitch. The self-righteous indignation.
She was just like the rest of her kind—a spoiled baby
idealizing a world of unicorns and rainbows and pink and
blue cotton candy for everyone after the General Strike . . .

Her best martyr routine, Nathalie stared me down. But
she, like Nahui, was a most unconvincing saint. And, formal-
ities considered, if anyone was going to play saint, it should
have been me. Saint Francis of Assisi, specifically. Poor old
blind Saint Francis, crazed, all alone in the middle of the
forest, singing his Canticle of the Brother Sun:

. . . *my lord Brother Sun . . . how beautiful is he, how radiant in all*
his splendor . . .

Saint Francis's feast day. That was the day Nahui kissed
my father's mother at the fountain in Mexico. Nahui stared at
the sun. Her eyes burned. She kissed my very pregnant
father's mother. My father kicked. The baby's name was an
obvious choice. And Nahui earned a throne on a grafted
branch of my family tree.

Francisco: My father's name had such a handsome ring to
it. But names are disasters waiting to happen. One need give
care when choosing names. Just ask my father, he could have
told you. He took after Saint Francis in ways no mother would

ever wish. And then, when his only child was born, the legacy continued.

Frank. Born Francisca. The three of us: Father, the Son-to-be, and Nahui, the Holiest of Ghosts. A most unusual trinity. I wished I could have been lucky like a nun and had my true name whispered to me by God. But I had no god. And so I was never the beneficiary of such convenient divine intervention. I chose my own name, both in honor of my father and for its function as a verb.

"Verb? *Frank* is an adjective, not a verb," Nathalie once challenged me when I explained.

In response, I'd told her to go look it up. She did.

Webster's, definition 11: *To enable to pass or go freely.*

To live without the curses and consequences that crippled my family before me, to break free of a life I preferred were not mine, to pass without constraint through the world . . . as a man, a good and decent man—to this I aspired.

"Wish?" Nathalie broke my silent thoughts.

She held the lit Virgin Mary candle close to my lips. Still rubbing the slight warmth where she'd slapped me, I closed my eyes and concentrated. I'd learned the hard way with the birthday cake my dad made me that I should phrase my wishes carefully. So I thought for a good long minute. And then I opened my eyes and blew out the candle. Nathalie swiped her thumb across her tongue and pinched her fingertips against the candle's dead wick. Gray sooty flesh, she reached toward me.

"Thou art dust and unto dust thou shall return," she said, and marked my forehead with her thumbprint.

Her touch was electric. Head to toe I was flame hot lit.

She stood and planted her lips on mine to seal the deal. The intensity of that simple little kiss was indescribable. Everything turned heavy and earnest all of a sudden. To be honest, I got sort of worried. Was Nat taking this repenting thing seriously? Were we supposed to act all saintly now? Maybe we'd crossed some line. Maybe we'd ruined everything.

She saw my concern.

"By the way, you are devilishly handsome in that suit."

"Thanks."

Smile shining bright, she winked and took my hand.

"Ever heard the saying, *No rest for the wicked* . . ."

We were a busy pair.

PART TWO

CHAPTER ELEVEN

2 November 2002. Day of the Dead.

Nathalie woke screaming at precisely 8:45 A.M. Her internal clock was set quartz precision accurate, and her guttural, muffled screech was, as usual, both a terrifying shock to the senses and entirely unsurprising. For over a year, more mornings than not, she woke us this way. She and I were spiraling. We were going up in smoke. Insert here any other tasteless disaster metaphors for a strained relationship—adore each other and try as we did, our seventh anniversary looming large, Nathalie and I reeled from unexpected turns.

Six years had passed between us and everything had been almost obscenely good. Seriously. I mean, sure we were imperfect humans and we had our flare-ups and spats and foot-in-mouth moments. But whatever, by and large we were stoked for every free minute we got to spend together. And as for work, even that had been painless enough—random temp shit for me; same plus occasional nanny gigs with old family friends for her. We made ends meet no problem. Rent checks were mailed. Habits formed. Routines were established. And through it all, we remained fucking giddy to be with each other. Tick tock, one year passed. And another. Plus four more. But then we woke one day to find that the fantasy fort we'd built and mortared with repetition had been smashed by a wrecking ball as we slept.

September 11, 2001. The crisp blue sky came tumbling down and yet, somehow, Nat and I slept like babies well past noon. Neither of us had jobs to head off to that day, so we remained asleep and comfy cozy in bed as the southern tip of what was arguably the country's most important city collapsed less than three miles south of our repose. How we didn't hear the sirens and helicopters and neighbors' screams of shock as they watched the news, how we'd dreamed of sugar plum fairies through it all, I'll never understand. But we did. We slept. Beautifully. Peacefully. And it was a good thing we did, because that would be the last time we'd wake rested for a very long time to come.

I'm ashamed to admit this, but it wasn't until we'd been awake for a while—when I was in the shower and Nathalie was whipping up some breakfast—that we even realized anything was wrong out in the world. Nathalie had just turned on the television to keep her company as she cooked when she saw. She called for me to come quick, "Frank, hurry, something awful happened!" I ran out of the bathroom wrapped in a towel, expecting to find Nathalie with her hair on fire or a finger cut off. Although the tofu scramble she'd been cooking burned and sat uneaten in the pan for the rest of the day, our immediate reality remained, almost shamefully, unaffected.

Not sure what we should do, what was safe, what might come next, we sat on the floor directly in front of the television and watched the news. Nathalie leaned on my side, she huddled into me. And she shook. She rattled, actually. And sobbed. She cried enough for the both of us. This was her job, I guess, because I couldn't cry. Tears and emotions were nowhere forthcoming for me. So, Nathalie a bundle of demonstrative emotional response and me a stone statue, together we sat in our opposing states of shock and we took turns cradling what little crumbled gritty brick evidence remained of our bliss heaven fort.

By the day's end, what to do with the bricks preoccupied

Nathalie. She took to throwing them against the walls, out windows, and in my general direction. Quite simply, Nathalie freaked out. She kept saying, a panicked wildness in her voice, "There isn't enough oxygen. I can feel it. Seriously, I can't breathe."

Nathalie kept breathing. And, furthest thing from what I would have anticipated, the next day she said: "St. Paul's is organizing volunteers. I'm going."

I watched as she threw things in a purse for her planned trip down to the site. And what does a person pack for such a trip? Apparently lip gloss, a small bottle of water, and chewing gum are the only sundries needed for an emergency-response kit. Nathalie snapped her purse shut, her hands trembling in unison with the length of her arms and up into her shoulders and down into her torso and through her central nervous system to the entirety of her body and mind and voice. My contrasting robotron state had, luckily, at least been programmed to include activation of an empathy chip. I felt a rush of intense need to protect my girl.

"Nat, maybe you shouldn't go."

"I'm going."

"I'll go with you."

"No, Frank. I want to go alone."

And so she did. To be honest, seeing the site was the last thing I wanted to do. So in some ways I was glad she didn't want me to go. But when she came home later that afternoon, I knew I'd been wrong not to insist I go with her. She'd stopped shaking, but her somber stillness was somehow even more disquieting than the shaking had been. She wouldn't tell me what she'd seen. She wouldn't tell me anything. And, really, she didn't have to. The horrible weight of it all was visible in her eyes.

That was the first night she woke us with one of her hell screeches. Both of us sound asleep, her scream started as something that sounded like a cement mixer stuck in her throat, a gravelly moan, and expanded and deepened into a reverberating bear's growl. It lasted probably a total of half a minute, but in an instant I was awake in the dark room and every childhood *Exorcist* fear I'd ever had hit me full force. I swear I almost pissed myself I was so scared. And poor Nat, she looked even more spooked than me. It was like she'd heard the tail-end of the scream and hadn't known where it'd come from.

"Did I do that?"

"Yeah. You okay?"

She was shaking even more than when we'd been sitting in front of the television the day the towers collapsed. Eventually, we sort of fell asleep again. But you should have seen the dark circles under our eyes the next day. It wasn't pretty. I was relieved when she turned on the radio in the morning and we heard that pedestrian traffic would be restricted south of Canal.

I didn't ever want Nathalie to go back to that place again.

Yet for months, Nathalie jolted awake in the middle of the night with cold sweats. She stocked up on valerian root and a prescription her doctor gave her but that she never used. I encouraged her to take the pills. I wanted us to sleep. I wanted the haggard look shading her eyes to fade away and the sparkle to come back. I wanted her to be her spasmodic witty self again. But, honestly, more than anything I wanted her angst to mellow out so I wouldn't feel so goddamned numb in comparison. Because for all her histrionic grief, I was twice as much on autopilot.

I mean, I still tried to be everything Nat could ever want or need. I comforted her. I brought her cups of tea with huge spoonfuls of honey stirred in when she'd wake in the night, and I'd hold her and give her little kisses on the back of her neck and smooth her hair and rock her until she went back to sleep. I tried to keep her days light and upbeat, but inside I felt like a vortex void. I hate to sound so fucking cliché, but I know my emotional reaction, or apparent lack thereof, came about, as paradoxical as it may seem, exactly because I could get through any trauma the world threw—so long as I didn't have to *feel*. Any fucking moron could tell you it sucked and was totally terrifying to have that much death and destruction so close by. As it was, I was having a hard enough time just being around Nat's misery.

I started taking Nathalie's sleeping pills—the prescription ones from the squat little rectangular white bottle that had sat untouched in the kitchen cupboard next to the drinking glasses, the pills that were a creepy shade of pink and reminded me of a Barbie doll or a "flesh-tone" Band-Aid. At first I took half of one maybe every three nights, but soon I was taking two each night and getting the prescription refilled once a month. For at least eight hours each night I sunk into a deadening sleep. And each morning, I woke hazy-brained and even more numbed-out than before. This kept me going. What I didn't realize was that it was becoming difficult for Nathalie to be with someone who refused to feel anything. Because feel she did. Very much.

When the city organized public ceremonies for the one-year commemoration of September 11, Nathalie attended and cried for days after. I don't know if that's when she got the idea for the Day of the Dead altar, but it was her idea entirely. Closest I'd ever gotten to a Day of the Dead altar was at Bowers Museum in Santa Ana when my mom dragged me to a fund-raising festival the year she was on the Board of Advisors. Untraditional Mexican-descendent jerk that I was, until Nat brought up the idea, I'd never even thought of making an altar for my father. Nathalie, unlike me, was getting wings for sure. She wanted to set up an altar in our apartment for people she didn't even know. And so, come November 2, we did.

The altar was elegant in a homemade kitsch sort of way. Nathalie covered one wall with taped-up tinfoil and pasted onto it swirling patterns of bright plastic gemstones she bought at the 99 cent store. We got out our one lace tablecloth—scarred with oxidized maroon wine glass rings and curry stains, but pretty nonetheless—draped it over the kitchen table, and pushed the table up against the sparkling and bejeweled foil wall. On the table edge closest to the wall, we placed our only non-chipped turquoise blue vintage Fiestaware plate. The plate cradled a selection of the best persimmons, pomegranates, and pears from the Union Square farmer's market. Nathalie set a clunky glass vase next to the fruit and arranged a bouquet of the glittery plastic flowers she usually tucked in her tangled hair. Our makeshift altar glowed with a trillion little tea light candles.

And at the center of the altar table, I placed the retablo of Nahui that Nathalie had framed for our first anniversary—*Happy Paper Anniversary*, Nat had said when she presented me with the gift. *Nahui will stay safe this way*, she'd said. To me it had sort of felt like Nahui was jailed inside the intentionally gaudy gold frame and its thick glass pane, but the gift was given with good intentions, so I took it as such. Not that Nat could have predicted this result six years earlier, but the campy tacky gold frame looked perfect on our altar.

Still, Nat asked: "Isn't it strange to put her on the altar?"

"I don't have any pictures of my dad," I said by way of explanation.

I lit even more candles and added the following to the table: a box of Wheaties, a can of chili beans, stalks of green onion, pints of coffee yogurt, cranberry and grape juice, three scoops of rocky road ice cream in our best jadeite bowl . . . the favorite foods my father's cancer belly hadn't allowed as his final meal.

As I sat admiring the altar, Nathalie went to the closet and came back with what appeared to be a fragment of concrete and a few shards of tinted window glass. With a very delicate and reverent touch, she placed these items on the altar.

"What's that?" I asked, even though I was sure I knew the answer.

"They're from South Broadway. Out front of St. Paul's."

The broken glass caught candlelight and bounced tiny white prisms of radiant matter throughout the room like shooting stars. Part of me wished Nathalie and I could be under actual stars that night, that we could go to a cemetery with armfuls of bright orange marigolds wrapped in newspaper cones to lay on gravestones, to picnic and drink and play music in distracted celebration of the dead. But, clearly, that was not likely to happen in Manhattan. So Nathalie and I sat on the floor in front of our apartment altar, listened to music on the radio, and ate a Thai takeout dinner.

"This is really nice, Frank," she said.

I agreed.

But sometimes even when you've put forth a great deal of effort to pay your respects and move on, grief sticks with you. I took my sleeping pills before we went to bed. Nathalie woke screaming. I stumbled to the kitchen for glasses of water. I handed Nathalie valerian, and I took more prescription pills.

Two mornings after we'd set up the altar, I awoke a total zombie from the pink sedative I could still feel coursing through my veins. I took a cold shower to try to come back to the land of the living. I was moving so slow that by the time I got dressed, I was already late for work. I grabbed a pear from the altar's fruit plate to take with me so I wouldn't starve before lunch. A quick stab of guilt hit, and I felt like maybe I should light the altar's candles—if for no other reason, then as payment for the pear. I took a match from the box we'd left on the altar, and as I struck it, sulfur spiraled up. My nose stung. My eyes watered.

Through my induced tears, I could practically see the candlelight licking the wall. The whole building would go up in flames before the fire department could respond. And all doped up on hippie sleep-inducers like she was, Nathalie would die in the fire. She wouldn't even realize she was inhaling smoke. She'd sleep right through flames consuming the bed and turning it all charred box-frame and blackened metal springs. I'd spend the rest of my life in mourning, refusing to love again, refusing to sleep, refusing ever to eat another pear.

Okay, maybe I really *was* Mexican after all.

Mental note made to give Nat a call when I got to work, to ask her to blow out the candles before she went anywhere, I tiptoed back to our bed. Clumsy puppy paw hands, I pulled the covers up around Nat's shoulders as gently as I knew how. I leaned over and kissed her forehead. The crease between her brows—a deep ridge that had etched itself into the permanent composition of her face the day the sky fell and had deepened progressively ever since—relaxed. Nathalie, still sound asleep, sighed, shifted slightly, and dug her head deeper into her pillow. And then her frown returned. She nearly scowled as she continued dreaming. I plumped my pillow and wedged it behind her back so she'd have something to lean on even though I wasn't there. I did these things, but if I'd realized what would unfold later that same morning, I would have done more. I would have climbed back in bed with Nathalie, and I would have wrapped my arms around her. Tight. As tight as I could without hurting her.

CHAPTER TWELVE

That night, I stopped at the bodega on Avenue A between 6th and 7th, the one with the really nice flowers, to get a fancy bouquet for Nathalie. Actually, I ended up buying a dozen cheapie marigolds, but those deep orange flowers were absolute pristine perfection. I knew Nathalie would love them and, bonus, she could even add them to the altar if she wanted.

To be honest, I wasn't sure if it was disrespectful to add stuff to the altar two days *after* the Day of the Dead—I mean, was it rude somehow, like you're emotionally manipulating the dead into hanging around when they just want to rest in peace again after partying so hard? I figured Nat would know. In our nearly seven years of being together, I'd come to realize she knew pretty much everything a person would ever want to know. And if she didn't already know something, she knew how to find out. So I'd just ask her. She'd be home; she always got home from work before me, and she'd probably be in the midst of cooking some fabulous meal for dinner, looking beautiful as always. Flowers in hand, I opened the door to our apartment.

"Nat, is it okay to put stuff . . ."

Are you familiar with the confusion and embarrassment that accompanies speaking aloud and then finding that nobody is there to hear you? That feeling, a warm and tingling sensation along the neck and ears, flirted at me as I realized the apartment was too quiet. The room was empty. And dark. I flipped on the light switch closest to the front door. A silver envelope on the kitchen table, propped up against the plate of fruit in the midst of the altar, caught the overhead light and glimmered. I closed the door behind me, walked over to the table, put the cellophane-wrapped marigolds down on top of the altar's unlit votives, and picked up the silver envelope. It contained a note, written on matching silver-tinted cardstock.

Sweetness,
I need to go. Don't know for how long exactly.
Please, please forgive me.
I'll call soon. I love you. Endlessly.

Your girl,
N.

Maybe I'm hopelessly dense, but at first I couldn't comprehend the note. I mean, who ever comes home prepared to find a Dear John "I'm leaving you—well, at least for a while" letter? I really just figured Nathalie meant she needed to run some errands or something. Like she wasn't sure if she'd make it back by the time we usually ate dinner. But three hours later, no call to ask if I needed anything on the way home, no keys jangling at the front door, reality sunk in. Snap to, knucklehead. Your girl is gone. Like *gone* gone.

And I thought:

So, Dad, it's like this, is it?

I stood alone, Nathalie's heliotrope perfumed letter in hand, holding what felt to be the final remaining brick of our fantasy fort. I had no clue where she might have gone, but the urge to search for her was maddening. Out of what I suddenly considered a totally lame and misguided neo-Luddite rebel stance, she'd—same as me—always refused to own a cell phone. There was absolutely no fucking way for me to reach her. Frustration, sadness, anger, longing, fear, and loneliness crashed against my skin from the inside. No fucking way was I going to sit alone in that murky mess of emotions. I pulled on a jacket, and I walked.

The night sky was crisp and clear, evidence of winter knocking on the door but not quite at the party yet. Cold air pinking my face, I walked at a frantic pace with no clear destination in mind. Clammy sweat bunched my socks and slicked my skin. My shins felt like they might splinter into shards, and my heels ached from how hard I hit the pavement with each step. The constantly changing sidewalk landscape became heaven-sent preoccupation—*watch out for that dog shit, avoid the puddle, there's a piece of gum, extinguish the cigarette that jerk who's been walking in front of you for five blocks just flicked back toward you.* I headed west and eventually up toward Union Square.

Winded from speed-walking block after block, I stopped at the rolling bookshelves outside the Strand Bookstore to catch my breath. The Strand. It was a place I knew very well. The first time I'd been there was on a bookstore date with Nat early in our relationship. She had suggested we go to the Strand, and I replied: "A bookstore on a Friday night? Ha-ha. So, really, where do you want to go?" Somewhere they sold vinyl, an old movie house—those places made sense to me. But a bookstore? Lame.

"Have you ever been to the Strand?" she asked.

"You're serious?"

"The Strand is super cool. Trust me."

And so I'd gone with her. Reluctantly. At worst, I figured it'd be a super-sized mall-style store with a café, and at best it would be a boring little place stocked with antique books. Instead, as Nat walked me through floor after floor of warehouse-tall stacks, the store's motto promising miles and miles of books ceased seeming like pumped-up hype. The place was like a fucking labyrinth of books in endless categories: *Literature, Film, Science, Architecture, Religion, Americana,* and on and on. So, yeah, the selection was impressive, and I guess arguably "cool," as Nathalie had promised, but it wasn't until we went to the furthest southeast corner of the basement that I found what was truly awesome about the Strand.

Yes, the less-than-a-dollar pre-publication book galleys they kept there were pretty great, but what I dug was how desolate that dimly lit and slightly musty corner of the bookstore was. It was like finding an old bomb shelter in your neighbor's backyard. Better yet, it was like finding the bomb shelter with your foxy neighbor girl in tow. Nat and I made out in that basement corner for a very long time. Every now and then a weirdo book-freak with duct-taped glasses or really greasy hair would wander back there and try to ignore us as he scanned whichever shelves we weren't leaned up against and knocking askew with our fun. But other than that, nobody bothered us or told us to stop or really seemed to mind our bookstore recreation. The smell of old books has been a turn-on for me ever since.

Clearly, I was converted. Now I fucking loved bookstores. Over the years the Strand became a habit for us, a favorite place to go on a date. Lately, we'd started heading over to the pommes frites place on Second Avenue afterward, and Nat would order a huge paper cone of thick fries and we'd sprinkle vinegar over them and eat them as we walked home.

So, considering the Strand was one of *our* places, stopping there the night Nathalie took off probably wasn't the best idea. The crap pulp novels and science textbooks on the discounted shelves outside the store cleared my head for a few minutes, but too quickly my hurt and confusion caught up with me and swelled in huge giant waves and crested bigger and bigger in my chest, pushing up against my lungs, compressing my breath, making my heart pump too much blood. I thought about Nathalie and how she was gone and fuck, I was so goddamned pissed at her, how could she just up and leave like that . . . Total contradiction, I practically ran inside our bookstore in search of distraction.

For a good hour I walked the towering stacks—up and down one aisle after another, from the west wall to the east and then up and down aisles back to the west wall again, my fingers dragging along the shelves—just to keep moving. I felt totally catatonic, undead really. I was just about to go off in search of a pretty little virgin whose blood I could suck to stay alive—a legal and willing virgin, of course; I wasn't some sort of monster, for God's sake—but then I remembered that one scene in Warhol's flick *Blood for Dracula* where the Count hooks up with that hottie chick who swears she's a virgin but then, when Dracula sinks his teeth into her neck, he heaves like he's shot up some crazy-bad junk. Obviously she wasn't a virgin. I mean, that movie took place in the 1970s, what was he thinking? But still, poor dude. Sad and scared that I too might be love-hungry for all eternity to come, craving the strange funk cryptlike comfort of dank, dusty, recycled air, I went down to the basement. I leaned in the southeast corner, our corner, and willed tears to come, but fuck if anything could go the way I wanted. So I stood there mopey-faced and bummed and hurting and totally dry-eyed.

Eventually, I walked up two flights of stairs to the art section. If I couldn't have Nat or some yum-blood virgin, maybe at least Nahui would be seen in public with me. I was looking for a Weston monograph, scanning rows of oversized books with my fingertip, eyes focused on titles, when I stepped on a small hard book. A hot pain shot up my leg to my lower back. My spine ached momentarily. That may have been one of the first times I cognitively realized I wasn't a kid anymore. I mean, it used to be that I could stay up and party and do whatever the fuck I wanted all night long and wake after barely any sleep, and I wouldn't feel pain, not then, not the next day, not ever. Now, simply pounding pavement hard for twenty minutes—just fast walking, really—had left my body sore.

The book. I still stood on the book. Strand protocol allowed that I should have ignored it or maybe paused momentarily to push it under a bookshelf with my foot. But the concentrated dense pressure of the small rectangular book under my left foot was the closest I would get to receiving a comforting hug that night. So I stayed standing on it. I shifted my weight back and forth. And switched feet. The binding wiggled and cracked under my weight.

After a few moments of this pathetic solo dance, I picked up the book and opened it at random. I read:

> The only hero able to cut off Medusa's head is Perseus, who flies with winged sandals; Perseus, who does not turn his gaze upon the face of the Gorgon . . . supports himself on the very lightest of things, the winds and the clouds, and fixes his gaze upon what can be revealed only by indirect vision, an image caught in a mirror . . .

Italo Calvino. "Lightness." *Six Memos for the Next Millennium*. I hadn't located a book of Edward Weston's photographs. I hadn't found his portrait of Nahui. But with Calvino's misplaced book in hand, I couldn't help but think Nahui had found *me*, that she'd managed to send me a gift. To keep me company. To help explain, maybe.

Nathalie was lucky. She had the gift of flight. And, vain girl that she was, never without a mirror, maybe she was in her own indirect way facing demons. Maybe she'd explain when she called . . .

Oh shit. She'd said in the note that she'd call soon. What if she'd already tried to reach me? She would have expected I'd be home. My Perseus flown away, all I could do was run.

* * *

I sprinted up the stairwell, scurried into the apartment, and ran to the answering machine. The light wasn't blinking. Damnit, maybe Nathalie had called but hadn't left a message? Okay, breathe, breathe, she'll call back soon.

Unable to sit still, I paced the apartment as I waited for the phone to ring. My aimless pacing quickly turned into a detective's hunt. If Nathalie had packed anything, it hadn't been much. The apartment seemed pragmatically unchanged. I studied the closet. I knew Nathalie had a red dress, but there was no red dress in the closet. She must have packed it. Or maybe I was remembering wrong and the dress I was thinking of was actually the pink one still hanging next to the gray evening gown? And didn't we have two umbrellas? There was only one in the closet. Wait, had we lost one of them? I remembered walking home from a movie with Nathalie the last time it had rained—I'd shared my umbrella with her, but it was totally possible we'd had two umbrellas that night and that she'd simply tucked hers in her purse. Was she going somewhere it rained? Fuck. It was useless. I was no good for this sort of work.

Sentimental fool, I continued searching in all the places she might remain. The girly fragrant lotions she'd left at the bathroom sink failed to conjure her. Her fennel toothpaste was only pungent chalkiness, not her full lower lip and teasing bites. The fancy slab of honey and oatmeal soap she'd bought at a SoHo boutique sat in a slight milk puddle of its own dilution and probably offered her DNA to be retrieved by those with the proper tools, but not by me. If only I'd held onto the recreational junior scientist kit I'd owned as a geeky kid: thin-walled glass vials and semi-combustible powders in flip-lid squat containers, a miniature Bunsen burner, flimsy tin clamp-teethed prongs, and a length of frayed wick. I'd never known what to make of the wick. A wick? To craft explosions? To create a candle? For what? Really, why was there a wick in a junior scientist kit? I remember one day a friend came over after school to play mad scientist. She saw the wick and seemed as confounded as I was. And then, pretty much out of the blue, she told me that she lit candles to Saint Jude.

"Why?"

"For faith," she'd said.

As I stood in the bathroom, sniffing Nathalie's fancy lavender soap like some hunting dog desperate to pick up a scent, resisting the urge to bite into the soap, it occurred to me that I had no guarantee that Nathalie would find her way home, or that she really wanted to, for that matter. I needed to do something about that. And so I went to the kitchen and filled a mason jar with water. I took the bouquet of marigolds I'd left on our Day of the Dead altar, transferred them to the jar, and put them back on the altar next to the framed retablo of Nahui. Then I lit all the votives. Whining pleas to Saint Jude, I begged for Nathalie to call, for her to love me still, for her to come home.

Hours later, I forced myself to try to get some sleep. A glass of water from the kitchen and two pink pills swallowed, I got in bed. It was the first night since I'd met Nathalie that I was in bed without her at my side. And it fucking sucked. I tried to close my eyes, but they just wouldn't cooperate. As I lay on my side of the bed, exhausted but sleepless, I stared at the altar. Candlelight bounced off the glass of the framed retablo, and Nahui's silver eyes seemed to glimmer as she stared in my direction. Maybe I just needed glasses; I know I needed sleep, but I swear it looked like Nahui was weeping. Shimmering sepia tears trickled down her face. She felt my pain. She took my pain. Soothed, I watched the candles die down and extinguish themselves. And as I fell asleep, I promised myself that first thing in the morning I'd collect the burned-out wicks and keep them in my pocket for good measure.

CHAPTER THIRTEEN

8 November 2002.

The phone rattled on the kitchen table. Telephone wires outside the window unfurled from their post and wrapped themselves thorny binding around my chest. Another ring. I wanted to pretend I didn't know who it was. I wanted to screen the call and not answer. But even though it'd taken Nathalie nearly a week of being gone to finally fucking call, and even though I was beyond pissed, I still wanted to talk to her. I missed her. Horribly. And so, on the fourth ring, the machine about to pick up, I pushed myself out of bed, turned off the stupid afternoon talk show I'd been sort of watching on television, and made quick of the ten steps it took to cross the apartment to the phone.

"Hello?"

There was a pause. And then:

"Hey," Nathalie said all monosyllabic monotone.

That was all she could say—"hey"? It was so obvious she hadn't expected me to be home. She'd probably figured I'd be at work and she could just leave a message. Nice, Nat.

"How are you?" she asked.

"Sweetheart, where the fuck are you?"

"This horrid town called Shamrock," she said. "The McDonald's here has a bathroom sink the shape of Texas."

She said it so matter-of-fact, just like that, like a trip to Shamrock, Texas was one she'd been planning forever, and that I'd known she was going on. What I wanted to know was if Shamrock was so goddamned awful, why was she there?

And McDonald's? What was she trying to prove? She didn't even eat fast food. Hello, and why the fuck had she gone off in the first place? Was she going to apologize? Explain? I wanted to demand answers. But more than that, I wanted Nat to come home. And so I tried to be patient. My ear burned from how long I'd tightly held the phone to it, listening to total silence.

"Nat, are you coming back?"

"Of course. And I'll explain when I get home, okay?"

I didn't respond.

"Frank?"

"Fine," I said.

I hated myself the moment that answer left my mouth because it wasn't fine, nothing about the situation was fine. In fact, everything I'd thought I'd known had been royally screwed. I had absolutely no clue how to deal with the intense misery her departure made me feel. Gun to foot, ready to shoot—and why not, my heart was already ripped apart—I started in on surface bullshit.

"I saw Johnny yesterday."

"Oh, that's nice. How is he?" I could tell Nathalie was grateful for the deflection of drama.

"He's fine, I guess," I answered.

Fine. Yup, I'm fine. And he's fine. We're all just fucking fine.

Really, on the matter of how Johnny was doing, I wasn't trying to be flip or obtuse. I just didn't know. In fact, I could count on less than two hands how much I knew about Johnny:

1. Johnny lived in our building.
2. He was an ancient WWII vet.
3. He rented the apartment directly downstairs.
4. He had inhabited that apartment for centuries probably.

5. He watched TV loud enough to hear the commercials through our shared ceiling/floor.
6. Each night he went to the corner bar for as many beers as the money in his wallet could buy.
7. More often than not, a lit Camel hung from his craggily thin-lipped mouth.
8. I liked Johnny.
9. And Johnny liked me.

With his irony-free meticulous flattop, flannel shirts, and pressed jeans, at first I'd dismissed Johnny as some sort of redneck throwback who'd love to beat the crap out of me if he still had the wherewithal. But then one night I held the vestibule door open for him, more automatic gesture than intended courtesy, and he responded with a wink and a heavily laced, "Thank you, *young man*."

The wink. The knowing smile. His tone of voice, like we were in on some shared secret. Were we? Just how much had I misperceived the dude? Was he one of the neighborhood's leftist rebels of yesteryear? Could it be that his lumberjack style was more Village People than Midwest hick? It would have been insane to presume anything, but *exactly* how much did we have in common? That smile. The look in his eyes. We never spoke about any of this directly, but over time he took to chummy hellos with me and exaggerated flirty winks with Nathalie when we'd see him around the neighborhood. I don't know, the whole thing was sweet somehow. And strangely comforting. Only a few feet of concrete and drywall between us as we slept and shit and ate, we were nearly complete strangers, but I liked that there was a shared membrane of building and routine connecting us.

I'd seen him the day before when I was getting the mail. Johnny had made his way down the stairwell, his walking stick one step ahead of his house-slipper feet, his drooping face looking particularly tired, his gray flattop not as military precise as usual. I watched to make sure his pajama pants hem didn't catch on his feet as he took the final steps to the mailboxes. I hadn't seen him dressed in his dark jeans and red plaid shirt in weeks. He seemed utterly drained.

"Where's that firecracker of yours been?" he asked.

"She'll be back soon," I said. And tried to convince myself it was necessarily true.

"Lucky dog," he said, and laid an unsteady slap on my back.

I told Nathalie: "He said to tell the *firecracker* hello."

"Tell him I send hugs . . . So, what else is up?"

The woman I thought would be with me always is gone, that's what else is fucking up.

"Nothing major," I said.

"You been working hard?"

What the fuck?! Could we please have a real conversation already?

And, as for me working hard, until Nathalie gave a little on her end of the line, there was no way in hell I was going to confess that I'd been calling in sick to the temp office each day since she'd left. I'd spent all week just like I was spending that particular day—in bed, wearing pajama pants and a hoody, hood up, slumped down in blankets, and staring at the television I'd dragged over and put on the nightstand. I was living a parallel life to Johnny's, slightly cooler dressed and without the evening forays to the corner bar, but still.

In all my moping about, I hadn't even taken down the Day of the Dead altar. Well, I had managed to deal with some of its edible parts. The fruit was first to go, then I made my way through the final meal I'd left for my father. Box of Wheaties: eaten dry, box to hand to mouth. Can of chili beans: opened, scraped from the can with a fork, and washed down with alternate swigs of cranberry and grape juice. The three scoops of rocky road ice cream had melted into a thick sludge moldy mess I wouldn't eat no matter how hungry I was, and the wilted stalks of green onion had turned dark slime and stuck to the lace tablecloth. The unopened pints of coffee yogurt bulged with gassy rot.

The apartment smelled sour and totally stale, and I didn't fucking care. All in all, I was useless. Other than my one night at the Strand and a few quick trips downstairs to get the mail, I'd pretty much lain in bed for a week straight.

Was I working hard? Well . . .

"Frank?"

"Nat, are you really coming back?"

"Of course, love."

"*When?*"

"Soon. I promise."

There was something in her voice that told me not to push for more answers. I could tell she meant it, she'd be back. So that was that. She said she loved me. I said the same in return. And it was true. I did love her. More than I'd ever loved anyone. But I also sort of hated her. That night, I hated her for not immediately running back home and throwing herself at my feet and groveling by way of apology for leaving me.

After we hung up, I felt like I'd go crazy if I stayed alone a second longer. At the same time, I didn't want to be around anyone. Unless Nathalie walked in the door, that is. But, although she'd said she'd be back home soon, I knew not to expect her to walk in the door that night. So, naïvely hoping to cure my anxious loneliness, I went to the closet, reached to the top shelf, moved a stack of extra blankets and towels, and retrieved my father's briefcase. My fingerprints marked the dusty black leather. Briefcase balanced on my knee, I used my sleeve to give the CIA-man case a quick shine. Clicking open the gold clasps was such a satisfying feeling—the metal spring lock giving way, pushing up into the pad of my thumb.

Pathetic, Frank. Totally pathetic. I needed Nat back. Tough beans, kid, she won't be home tonight. Deal. I sat on the bed to give the briefcase a thorough look-see.

The wad of bills my mother had given me the day she closed her front door on my face was long gone and used up, and Nahui's retablo had been promoted to formal framed display in the apartment, but the rest of the briefcase's contents remained almost exactly as they'd been the day I left Los Angeles. My father's dark glasses. His folded-up walking stick. Little pebble worry stone his mother had given him. Two safe deposit keys I'd taken off my keychain and stashed inside the briefcase for safekeeping. A padded manila envelope with *Paquita, Birthday Girl* written on it. And in that envelope: the disintegrating clothbound book whose yellowed pages barely clung together by patches of torn fabric and rotted thread. *A dix ans sur mon pupitre.* Inscribed to my father's mother. Given to me by my father. Ignored by me for nearly seven years.

"I'm so sorry," I said.

To Nahui, I guess. Maybe a little to my dad and his mother, too. I really was sorry. Nahui's book deserved to be revered by white-gloved researchers and stored in an archival box somewhere climate-controlled and protected. My lazy-ass possession of her book was practically sacrilege. Out of guilt and curiosity, I decided finally to read her poems.

Nahui's book and Nathalie's pocket-sized Spanish/English dictionary in hand, I cleared off a corner of the kitchen table altar and pulled up a chair. Nahui watched me from the retablo at the center of the table, her serious stare now stern schoolteacher as much as seductive vixen.

Trying not to damage the book any further, I opened it flat on the table and read. Esoteric incantations of cosmic truths and revolution pulsed on page after page. My frequent stops to look things up in the dictionary were welcome breaks. To say the stuff Nahui wrote was convoluted and dense is just the half of it. Her words were overwhelmingly hot and brilliant—something like combining all of Patti Smith's *Horses* lyrics and Gertrude Stein's *Tender Buttons* rants and Albert Einstein's theories into a single condensed form. It fucking rocked. I read for hours but made it only halfway through the book before my brain started to ache.

The sun set outside and the apartment turned dark. I opened the book to the peeling deco plate on the back cover. My eyes strained, I lingered over the inscription written so long ago:

> My love,
> "*She went through me like a pavement saw.*"
>   *Yours as ever for the revolution,*
>   *Nahui*

Wasn't no way to top that. Exhausted and wired all at once, I couldn't read anymore. Totally ready to put the book away, but wanting to honor it, at least to protect it somehow, to keep it from falling apart outright, I wrapped it in an old soft T-shirt before gently nestling it back in the briefcase. I was extra careful not to tilt the briefcase as I placed it flat on the closet's top shelf. Maybe I should have lit some candles on the altar again? Hell, I had no clue. I really wasn't a natural at these sorts of things. Nathalie would have known what to do, but I didn't.

Strange voodoo twist, minutes after I'd put the briefcase away, ants invaded the apartment like a heat wave had come. They arrived in drunken groups of three and four. Too frenzied to walk in tidy lines, they stampeded each other in their excitement. I watched as some gathered the dead upon their backs for eventual return to the farm. And inexplicably, the room suddenly smelled of Nathalie—of sugar, cloves, and ginger. Her warm sweet spice self detectable in the air, on my clothes, on my very skin, she was a hypnotizing force even in her absence. It was like the ants had arrived in a mad hunt for Nathalie, our candied queen, our sweet heaven. But armies of ants and traces of Nathalie or not, I remained alone. Well, maybe not entirely.

I turned off the lights and picked up the retablo of Nahui from the altar. Even through the darkness, her stare punctured me to my core. She was mine. Or maybe I was hers. Either way, for better or worse, through thick and thin, Nahui had stayed with me like no one else. Of course, I would have preferred Nathalie's company instead of a paper ghost. For the moment at least, I took what I could get.

CHAPTER FOURTEEN

9 November 2002.

I woke totally buzzed and bright-eyed with a cultlike "I adore life" and "The world is love" sort of optimism. Fuck knows where the burst of energy came from, but I was stoked for the change. For the first time in days, I showered and combed my hair and dressed in clean clothes that weren't designed to be slept in. Gliding around all giddy with my feet barely touching the ground, I tidied up the apartment. I opened the windows wide for fresh air and leaned out to take in the view. *Hello Gorgeous Autumn Day! And greetings to you, Mr. Bluebird sitting in your tree.* Then I moved the tiny television from its depressive-viewer position on the nightstand and put it back on its typing table home near the kitchen. *What a good little television you are, thank you for taking such good care of me.* I picked up dirty clothes off the floor and even dusted some surfaces with a more or less clean sock. *Look at you, you pretty little counter, all nice and shiny!* Careful to not tear it—*Don't worry, this won't hurt a bit*—I peeled the jewel-encrusted altar foil from the wall. I'd just started scraping the nasty food remains from the altar plates into the garbage, when the phone rang.

"Hello?"

"Frank, I'll be gone longer than planned," Nathalie said.

Wait a minute, there was a plan? I didn't recall being included in any planning. Had Nathalie shown me an itinerary or projected goals or whatever would go into this sort of plan? Just like that, piss on the parade, my fizzy pep burned out.

"I went grocery shopping this morning," she said, and paused for effect.

By "shopping" she meant that she had wandered up the delivery dock of a health food supermarket and filled her bag with produce and deliveries—she was genius at this, at being so obvious and outrageous that she was beyond reproach.

"So I was shopping," she continued, "and then I realized this other kid was shopping too . . ."

I resisted reminding Nathalie she hadn't qualified for the moniker "kid" in many years.

". . . we wandered off in the same direction and started talking. He's meeting up with some friends tomorrow and they're headed to Tennessee . . ."

Just to torture me more, of course the other person had to be a dude.

"I've always wanted to go to Nashville," she added.

Nathalie wouldn't make it to Tennessee. She'd end up somewhere else and I wouldn't know where she was. I was beginning to realize this was part of the plan.

"Nat, you realize Thanksgiving is coming up?"

"In two weeks."

"It's our seventh anniversary."

"I know."

My silent *and?* sat heavily on the line.

"You plan to be home by then?" I finally asked.

"Promise," she said.

Swing music played in a faint echo through the phone.

"Frank? What's that?"

"Just the phone," I said.

"It's spooky."

"Not really," I said.

"I love you."

"Love you too."

I kept the phone to my ear long after Nathalie had hung

up. And I stared blankly at the retablo on the kitchen table. Nahui had been witness to everything that happened in the apartment. I wished she could speak.

"Come on, can't you say something? Just one little thing?"

Of course the retablo didn't respond.

Stuck, unwilling to move quite yet, I continued to hold the phone to my ear. No dial tone or operator came on. Music continued to play faintly over the line, one scratchy classic tune after another. It might have been the result of a cracked telephone wire somewhere picking up the wrong signal, but I was pretty sure that if I listened hard enough, I'd hear it was Nahui doing the singing.

Even though Nathalie wouldn't be coming home as soon as I'd hoped, I was still showered and dressed and more socially presentable than I'd been in days. And so I headed to the coffee house on 9th Street. Baby steps, you know? At least I'd be out in the world, breathing cool crisp air. In fact, by the time I walked up Avenue B to 9th, I had a slight bounce in my step. And when I walked under the weeping willows at the community garden on Avenue C, long delicate tree tendrils reached down to bless my journey. Determined to stay in my good mood, I even stopped to pet this fat golden retriever tied to the benches outside the coffee house. Inside, I pulled a stool to the clunky wooden bar and said a friendly hello to the cute anarchist-squatter-chic girl working behind the counter. She took my order and brought me a pile of little brown napkins, two sugars, and a wooden stirring stick with my coffee. And she even smiled. Sort of. I mean, as much as an anarchist-squatter-chic girl can smile without blowing her cool.

I sipped my coffee and flipped through a *Village Voice* someone had left lying around. Black ink smearing my fingers, I read my horoscope. Nothing good there. I kept cruising the back pages aimlessly. And that's when I found the announcement:

Estate Sale!
BUSHWICK, BROOKLYN
Saturday November 9th, 8:30 a.m.-4 p.m.
1938 Gaffer & Sattler stove, 1940s movie magazines and books
and family photos. Sofas, assorted chairs, coffee/end tables,
dining room table, king bed, 6-piece full bedroom set, desk, many
cabinets. Vintage jewelry, furs, linens, TVs, trunks, oils, kitchen
banquet set, refrigerator, washer/dryer, assorted pots/pans/
glassware. Wood working stuff, yard/garage tools, used bricks.
Cash only!
Look for red balloon and signs at L train Montrose exit.

What a fucking wonky mix of old-school stuff. And it was
up for in grabs in the middle of barrio Bushwick? There would
be a red balloon? It was all too strange and cool to be true. I
left a tip on the bar for the barista and I walked to the L.

A four-year-old whiner sat next to me, squirming and picking
his nose the entire ride from First & 14th to Brooklyn. He stared
at me. And I stared at him. By the time the train had crossed
under the river, it was like we knew each other. I hated that
kid. I wanted to bite him. But still, since no other commuters
seemed in the mood to be decent, when he and his young mom
got off at Montrose Avenue, I took pity on them and helped
carry his condo-sized stroller up the stairs to the street. Out on
the sidewalk, the kid waved goodbye to me as though we were
best friends. And—like suddenly being caught in a little fox
trap, the kind that gets your ankle in its metal razor jaw teeth—
my flesh ached.

Trust me, it wasn't that my interaction with that little
monster made me long to be a parent. No. Old-fashioned as
maple syrup, I craved the consuming thrill of what so often
preceded the creation of life. I wanted sticky fingers and muddy

boots, a reason to slip under the covers when the sun was still shining. Pure and simple, I wanted to tumble with Nathalie. Or with that anarchist chick at the coffee shop. Or Nahui, for God's sake. But, faithful sort that I am, I took an imaginary cold shower, chilled the fuck out, and looked for a red balloon.

And there it was—there were two balloons actually, but only one was still inflated—on the lamppost nearest the subway exit at the corner of Montrose and Bushwick. A sign was attached to the balloons: *Estate Sale This Way*, with a big arrow pointing up Bushwick. I followed the arrow and eventually found another red balloon and sign tied to a stoop fence: *Buzz #2*.

For a minute I considered that maybe the whole estate sale thing was a hoax. Maybe I was inadvertently about to enter one of those crazy setups you hear about all the time where a crime ring lures a person into a room under false pretenses and then five days later the sucker is found bleeding to death in a bathtub of ice, naked with their kidneys missing. I mean, who the fuck goes off in search of red balloons in Bushwick? I do, that's who.

And so did other people, apparently. I buzzed the intercom and landed in a dank fifth-floor walk-up three-bedroom apartment amidst a hoard of bargain-hunting vultures. I walked down a narrow hallway made even narrower by stacks of old chocolate tins used for storage and clusters of satin-lined hatboxes bursting with ill-fitting contents—a lifetime packed up and priced and ready for purchase. I watched people fight over deathbed linens and wedding bands barely removed from rigor mortis hands. They wanted the goods, but they couldn't have cared a piss about the corpses they stole from. I did. And so, alone in a corner of the apartment's dining room, I searched through messy stacks of old yellowed photographs, looking for the dead people's portraits, for their eyes, for the most beautiful dead girl wherever she might be hiding. The task at hand was not an easy one. There were simply too many choices. And, awesome but unsettling surprise, as I flipped through photos, I swear I started to see Nahui in each and every photo. All the faces started to look like hers in the retablo portrait. Her fiery essence, her scalding stare, her come-hither tease. She was haunting me something good. She was everywhere.

In one black-and-white, a Nahui-wannabe posed on a boardwalk. Gleaming roller coasters behind her, she leaned against a lamppost in a bathing suit and platform esplanades. *Isabella at Coney Island, 1946*. In another photograph, a Nahui-esque woman stood several rows deep in an orchard of sturdy fruit trees, striking a Botticelli pose in an evening gown, her sumptuous arms raised ever so slightly to set shadows in service of her gloriously curved hips. *Tenth Anniversary, Martha's Vineyard, 1957*. In another photo, coated with the powdered blood of a cutlery case's disintegrated red felt lining, a poseur Nahui wore a maid uniform and held a sparkling clean baby boy in front of a birthday cake. That one was inscribed across its back with no more hint than *1905*. And then, fate hit hard:

Photographic silver luster fading, the spark of her serious eyes remained vividly present nonetheless. Gleaming pearls the size of kumquats hung from her neck in long strands. She wore a mink stole, short dress, set-wave bob, and a smug smile.

I took my darling to the bedroom furthest down the hall. Hidden from the probing eyes of the estate sale staff who sat at the apartment's front door waiting to catch people sneaking items, I tucked the photograph up my sleeve with a single swift gesture. A couple meaningless small items purchased at the front door to ward off suspicion, my affair began.

Paper cuts on the underside of my left wrist, the excitement of my heist making my hands tremble, safe out of sight from the apartment, two blocks away, I took the photo from my sleeve and wrapped my girl in the softest material I'd come to own that day, an embroidered handkerchief marked with a cigarette burn from fifty years before.

As I rode the train and walked home, one stolen moment at a time, I searched the photograph for clues. Draped in flapper threads, this Nahui was posed in, of all places, Tompkins Square Park. She'd been so close. Eighty years earlier, she'd stood dolled up within sight of my apartment window. Chances were she'd just come from Lansky Lounge on Norfolk with her gangster boyfriend. Her satin high heels were stained at the toe. Tipsy from all the brandy she'd sipped out of dainty Prohibition teacups, she'd splashed in a puddle in the back alleyway exit at Lansky's. In the getaway car, she'd worn a platinum wig disguise over her auburn bobbed permanent waves. She was dangerous perfection.

Cherry on top, she'd posed for her photograph near the park's entrance at Avenue A and St. Mark's—at the Temperance Fountain. Drunk off her darling little ass, she'd leaned against the marble pillars of a public monument dedicated to the virtues of sobriety for her picture pose. It was all too fucking good. As I squinted to admire more closely my flapper, I noticed a slightly rusty indentation on the upper left corner of the photograph. The mark appeared to be the swirling pattern of a paper clip long ago removed. A relic if ever one existed, more precious than a drop of milk from any virgin's pert breast, the missing paper clip likely sat upon a velvet cushion on an altar in some cathedral somewhere.

I almost could have wandered off in search of that damned paper clip. I would have loved to pack a bag and head out, stopping at every goddamned church from New York to California and down to Mexico, across all of Latin America, and through Europe. Why the fuck not? (The dough required to globe-wander was one issue, but money shouldn't factor in escapist fantasies, so *whatever*.) In all seriousness, I probably should have gone off to find that Holy Grail paper clip, because the second I got to my empty apartment, I remembered. I was so fucking lonely.

In search of some perverted fun, I lay my flapper date face up on the kitchen table. Nahui, the *real* Nahui, watched from her framed retablo as I, with a single steady push of my palm, smoothed the flapper's curling body. Photographic image and paper peeled away from one another. Corners of the flapper's dress and bits of her face clung to my nervous damp skin— together she and I were exquisite ruin. I tucked what was left of the photo in my wallet. When I saw the flapper smiling her sultry smile at me from the wallet's clear plastic pocket—that standard billfold feature designed for proud daddy photographic displays of wife and babies—I felt a momentary pang of guilt. But it wasn't like the retablo of Nahui would have fit there anyway. And as for Nathalie, it was becoming clearer and clearer that the only accurate sweetheart portrait of her might be an empty frame.

CHAPTER FIFTEEN

27 November 2002.

In traditional Japanese movies, ghosts hop, they don't float—this thought came from some obscure fold in my cerebral cortex as the front door opened and closed and a nearly silent stride made its way into the apartment and stopped directly behind me.

My brain had begun to do tricky things while Nathalie was gone. By the second week of her absence, when I tried to imagine her in my mind's eye, the focus was fuzzy. I couldn't recall specific details of her person, like which side of her lip had freckles and what her skin smelled like when we fucked. Losing her so quickly in my memory was unsettling. Especially because, at the same time, I could clearly imagine Nahui-the-flapper, my make-believe girlfriend, pinned under me, my hands slicked with her metallic sugar.

So, yes, when Nathalie entered the apartment and approached, I jumped, startled out of what had become nearly constant daydreams. I stood frozen, facing the sink of dishes I'd been washing. My pants grew tighter at the thigh. Heavier and heavier, dead weight pulled on my pocket lining. Solid clanking sound. Rocks. From the places Nathalie had been. Rocks she had collected for me.

"To ground you," she explained.

Pretty fucking funny.

To let me know she thought of me always, she said. Little earthly delights. All the souvenir rocks transferred to my possession, Nathalie curved her body up against my back and pushed her mouth to my left ear.

"Happy anniversary, love," she said.

It's tomorrow, I wanted to correct her. To scold her. Shame her. Punish her.

"Happy anniversary," was all that came out of my mouth as I turned around to face her.

She'd been smoking again. Lots. The first cigarette of her renewed habit had most likely been justified as a well-deserved end to a particularly tough day. But that was just the first cigarette, probably smoked at some Greyhound station equipped with a snack machine that stole her quarters and a soda machine that would only give Mountain Dew. Blotches of deep violet shaded the thin and finely lined skin under Nathalie's eyes. A matching set of bruises fanned out from near each tear duct. Allergic shiners. Self-inflicted lavender.

Lavender. Before Ivory existed all individually paper-wrapped on store shelves, people smelled a little less human by rubbing themselves with lavender. Filling large tubs of hot water with the herb, they seasoned and marinated themselves like the edible mammals they were. Lavender. Nathalie's lavender was different in that it was caused by the inflammation of her ethmoid sinus cavities—the honeycomb-intricate hollow pockets of warmed air in the moist patch of skull between her eyes had been strained by too much smoke. I knew this geeky factoid tidbit from back in junior high when my mother began her fright tactics to make sure I didn't start smoking: *I'll know just by looking at you if you've been smoking, Francisca*, she'd say with a totally serious and intimidating tone. Anyway, Nat on occasion gave herself temporary black eyes. I saw her dark circle bruising and wished I knew exactly what she had done while she'd been gone. All I really knew was that she'd been smoking again.

I hated feeling so shut out of three weeks of her life, but I feared if I let my discomfort show, she'd misunderstand my pain and think I wasn't happy to have her home. So I played it cool. I put on my best Humphrey Bogart smooth attitude and fed her the in-control charmer line I'd prepared for her return.

"Doll," I said, "I'm going to plant a forest for you."

"You're what?"

"There's a pothole at 7th and B."

"Okay . . ."

"But the forest will need your supervision."

"I think it'd be fine without me," she said, laughing.

I had missed that laugh so goddamned much.

I wished for a reality in which Nathalie and I could sit on the fire escape with our toes dug into the leaves of an evergreen forest I'd plant for us; together we'd watch it grow one inch, then one foot, then one story, then one mile up into the air.

"Seriously, I'm going to plant a tree," I said.

"That's sweet, Frank. Strange, but sweet."

Nathalie didn't believe me. She was humoring me. But I was absolutely serious. I would plant an entire forest if it would keep her home with me.

She reached behind me and searched through a bag of groceries I'd left on the kitchen counter from errands earlier. One skinny arm wrapped tightly around my ribs, she held a box of pink cake mix close to my face.

"This shit is poison," she whispered into my ear, and pushed me hard against cheap cabinet compressed wood.

My lower back ached and my heart rattled. My girl was home again. And for that very second at least, every molecule of her imperfect being was all mine. Instant cake powder perfumed the air around us. The effect was stick and carrot combined. Right there at the kitchen sink, I fucked Nathalie. Hard. My skull crashed into her tangled crown. We bruised elbows and knees and pinched fingers in sliding drawers. A glass shattered on the floor. Nathalie nearly made me deaf with her screaming. I fell in love all over again. And in the midst of it, I cried.

Only two things had ever brought me to tears. One: my father's death. And two: the way the three freckles on Nathalie's left lower lip disappeared into a flustered blush when we fucked. Sick triggers to mention in the same breath, I know. But so be it. Those were the two things that made me cry. Nathalie. The only person I'd ever been able to imagine myself all shriveled up and gray and slow-walking old with. She was the one.

And so, her complicated self in my arms, I cried. I tried not to let her know. I think I got away with it. Maybe she didn't know. But I did cry. And I willed my tears to stain. I wanted to claim her as exclusively mine. Properly embarrassed by this canine desire, I resisted leaving any literal mottled evidence on her willing neck. I wanted to mark Nathalie in ways regenerative white cells and oxygen would never erase.

We fucked. I cried. And then:

"Darling, I need a bath," she said. And walked away.

Puppy me, I was loathe to lose Nathalie's scent, her muddy hair and the bitter grapes behind her ears, the tart fresh-cut cactus taste she left on my hands. I detested that Nathalie would wash so much away.

That said, the heaven excellence that soon followed—days of road-travel scrubbed off, auburn locks slicked wet to her shoulders, her entire body streaked with beading water and ready for more adoration—was consolation aplenty.

You have your father's blood in you.

Rude interruption, my mother's words echoed in my thoughts.

Nathalie stared at me with the slightest of smiles, her eyes relaxed and tired. Water dripped off her and onto the wood floor, her majesty warping the forests that lay themselves at her feet to be walked upon.

You have your father's blood in you.

"Frank?"

I'd been staring at Nathalie for who knows how many minutes. The girl got me directly in my chest. Ribs simply shouldn't be cracked open and separated by a layperson. Cardiac matter shouldn't be touched but in the most pristine environments. Even then, complications are likely to occur.

"Nat, you've got my heart on a silver platter."

Shy girl all of a sudden, she just smiled bashfully and tapped her toes in the micro-puddle that'd formed narcissus pond around her as she stood there goose-bump chilled and admired.

"Wait just a sec," I said, and retrieved the thickest and softest towel we owned. I patted my darling dry. It was the least I could do. Whereas some might have found this sub-servient devotion pitiful, I knew that at least my father would have understood.

You have your father's blood in you.

Duh, mother.

Damp bath towel dropped to the floor at Nathalie's feet, I kissed the girl's jagged skinny hipbones. I kissed her where the baby down hair of her belly turned coarse. I kissed the smooth skin of her thighs and trailed kisses to the crook of her knees. Kisses upon her feet, I bowed down before her in the only manner she deserved.

And I asked: "Nat, why'd you leave?"

"I love you, Frank."

"Seriously, please . . ."

"Can we talk after I sleep a little?"

From her non-answer I knew that if I'd ever hear directly from her mouth why she'd gone, it wouldn't be for a long time to come, much further into the future than the culmination of her nap. I tried to remind myself that three weeks of relationship breakdown in a span of nearly seven years wasn't inherently some sort of deal breaker. I mean, really, what was I aiming for, prescribed *Leave It to Beaver* bullshit? The girl had needed time away. She hadn't gone about getting it in the most considerate way, but she loved me, I'd get over my hurt, and she'd make it up to me. Mostly, I was relieved she was home again. I just wanted to get on with our life. So, we'd talk when we talked. There was no need to force anything. True, I could have insisted we have a marathon processing session without further delay. I could have said she had no right to make me wait for an explanation. But I didn't. Instead, I tucked my girl in the narrow mess of our bed with a kiss. Back home after wandering to exactly where I didn't know, finally home, mouth open and quiet rasping breath, Nathalie quickly fell into a deep sleep.

Not tired, I sat and watched her sleep for a long while. At one point, someone cruised by on the street in a pumped-up low rider and rattled me out of my daze. The roaring engine and rumbling bass triggered car alarms and our windows turned kinetic like marbles in a coffee can rattle. Sudden shallow breath and sharp limbs all frenetic, Nathalie tossed and turned momentarily before settling into deep sleep yet again.

Wanting to hold her, to crawl in bed with her and let the day be done, I went to the kitchen for a glass of water. When I reached into the cupboard for my bottle of pink pills, I found that it was empty. How that had happened without my noticing, without my realizing I needed to get a refill—well, I took it as a sign. I got dressed for bed and, although it took a long time, eventually I fell asleep holding Nathalie tight to make sure she wouldn't disappear in the middle of the night.

CHAPTER SIXTEEN

28 November 2002. Thanksgiving Day.

My darling dearest woke me the morning of our seventh anniversary by perching on my lap and planting endless kisses upon my brow. This gesture had once been a familiar comfort between us. As was our old routine, I responded by rolling Nathalie up against the wall and fucking her quick and sweet. And then we lay on the bed sweaty and tired. I held her bony beautifulness. Even after what had been a miraculously long and peaceful night of sleep, we fell into a midmorning nap we barely intended to wake from. Then Nathalie decided she needed a coffee from down the street.

"Babe, we have coffee here."

"I'd love a bodega coffee, light and sweet."

And so I threw on clothes and headed off to run the errand specifically assigned to make sure I knew good and plenty who was in charge. After taking my time, I returned to the apartment with the bodega coffee. Nathalie stood in the kitchen holding a Mason jar. I'd left the jar in the cupboard for her to find.

"What's this?"

"Your anniversary gift."

"And what exactly is my anniversary gift, dear?"

"'Shrooms. In honey. For my sweet," I said as casually as possible, and left her cup of coffee on the counter.

"Seriously?"

"The honey's a preservative," I offered, even though I

knew she wasn't seeking further explanation on that particular detail.

"Frank, I know that. Hello, *'shrooms?*"

The quizzical look on her face was totally understandable. We didn't typically keep stashes of hallucinogens in the honey, let alone anywhere in the apartment. That's not to say that we shouldn't have considered the idea before, but we simply hadn't. So . . .

I explained. Rather, I told her the part I was willing to reveal at that point:

The Monday after she phoned from Texas, I'd called my temp placement office and said I was available for assignment again. The next day, I reported to the corporate insurance company I'd been at before my week out "sick." For eight hours a day, I entered data into Excel spreadsheets, ran a few interoffice hand deliveries, and did some copying like a good little trained monkey. It fucking sucked, but whatever, there were free bagels in the break room, and it paid well. Unfortunately, on the first day back I was in the Xerox room copying some account summaries when I ran into this one other temp dude. I'd made the mistake of going to lunch with him when I'd first been assigned to the company, and I'd since learned he was the sort of person who would corner you and talk at you with his bad breath for hours at a time if you let him. He was a totally self-righteous artist-wannabe type who was maybe in his early twenties, but who threw vibe like he was Malcolm X, Buddha, and Che all rolled up into a single slow-moving slim muscled body. One time he'd shown me the T-shirt he wore under his office drag. It was black and it said *Gun Club of Brooklyn* on it. The shirt would been cool except its wearer tried way too hard. For instance: Once, in that same Xerox room, Cool Dude parted his cotton-mouthed lips to tell me I needed to learn how to aim and shoot firearms.

"I don't like guns," I'd said.

"Neither do I, but come the revolution, you will need them," he'd replied with barely a smidgen of irony.

So anyway, there we were in the Xerox room again. And I still had several stacks of copies to make. I was stuck. For reasons unknown, he asked if I'd be interested in buying some 'shrooms. He said his hippie parents had given them to him during a visit to their recently acquired New Mexico retirement adobe.

"I've never seen so much goddamned turquoise jewelry. And all the strung-up red chiles in adobe doorways . . . God, I fucking hate the Southwest," he'd said.

I tried to change the subject. He asked again if I wanted the 'shrooms.

"He wouldn't quit pestering me," I told Nathalie.

What I didn't tell Nathalie was that I took Cool Dude up on his offer because of her. I figured if she wanted things to be an adventure all the time, then fine, I'd buy the 'shrooms and give them to her when she came back. Maybe then she'd realize she didn't have to leave to escape. I was plenty aware that Nathalie was handful enough without the added benefit of hallucinogens, organic or not, but if she was determined to put on a show, not only was I game, but I could match her and up the ante some.

"He said they're really good," I added.

Jar still in hand, Nathalie smiled.

"Let's eat them," she said.

"They're for you, sweetie."

"You're not going to do any?"

"Nah, not my thing."

"Come on, Frank."

"They're all yours."

"I want to do them now."

"Okay," I said, pretending I couldn't care less one way or

the other, knowing full well my seeming indifference would push her in exactly the direction I was hoping she'd go.

It was all perfect, really. Truly. I had such a fucking perfect plan.

I took the Mason jar from Nathalie and sat at the kitchen table. Nathalie grabbed her coffee and joined me. Vacuum-sealed golden lid unscrewed, I dipped my right index finger in the jar and coated it with honey.

"They used to do this at flea circuses," I said.

Messy sticky finger, I wrote N-A-T in cursive on the tabletop. A cluster of the ants—relatives of those that had arrived the night Nat first called from the road—bolted from their tidy marching line along the wall to eat the bounty. Within minutes, Nathalie's name appeared in pulsing, living script. As the ants then carried the honey away on their backs or antennae or however it is ants transport such things, we watched Nathalie's name disappear like some Seurat pointillist print turning to ash. Best part was knowing that, trace amounts of the 'shrooms in each molecule of the honey, those ants—same as me—would be forever changed after their first taste of Nathalie.

"Be ready in an hour," I said.

"For what?"

"We're going to the forest."

I handed her the jar of 'shrooms and left.

By early afternoon, we were in a crappy rented station wagon at the gas station under the FDR at East 23rd. Faux bored expression, Nathalie sat on the passenger side of the front bench seat and pretended not to watch as I maneuvered a squeegee with refined show-off skill.

"No point in a pleasure drive if the windshield is dirty," I said—this bit of advice once sarcastically offered to me by my blind father himself.

After each stroke, gray soapy water dripping down the windshield, I wiped the squeegee's rubber blade across a stiff tree-bark paper towel. If all I could do was provide Nathalie a clear view, I hoped that this in and of itself might just be enough to keep her by my side.

Our station wagon's failing automatic transmission lurched into high gear as I pulled out and headed north on the FDR. Nathalie turned slightly green as her stomach acids went on overdrive to digest the hallucinogens into little particles of sugared brain-trick. She curled into a legs-up and chin-on-knees position.

"We're really going to the forest?" she asked.

"Where else would I get a tree to plant on Avenue B for you?"

"No joke?"

"No joke."

"Cool."

Really, my plan was a joke, a pathetically comical excuse to make sure I got to spend the day with Nathalie, alone, in situations—driving along the highway, stopping deep in the forest—that she couldn't easily leave. So why didn't we just go for a drive to Maine for some lobster dinner or something? Well:

1. Lobster smells like piss, it's no good without melted butter, and dairy gave me the shits.
2. Have you ever heard a lobster scream when it's boiled?
3. No lobster place would be open on Thanksgiving night.
4. Nathalie would never have been into such a conventional trip, even if it had been a good idea.

Put simply, our anniversary celebration had to be outrageous and unexpected. Self-consciously so. Or else

Nathalie would find it drab. And really, what could be more outrageous or unexpected than driving out to the forest on Thanksgiving to steal a tree to plant in a pothole in the middle of the East Village as a declaration of love? It was perfect. Or so I hoped.

Nathalie groaned and I looked over to see that not only had she turned even greener from carsickness, but she was now shivering, and her face glistened with a light sweat.

"Nat, should I pull over?"

"No. Thank you," she answered haltingly.

She rolled down the passenger window and closed her eyes. Late-afternoon sunlight, diffused into patches of crimson and bright gold, pulsed through the windshield. Within fifteen minutes, Nathalie was asleep.

Two hours north of the city, I parked on the side of a deserted woodland road and turned off the station wagon's rattling engine. Nathalie didn't yawn, wake up, or even move. I returned to the car twenty minutes later, dragging my plucked forest prize. Scratching struggle, I tucked the evergreen sapling into the station wagon's flat bed. Nathalie still slept.

An hour into our drive home, an SUV abruptly pulled across my lane in an ill-conceived effort to get to his exit. I slammed on the brakes. No crash ensued, but I cussed plenty and the sapling shifted audibly. Nathalie finally opened her eyes. Even in the dark of night, I could see her pupils were like pixilated sequins, all shifting and watery.

"Honey," she said, very quietly.

"Yes?" I asked, touched by the unexpected nicety.

"I mean I taste honey," she said.

"Oh."

"She cut through me like a pavement saw."

Fuck left field, I swore sometimes Nathalie came from outside the stadium entirely.

"'Shrooms kick in?" I asked.

"No," she said humorlessly.

"You got a good nap at least."

"The 'shrooms were bunk. I crashed from all the honey." And then she said again: *"She cut through me like a pavement saw."*

Silence.

"It's Nahui's inscription. From *A dix ans sur mon pupitre,* remember?" she asked.

Maybe the 'shrooms were working just the tiniest bit.

"Of course I remember," I said.

"I like it."

"Me too. In fact, maybe . . ."

Before I could finish my thought, Nathalie blurted out, "Frank, pull over, quick."

"You okay?"

"Please, pull over," she whined through clenched teeth.

I jerked to the gravel side of the highway. Nathalie threw her door open, bolted out, and puked next to some trash-clotted shrubs. I rushed to her side.

"Baby, can I do anything?"

Embarrassed, she waved me away. And I hate to say this, but thank God she didn't want me there. The smell of her toxic vomit made me gag. I waited for her in the station wagon.

"Feel better?"

"Not really."

We drove across the George Washington Bridge just as the digits on the station wagon's dashboard clock reconfigured to read 7:00. Nathalie would have under ten hours to hydrate, rest, and prepare herself properly.

4:45 A.M. Tompkins Square Park and the entire East Village the quietest it ever got, in the sore strip of East 7th Street at Avenue B, out front the newest crappy boutique with the vaguely plastic name, an evergreen tree was about to appear.

I located the deepest of metropolitan potholes in said intersection and asked Nathalie for her assistance. As she leaned the delicate sapling against her shivering body, its trunk soiled her winter coat, and its fragile upper branches tangled in her hair. I bowed down on my knees with tools at my side.

The asphalt was fucking freezing, but I didn't care. Barehanded, I centered the sapling's roots in their pothole cradle and unloaded a bag of soil and some heavy rocks to make a tight and solid base. My victory garden firmly anchored, I secured a gold glittering craft-store bird, all spray-painted cheap chicken feathers and Styrofoam core, to the sapling's uppermost branch. I felt a tension in my chest I didn't even know I'd been carrying with me loosen. I could breathe. Deeply. And so I did. Breathe. Deeply. A brisk green scent filled my lungs and sparked the most fantastic mood. I beamed a smile at Nathalie. She smiled back, though with considerably less exuberance.

The police didn't come. Nobody walked by or yelled reprimands from their apartment window. The few cars that drove past were careful to not hit us, but didn't acknowledge our existence otherwise. Encouraged by what seemed to be a late-night downtown superhuman cloak of invisibility, I added the final touch with particularly careful and loving calm.

Billy the Kid, that pimply faced boy in tight cowboy regalia, always wrote press releases to leave at his own crime scenes. Inspired by his ingenuity, I hung a gold picture frame from the sapling's strongest branch. Penned in gold ink, the press release simply read:

She cut through me like a pavement saw.

A love letter. From Nahui. To my father's mother. From me. To Nathalie. For the entire world to read.

* * *

As the sun rose and we sat at the kitchen table drinking mugs of hot carob soy milk, I gave Nathalie my hand.

"Splinter," I said.

Thrown off for only a second, Nathalie walked to the kitchen and took a small safety pin from her ancient dress's fallen hem. She lit the stove's pilot and held the tip in the orange flame until silver turned black and then red and glowing hot. Seated in her chair by my side again, she took my hand and, austere surgical grace, pushed pointed metal through the top layers of my thick skin. Her pupils huge in the apartment's dim light, she asked if the pin hurt.

"No," I replied.

She smiled quietly and applied more pressure. When I finally flinched, she waited a moment before removing the pin and pulling the splinter from my skin. Pin wiped clean and the hem of her gown refastened, she took my finger to her mouth. I watched as she sucked a single drop of blood from my fingertip. The dull ache in my finger disappeared.

"Thanks," I said.

"Thank *you*," she said, and licked her lips.

CHAPTER SEVENTEEN

Nat and I eventually crashed around seven that morning. When we finally came to and peeled our dry eyes open again, it was late afternoon and we were wicked hungry. *Hungry*—like if a small child had entered the apartment we just might have Texas-barbequed him and served him up with a side of slaw. In search of comfort food, something soaked in grease and bathed in salt, something that would stick heavily to our insides and ground us, we tugged on clothes and headed out to 2nd Ave Deli. But first we detoured to Avenue B. Of course, the tree and gold-framed love letter were already long gone. Even the pothole was back to its original deep-pit state. In fact, we were only able to find the tiniest tidbit of evidence that Project Evergreen hadn't been some sort of mutual hallucination. A few gold feathers from the craft-store bird I'd secured to the tree lay wedged in the cracked asphalt near the pothole. As we left, I picked up the feathers and put them in my pocket.

We made it to 2nd Ave Deli and happily suffered customary abuse from the helmet-haired hostess and our probably once-vixen eighty-year-old waitress, Daisy. Buckets of bitter deli coffee and mounds of potato pancakes with applesauce and ketchup later, stuffed to the gills and moving even slower than when we woke, we eventually moseyed back home, hand-in-hand, neither of us in any particular rush. We were on 9th Street, just past First Avenue, when someone called out Nathalie's name.

We stopped and stared at each other, not sure where the voice had come from.

"Up here, silly!"

We looked up to find the singsong interruption lilting out from a fourth-floor apartment window. A pretty little fag in a striped polo shirt and jeans was posing at the windowsill like the parade had taken a side route and the float had gotten stuck four floors up. Princess kept waving and smiling—so many teeth, such a pearly smile—and I had absolutely no fucking idea who he was.

"Georgie!" Nat squealed up at him.

Georgie?

"Get up here this instant, missy," he commanded, planting his hands on his hips and scowling.

Nat giggled like a schoolgirl.

"And bring that yummy creature with you," he purred, peering down at me.

"Nat?" I asked through a polite smile.

"That's George."

Uh, okay. And?

"He's from the ad agency I worked at a couple months ago."

"Buzz number five!" he called down to us, and disappeared back into his apartment.

"Want to go up?" Nat asked.

"Not really."

"Ah, come on, he's really sweet."

"No thanks."

"Okay, love. I'll be home soon." She gave me a peck on the cheek and skipped off to buzz George's number five.

I continued onward until, six doors west from Avenue A, on the north side of the street, I saw a red and white rental sign propped in the window of an empty storefront. Instead of heading off to the warmth and comfort of home,

I found myself staring in through the empty storefront's smudged windows. It was one of those moments that will never make sense to anyone else no matter how many times I try to explain it. For some reason, as I stared into that tiny and sad-looking space, it hit me that I was thirty and that I didn't want to be a temp for stupid fucking corporate America anymore. Maybe Nathalie's return activated some primal desire to make a life for us. I don't know, but as sudden and totally illogical as it may have been, I knew I wanted to rent the storefront. I wanted to open a little shop and be my own boss and set my own hours and create a livelihood of my own from the ground up. Yes, just like that. Out of fucking nowhere. Told you it didn't make sense. But that's what happened. Some sort of rattling alarm went off inside me, and there was no going back to sleep. I memorized the phone number on the sign and went home.

It wasn't until later that night that I got up the nerve to call the number. Nathalie was cooking dinner and pretending to not listen as I talked to the property owner.

When I hung up, she waited several minutes before finally asking, "Anything you'd like to tell me?"

"There's a *For Rent* sign on 9th."

"A *For Rent* sign?"

"I was thinking maybe I could open a shop."

"A shop? What kind of shop?"

"I don't know, like cool vintage stuff or something."

"Babe, where's this coming from?"

That was the first time I tried to explain. I could tell from the look on Nathalie's face that my newfound goal sounded insane.

"Okay, first of all," she said, "there are already tons of shops like that in the neighborhood."

"I know, but mine would be better."

"It probably would be, but seriously, since when did you want to open a shop?"

Why did Nathalie have to get so damned sensible all of a sudden?

"I just thought of it today."

"Maybe you should think about it for a little longer?"

Of course, Nathalie was right. And so, her bewilderment and my own self-doubt combined, I agreed to sit on the idea. But I thought about it constantly—as we ate dinner that night, in my sleep, the entire weekend through, on my walk to work, when I should have been entering data into spreadsheets, all the fucking time. In fact, I even started cruising the Internet and found out which licenses a person needs to open a small business in Manhattan. I downloaded applications and jotted notes about required fees. I grabbed my checkbook and worked out numbers. I drew sketches of business-card logos and window displays and contemplated stupid shit like whether I'd use a cash box and calculator or a register. Night after night, I walked past the storefront on my way home from work, dreaming about all the cool things I wanted to sell. And, as if to keep me torn between hard reality and daydream fantasies, the red rental sign stayed in the window. The shop seemed to be waiting for me to come and take claim of it.

Two weeks from the day I first spotted it, Nat and I were eating dinner when she said, "I saw the rental sign is still in the shop window . . ."

That was all the encouragement I needed.

Even though it was after office hours on a Friday night, I called the phone number that still blazed brightly in the foreground of my mental Filofax. An old woman answered the phone this time. In the background, I heard what sounded like a football game playing full volume on the television.

"Hello, I'm calling about the property on 9th Street."

"Hold on just a second, dear . . . Harold, phone!"

And then the old man said: "Harold speaking."

The next morning, nine o'clock sharp, I met Harold in person. Luck shining down on me, he was a jovial guy with sparkling, kind eyes.

"Bet you didn't know this used to be a hardware store, did you?"

And so began the narration of his life story:

Born and raised, he'd lived his whole life downtown. Right out of high school, he'd started working in a hardware shop—this shop, the shop I now wanted to rent. Back in 1949, he'd met his wife in this same shop. She'd come in looking for a rat trap. Little did she know she'd end up with the rat. He nudged me and laughed gently. They married. Started a family. He kept working hard. They saved any money they could. Eventually, the owner sold him the shop. "For practically nothing. He was a good man, that one." Decades passed, and when it was time to retire, he and his wife decided to rent out the storefront. They moved to New Jersey. "So the grandkids would have a yard to play in," he said.

He asked me what my plans for the storefront were. I told him. He asked if I had the paperwork in order. No, I confessed, I didn't. "But my family had a little shop back in California. Running a business is in my blood," I said, padding the truth. He smiled. He said he liked me, I seemed like a nice kid, I had gumption, just like him when he was young.

"My nephew Sammy, he works at the Department of Consumer Affairs. Over on Broadway. He'll pull some strings for you."

I was given the necessary details and instructed to meet with Sammy on Monday morning.

"First and last, and the place is yours. Call me."

I practically ran home to tell Nathalie.

"No way . . . seriously?"

"I can't even tell you how excited I am, Nat."

"This is totally crazy," she sort of laughed, but there was a warm glow to her and I could tell she was impressed.

That Sunday night I called in sick at the temp agency. Bright and early Monday morning, I walked over to meet Sammy. He was as nice as his uncle—exactly where do these people come from?—and like his uncle had promised, he helped me with all the necessary forms. As I sat at his desk with a small Styrofoam cup of coffee he'd insisted on getting for me, he made several calls and arranged to put a rush on all my paperwork.

"You'll be up and running in four weeks, tops," he said, smiling.

The holidays were little more than a week away. Harold and Sammy would be receiving gift baskets of the nicest dried fruits, chocolates, and peanut brittle that Russ and Daughters' appetizing shop had to offer.

On the walk home from Broadway, I stopped at the bank and officially drained all my meager savings to obtain a cashier's check in the amount Howard had specified. The next morning, he met me at the shop, and I signed a one-year lease.

"Now, you can't sell anything until your license is in order, but you've got plenty to do in the meantime," he said, and handed me keys. "Good luck."

I called Nathalie, and she promised to meet me at the shop on her way home from work.

When she arrived, she said, "Oh my God, this place is such shit," and laughed nervously.

It was true. I'd spent the entire day sweeping and mopping and wiping things down, but the storefront was in need of some serious love. Over the next several days, the white on the raised numbers of my credit card began to rub off for how often I used plastic to buy supplies. I had no fucking idea what I was doing really, but, a growing lump of debt all mine, I'd gathered some supplies and was getting down to work. As other people did whatever it is they do at Christmastime, I wore my shittiest jeans and hoody and shivered with the door propped open as I painted the shop.

By New Year's Eve, the paint had dried and the space was immaculately clean, but still, other than permanent shelves and display counters, the place remained empty. Obviously, that was a problem. A big problem. I was sitting on the floor of the shop, head in hands, wondering what the fuck I'd gotten myself into, a pulsating knot in my chest feeling like it just might expand and become a full-fledged freak-out— when there was a tap on the glass of the shop door: Nathalie, with an immense cheapie bottle of champagne in tow.

"To all good things," she cheered, then popped the cork.

Champagne splashed on the floor. I cleaned up the spill with paper towels as Nathalie and I took turns drinking from the bottle.

Luckily, my ability to spot vintage kitsch gold amid piles of crap was Superman keen. To get my shop stocked, I made expert use of the thrifting skills I'd refined from adolescence onward. Each day for two weeks I rented a car and tore through every estate sale in the tri-state area. At night I returned to the shop to drop off carefully picked vintage clothes, jewelry, record albums, and other trinkets and enticing oddities.

Sammy called. He had my license ready for pick-up.

The shop was stocked.

All that was left to do was hang a shingle and pass out flyers.

"Nat, which do you like more, Frank's Finds or Curro's Curios?"

"What's a *Curro*?"

"Nickname for Francisco."

"How do you get *Curro* from *Francisco*?"

"Don't know. How about *Dick* from *Richard*?"

"Curro's Curios," she said. "Definitely, Curro's Curios."

And so it was decided.

Nat helped me Xerox flyers announcing the shop's grand opening—Saturday, January 18, 2003—and then she walked around the neighborhood, looking fabulous and charming people into promising they'd come check out the shop. The night before opening day, she even made batch after batch of chocolate chip cookies and bought tons of brightly colored napkins and plastic cups along with huge cartons of punch and lemonade from the grocery store. She was having a blast preparing to play hostess.

Opening day finally arrived. People trickled in, and slowly, too slowly really to be comforting, I began to sell some stuff. Nat, continuing in her role as the sensible one for the first time in our relationship, kept her temp gigs and offered to try to cover all our basic home expenses until the shop took off. She even threw down most of the second month's rent and utilities and offered to help out on weekends. For a while at least, I had hope.

CHAPTER EIGHTEEN

13 February 2003.

Given that it was smack in the middle of a brutally freezing winter and Nathalie had stayed home with the flu, I was more than a little surprised to come home and find her stark naked but for a rhinestone barrette pulling her bangs off her freshly cleaned face, broom and dustpan at her side. It seemed she'd been "cleaning" the closet—really just rifling through piles of clothes, dusty stacks of record albums and magazines, and, it appeared, my father's briefcase.

"Nat?"

"Hi, love," she said, and gave me a quick kiss.

"Shouldn't you be resting?"

"I did all day. I feel better," she said, sweetly and almost convincingly. And then: "By the way, you left your wallet this morning." She pointed to the nightstand.

"Thanks."

Nathalie responded with distracted nod and a pinched smile.

I found myself wishing she could afford a polite, *How was the shop today?* With meager sales those first few weeks the store was open, she probably figured it better not to ask. But why the strange vibe? She was clearly all worked up over something. Exhausted from yet another stressful day, I didn't have the energy it would require to get to the source of her bizarreness. Hoping to avoid the topic entirely, I took off my hat, scarf, coat, and shoes, lay down on the bed, and tried to distract myself with opening mail. At one point, Nathalie disappeared into the bathroom—and reappeared wearing something that momentarily stunned me.

My father's blind man dark glasses.

The stupid Dean & DeLuca catalog I'd been studying—glossy pages still open to the smoked salmon items whose descriptions I could recite by heart for how they suddenly stuck in my brain—slid from my hands and landed on the floor with a slick pathetic thump.

"Mind if I wear these?" Nathalie asked.

"You already are," I said, deeply uncomfortable but totally at a loss to articulate that discomfort, even to myself.

"So, it's okay?" she asked.

"They're for blind people."

My words were coming out too simple and slow. I sounded dumb. I wasn't angry exactly, but I felt violated on a cellular level somehow.

"Can I wear them?"

"Why do you want to?"

"Can I?"

"I guess."

"Good."

I was trying to figure out a way to tell her to please take off the glasses without seeming too sensitive, when, barely a beat later, out of nowhere, she said: "Frank, let's have a baby."

Mind you, she stood there wearing absolutely nothing other than a barrette and my father's glasses.

"Very funny, Nat."

She took off the glasses, left them on the kitchen counter, crossed the room, and lay on the bed next to me.

"Come on," she asked, "don't you want a baby?"

Sweet mercy—had Nat's fever finally gotten the best of her? No, she was serious. My brain struggled to catch up. If there was anyone in the world I would want a baby with, it would be Nathalie, but . . .

"It's not just if I *want* or don't want a baby, Nat."

I imagined checkbooks, science labs, fertility doctors, not to mention my father's blind eyes trailing along for the ride. Most importantly, I wasn't even sure I wanted kids.

"We'd figure everything out," Nathalie said cheerily.

Did she really want me to delineate the obvious aloud? First of all, we didn't have the money necessary to raise a kid responsibly. And even if we did, Nathalie knew that having a baby wouldn't be just prenatal vitamins from the corner pharmacy and don't use a condom for a few months. She knew it wasn't as simple as my saying, *Sure, sweetums, let's do it, we've got nothing to worry about and we'll have a perfect baby so long as you don't chug Wild Turkey or hit the Parliaments while you're pregnant.* She knew this.

But still she said, "You don't think we're a good family?"

Whatever came out of my mouth next needed to be damned articulate. I didn't respond.

"Frank," she said, "come on . . . tell me."

And so I said the only honest and kind thing I could at that moment: "I love you, Nat."

"Never mind," she said and play-slapped me. "I was just kidding." Her laughter was too loud, forced.

Sick twist was that if I had agreed with her and said, *Yes, heck, why not, let's have a baby,* she might have dropped the subject, never to pick it up again. But I couldn't just blurt out that I wanted a baby if I wasn't totally sure whether I did or didn't. That'd be plain wrong.

"We're going to the protest on Saturday, right?" Nathalie asked.

"I figured."

This new thread wasn't exactly a change in conversation. In our neighborhood, the upcoming protest at the U.N. had been on the tips of everyone's tongues for weeks. You couldn't walk through the park without getting at least four flyers about different groups organizing volunteers. NPR was constantly making announcements about whether or not the federal government was going to let the protest happen. Over two hundred thousand people were expected to show up at the U.N. to demonstrate against sending troops to Iraq. The topic was omnipresent; it pervaded even conversations that seemed to have no relation to it at all.

"The Socialist Party is meeting in front of the library on 42nd and Fifth at ten," Nat said.

Since when were we Socialists? I mean, I know marching with the proto-Commies sounded sexy, but wouldn't it have been more honest to march with Democrats or the Green Party or even just the Lower East Side contingent? Whatever. I figured we could be fist-pumping Socialists for a day. Why not?

"Sounds good."

"I have a surprise," Nathalie said excitedly, stood up, and walked to the closet.

I sat on the bed, tempted to curl up and sleep. If it weren't for the simple fact that being near Nathalie's bursts of energy felt like shots of adrenaline, I would have been the world's most exhausted man. A gust of cold air blew in from the window and chilled me. I thought: *This is what it felt like—the air turning cold so quick without her by my side to warm me. This is exactly what it felt like when she bailed.*

I watched as Nathalie took something from the closet and hid said wonder behind her naked back. Then, straddling me, her body so close I could smell the salty clean of her skin, she presented a gift to me.

"Ta-da," she said, and leaned forward to loop the softest of handmade angora scarves around my neck. The smoothness of her skin rubbed against my jaw. I wanted the scarf to stretch for miles and miles so she'd never stop wrapping it around me.

"Did you make this?" I asked, both touched and confused.

"Yeah, today."

"Since when do you knit?"

"I've always known how. I just had time today. So, what do you think?" she asked, and leaned back to survey her work.

I thought it was both thrilling and terrifying that even after seven-years-plus Nathalie could still so completely take me by surprise, that's what I thought.

"Beautiful, absolutely beautiful," I said.

And I meant it. Beautiful. Her skin flushed rosy, her limbs relaxed, her very being so present and still and close to me. That particular moment was so damned beautiful.

"It's too long. I made it too long," she said, and began unwinding the scarf from my neck.

"No, I love it," I said, holding the scarf and her hands in my own. "Please, it's perfect."

"It's not right," she said, and took back the treasure she'd made for me.

After you've dressed, remove at least one accessory or you're no better than common trash.

This was among the many commandments my Pilgrim mother taught me as a child. And that's how I knew for certain my mother's lip would have curled to watch Nathalie get dressed.

Soggy tissue in hand to catch frequent sneezes, after taking back my scarf and shoving it in a storage box of her things in the closet, Nathalie had reassembled the remainder of the closet to its pre-naked-girl-"cleaning" order. And now, slowly, deliberately, and slightly wobbly, she donned layer upon layer of silk organza, darned cashmere, and pizzazz. Busy clusters of rhinestones sparkled on her perfect little ears.

Brick red lipstick transformed her face from fresh-scrubbed to fuckably dangerous. Powder turned her sniffle-red nose porcelain pale. Her hair was tucked into a tangled French twist. She grabbed a sequined gold clutch to go, but not before adding the one accessory I wished she'd leave behind. To my annoyance, once again, she wore my father's glasses.

"Take me somewhere divine, won't you, darling?" she said in her best patrician accent.

"You should be in bed."

"Frank, come on, I'm stir-crazy. Please, let's go out," she said, and then let out an ear-piercing sneeze.

"Nat, you really should rest."

I may have been stubborn, but I wasn't dense. I knew what was going on. I might deny her the instant baby she was so convinced she wanted, but there was no denying how tantalizing she was even when in the throes of a flu. She was so foxy sweet that even just looking at her was enough to give a person cavities. She wanted to be arm candy that night. She wanted reassurance that all she had to do was bat her eyelashes to get me wrapped around her little finger. She knew I'd give in. To pretty much anything she wanted of me.

So, fine, if we were going on a proper date—which, clearly she wanted to—at least I could play my role well and present her with a token of my affection. I had no bouquet to offer, but I knew if Nathalie had been able to see herself in the mirror through those opaque blind man glasses, she would have wanted, in total opposition to my mother's rules, even more bling to set off her ensemble. In search of the one object I knew would be perfection, I went to the closet and took down the briefcase Nathalie seemed to have gone through too quickly earlier that night. Tucked in the interior leather pouch, I found her treat.

"Here." I placed the gift in her hand.

"What's this?"

"Walking stick. Goes with the glasses."

"Delightful," she said and smiled.

As Nathalie fumbled with the red-tipped walking stick and snapped it open to full extension, I noticed how damn sexual the thing was when in her hands. Blushing, I helped with her coat. In the kitchen, I placed a single orange in a paper bag to bring with us. I knew exactly where to take her.

Stumbling novice, tapping her walking stick in haphazard sweeping gestures and clutching my left arm with her free hand, Nathalie took forever to traverse the handful of blocks to our destination. The entire way I was terrified we might cross paths with an actual blind person. Obviously, they wouldn't be able to see us if we did, but man, talk about rude. It would have been a seriously shameful moment. As it was, I was embarrassed enough by the way people were staring at us, trying to figure out if Nathalie was really blind or if maybe we were doing some sort of lame performance piece. Let me tell you, I'd never been happier to arrive at the Village East Cinemas than I was that night. I paid our dues, guided Nathalie through the foyer, and led us up two flights of sticky handrail-lined stairs to the third balcony.

Movie theater third balconies were some of my favorite places in the world. True nosebleed seating, they'd originally been designated for colored folk and the poor. As far as I was concerned, there was absolutely no better place to watch the speckled black-and-white films of yesteryear. And from the third balcony of this Yiddish vaudeville theater turned revival movie palace, one could also mourn bygone eras' neo-rococo gilded ornamentation as it stumbled up the walls and onto the ceiling. Having existed for over three-quarters of a century just north of St. Mark's Church—but jammed between a storefront car service office and a unisex hair salon that no historic society or tourist association would ever recommend visiting—the theater was permanently streaked and stained by particles of soot. The third balcony was an antiquated and empty place, and, as usual, so was the rest of the damp, ammonia-soaked theater. My blind mouse Nathalie and I were entirely alone.

"Frank, I can't see anything in here," Nathalie whispered once I'd helped her to the seat beside me. She adjusted the oversized dark glasses, which kept sliding down her nose.

"Maybe you should take off the glasses," I said.

I really wished she would. Trust me, I know, taking her to a movie theater was more than a little passive-aggressive. But, whatever, I wanted her to put the glasses away. I wanted them back in my dad's briefcase. And I most certainly didn't want her wearing them. Seeing her with the glasses creeped me out. So why'd I give her the walking stick then? Fuck, do I have to be able to explain every little thing I did? Does it all have to make sense? Sorry, but all I knew was: 1) Seeing my father's glasses really upset me, and 2) I wasn't sure how to tell Nathalie that I didn't like her playing blind without it seeming like I was making a big deal out of nothing.

Glasses still on, Nathalie pushed herself up out of her rusted-springs sunken chair. Closed walking stick tucked under her left arm, she groped the backs of chairs with her clumsy blind hands and jammed her knee against the railing at the row's end. Cane snapped open and pointed into the aisle, she tapped the theater's matted carpet and walked in a slow straight line until she found solid resistance. The right side of her body flush against the wall, she slowly descended one stair at a time out of my sight and into the lobby.

When Nathalie returned, several long deafeningly quiet minutes later, the tart stench of melted artificial butter preceded her. She sat down, and I closed my eyes and listened to the muffled and wet sound of paper tearing between her teeth. I heard her spit out the paper and I strained my ears to catch soft sandy rainfall as she poured small packets of salt onto her popcorn. I opened my eyes when she pressed a few kernels to my lips. Being with Nathalie made my mouth dry, and like so much of the time when I was with her, concerns of unfulfilled thirst plagued me.

I leaned forward and reached into the soft and wrinkled bag I'd packed for us. Cool and dense comfort, I took out the orange. I balanced the fruit on my lap, peeled it, sectioned it, and cleansed each sticky wedge of its foamy white veins. Not hungry, I only sucked one wedge for its juice and then chewed particles of bumpy thick peel until a bitter chalkiness coated my tongue.

"Frank?"

"Yeah?"

"Can I have some orange?" she asked.

"Of course."

Nathalie reached a searching hand to my lap, took the fruit one section at a time, and ate.

"Nat, I think we should talk," I said. "I mean, do you really you want a baby?"

She rattled a paper cup filled with just a splash of soda and mostly ice cubes. I knew her ice routine from glasses of water in bed, at restaurants, in the park, wherever we went. The girl didn't sip daintily. Nathalie avoided the liquid soda in her cup, seeking out solids, stopping only once her Kali tongue found and retrieved the perfect ice cube to warm in her mouth. She'd told me once that she loved the feel of an already slightly melted-down cold square diminishing under the roof of her mouth, the crackling of its surface an audible popping sound. She was such a delicate girl in some ways, such a brute in others.

"Nat?"

She crunched on her ice, reveling in its decimation.

Torn and stained once-crimson curtains abruptly parted

in front of the screen below. The movie began. There was no orchestra.

"Nat, come on . . ."

"I don't want to talk during the movie, Frank."

She rattled another piece of ice into her mouth.

For the next one hundred forty-nine minutes, we sat in silence.

Trying to read between the lines without enough background information is fool's business. I would be a rich man if that business paid well. All through the movie I'd attempted to decipher what the hell was really going on with Nathalie. It wasn't until we got home that she finally gave me a decoder ring to begin unscrambling the mess. She explained:

That morning, after I'd left for work, she'd woken—totally groggy from cough medicine, too little sleep, and a raging temperature—to screams. From across the street. In the park.

Nathalie heard the noise, and she pushed her dizzy sick self out of bed and onto unsteady feet to investigate, to call the police if necessary. She stumbled over to the window, and what did she see but just a bunch of day care kids entering the park in tidy lines all chain-gang roped together. Eardrum-shattering communal screams, the kids were set free in the playground just three floors down and slightly east of our window. They swung from monkey bars, spun in circles, kicked each other, threw dirt at the bright yellow plastic slide. Their sugary morning-snack-fueled choruses were pure unconsidered truths: there-is-no-future, there-is-little-past, this-is-now and now is what I feel and it is a blue sky day and the air is shivering cold and I've been fed and I don't have to piss or shit and this kid is chasing me and the swings are calling my name. Their noise was absolutely pure primal joy and excitement, but the screeching chilled Nathalie.

She heard the kids and she remembered the screams of people jumping from fireball crumbling tall buildings. Screams on the television. Screams from flyers taped on lampposts and bus stops on every downtown street. The guttural screams that had escaped from her own mouth during so many lucid early-morning nightmares. Screams. She had run away for weeks to try to escape memories of screams. And now that she was settled at home again, children had woken her with their screams.

So why didn't she just close the windows and block out the racket, right? If only. It was too hot in the apartment with the building's heat blasting. The windows had to stay open. And hence the screams continued to filter in. Couldn't she have turned on the television or radio to cover the noise? Well, she did. But the first thing she heard as she listened to NPR was yet another announcement and reminder about the protest. It was far from the white noise she craved.

Restless and eager for distraction, but too tired and sick to go anywhere, Nathalie dragged out an old storage box of her things from the back of the closet. She pulled yarn and bamboo knitting needles from the box. And when she sat back in bed with her supplies, she noticed my wallet on the nightstand. In my cloudy-headed morning rush after a sleepless night spent taking care of her, I'd forgotten it.

Nathalie reached for the wallet—to pick it up and call me and tell me I'd left it behind, to put it on the kitchen table where it could wait for me until I got home. But Nathalie's inner-ear must have been swollen or whatever it is that happens to one's equilibrium when a person has the flu, because as she reached for the wallet, she lurched too far forward and accidentally pushed it off the nightstand. It fell on the floor, open. Nathalie honestly hadn't intended to snoop, but as the wallet lay there, she saw the estate-sale photo of the flapper. I'd all but forgotten the photo was there, but for Nathalie it was a brand-new discovery. She couldn't help but pick up the wallet and stare. Eyes fever blurred, Nathalie swore she saw the flapper hitch her dress a little higher and purse her lips in an extra slutty smile.

Forget rules clustered in twelve—those written in stone and otherwise—jealousy is the most honest of human states. Add to jealousy a touch of the emotional regression that typically accompanies being sick, and you've got the most uncensored and bluntly honest of truth serums.

"How about a photo of me, asshole?" Nathalie had asked aloud. If she could have slapped the flapper girl, she would have. Instead, she closed my wallet and slammed it back down on the nightstand.

The kids in the park screamed.

Fuming, Nathalie picked up her knitting needles and cast on the yarn. One tightly pulled knot after another, a scarf took shape and gained length in her shaking hands. Eventually she relaxed, the rows of knitting became looser, and she tried to laugh off caring so much about the photograph in my wallet.

Having depleted her limited reserve of energy, Nathalie stopped knitting mid-row, stared at her hands, and noticed the shallow wrinkles and sprinkling of pinprick age spots that grazed her skin. Green veins pushed up far more than she'd remembered ever seeing before. Accustomed to considering herself as barely not a teenager anymore, it was in that exact moment that Nathalie realized, equal parts thrill and disbelief: *These are hands of a full-fledged adult.* Then, radio news detailing the war our government was about to send troops to, and kids screaming happily in the playground outside in loud happy bursts—nihilism and idealism juxtaposed so vividly—something deep in Nathalie begged for recognition. Immaculate or however it had to be, she wanted a baby kicking her from the inside. My baby. Our baby. The thought persisted. Demanded to be acted upon. And now that it had found her, it would remain.

Though it made little sense on a purely logical level, Nathalie suddenly craved the tiredness that would accompany waking throughout the night to tend to a creature half her and half me. She wanted to suckle a little monster until her nipples ached. Vivid daydreams filled her thoughts, and she watched as she grew a big round belly and heavy breasts and, fire searing pain, she heard our baby's first cry. She saw herself wrap our son in warm blankets, highchair feed him, teach him to speak, she saw herself by his side when he lost his first tooth . . . and in that particular future conditional moment, she watched herself run out to the corner bodega to buy a wind-up blink-eye robot to put under our little boy's pillow as he slept, so he would find it in the morning when he woke, so he would believe that the tooth fairy really did exist—so that when he was full-grown and looking back on his childhood, he would know his mother had always loved him dearly.

As much as Nathalie would have preferred to stay in this happy dream, memories of a lurid event she'd read about years before in the library-loaned biography of Nahui interrupted her bliss. The story, the only one she'd learned about Nahui that she hadn't yet shared with me, was of Nahui's baby—a baby I never even knew Nahui had.

The children in the playground screamed again. Ecstatic joy and destruction—who could tell them apart by sound alone? All those pleased children's screams probably weren't so unlike the scream of my father's sister as she fell under the train's weight. Likewise, my father's sister's scream probably wasn't entirely unlike Nahui's baby's final plea.

1915. Nahui's little Ángel Rodríguez Mondragón was born. He was a striking baby with electric wild green eyes like his mother's. Nahui loved Ángel—a creature crafted of her own flesh and blood—in the way it is said Narcissus admired himself. Fully. Obsessively. Without apology or hesitation. But, same as with any new mother, taking care of Ángel made Nahui more tired than she'd ever imagined. Every night she woke in the predawn dark to her son's cries. She took him from his bassinet and returned to bed with him beside her. His mouth at her breast, the warmth of his body soothing her, she fell asleep. This was their routine.

Then one morning Nahui woke to find baby Ángel lying at her side peacefully, but far too still and cold. He was not breathing. He was stiff to his mother's touch. Nahui screamed. Loudly. For the entire city to hear. She screamed to the heavens. To the earth. The oceans. Fire and air. She had never wished to harm her Ángel. But she had hurt him. Irreversibly. Nahui had smothered him in her sleep.

Before you judge her, consider this:

When Ángel was pronounced dead, Nahui's heart shattered. She threw herself onto his infant coffin at the grave. People snickered and called her a scandalous whore. They whispered loudly that God had never wanted her to be blessed with a child. There was talk that her baby had been bastard devil spawn. And when her husband left her, neighbors said it was because of the baby's death.

If they'd only known that Nahui agreed with much of what they said. Because, yes, *their* Catholic God, she was sure, wouldn't have wanted more of her kind. And, yes, it was true, the wicked love only their devil approved of was exactly the sort she enjoyed most. As for her husband—still but a young man torn by his desire for adventure and lovers as handsome as he—Manuel's deep sadness for his son's death was only part of the reason he left Nahui. That aside, to all the other mean-spirited accusations, Nahui would have confessed. Readily. It made no difference to her if she was guilty of such things. But really, the pain she felt, her baby dead, it was cruel of people to torment her further.

Especially considering the truth she never admitted aloud:

She couldn't remember anything of the night Ángel died, not a single damned moment or detail. But she did remember the day her son was born, she remembered that with crystal clarity—terror had gripped her chest and made her hands tremble when she saw him for the first time. From that moment forward, she'd secretly feared she wasn't capable of being the mother such perfection deserved. But she tried. She tried desperately. Then when Ángel died, nightmare that the possibility was, Nahui feared she'd been awake when he died, she feared she'd known she was smothering Ángel, that she'd been aware of his fading life, that she'd needed him gone. Nahui's uncertainty haunted her to her final day.

Biting her nails, gold flecks of polish on her teeth, Nathalie tried to push away thoughts of Nahui's baby. She tried to think instead of my promises to plant endless evergreens for her, leafy pothole love letters unfurled for the world to crash into. "Each tree, my heart on my sleeve," I'd post-fuck whispered to her as I promised to tear down the universe one city block at a time and build it back up in her honor.

Nathalie wiped tears away with the sleeve of her bed dress. Damnit, she thought, like hell if she was going to sit and stew enviously over a stupid old photograph in my wallet when there was a simple solution at hand. She went to the closet to find a picture of us to replace the one of the flapper. She sorted through old envelopes stuffed full of photos and negatives, and soon she was going through everything in that closet. Her things. My things. All our skeletons combined. And that was when she found the blind man glasses in my father's briefcase. They were enticing and hot to the touch and she couldn't help but put them on. Instantly, Nathalie fell in love with the way they blocked out the world around her, the way they made things so dark that even sound was somehow muffled.

For a while she returned to her knitting and completed the scarf. But by the time I got home, she was futzing with the boxes of our personal history again. And she wanted a baby.

Nathalie waited until late that night after we returned home from the movie theater to tell me about Nahui's baby. Unfamiliar images of Nahui as a mother skipped in and out of my mind, and I found myself thinking about my own mother. Like Nahui, my mother had also somehow managed to sleep through the death of her only child. (Forgive my emotional heavy-handedness here; I was extremely tired when Nathalie told me the story, and exhaustion tends to cause hyperbolic sentiment in me.) Yes, of course I hadn't actually died like little baby Ángel, but an innocent and peaceful kid had been stamped out of existence just the same during certain miserable nights of my own childhood. To say I was deeply unsettled by the fact that Nahui and my mother had something so regrettable in common would be an understatement of vast proportions. I was horrified.

Trying to keep a logical cap on the situation, I calmly forced myself to ask Nathalie why she hadn't told me about Nahui's baby before. Forget just sooner that night; why hadn't she mentioned it on the Ash Wednesday years earlier when she'd told me everything else she'd learned about Nahui, when she'd taken on the role of Nahui and brought her to life?

She replied: "I didn't want to ruin Nahui for you."

I suspected Nathalie actually meant, *I didn't want to ruin us.*

CHAPTER NINETEEN

14 February 2003. Valentine's Day.

All morning at the shop, thoughts of Nahui's dead baby refused to leave me be. Little Ángel—inexplicably dressed by my imagination in a Victorian-era funeral gown, stiff lace ruffle collar pushing up against his pallid full-moon cheeks, lips and eyelids waxed closed for his wake viewing—accompanied me as I stumbled around, sold an antique celery vase to a boho-professorial dude, dusted knickknacks, and tried to convince myself I didn't really keep getting whiffs of lilies and smoky funereal candles.

By early afternoon, somewhat queasy from my morbid preoccupations, but aware I would soon get a headache if I didn't eat, I forced myself to open my bagged lunch. I wondered if it would be proper to give half my sandwich to Ángel. If it were appropriately reverent, I could make an altar for him in the store and leave offerings. But would he like grilled tofu on wheat with red leaf lettuce? Maybe he'd prefer a glass of soy milk instead?

Ángel's hungry ghost keeping me company, I had just taken the first bite of my sandwich when Nathalie's unmistakable scream, coming from somewhere outside, pierced the quiet. I dropped my sandwich, ran to the door, and scanned up and down the street.

A station wagon, seemingly the same one Nathalie and I had taken to the woods on Thanksgiving, idled one storefront over. From where I stood I could see that the vehicle's driver-side door was wide open, but nobody sat in the driver's seat.

In an accelerated split-second, a series of pragmatically useless questions swirled through my brain. Hadn't Nat said she was going to spend the day in bed, drinking herbal tea with lemon to kick the last bit of her flu? What time was it? Was the sun always situated so low in the sky? Had the sunlight been strange like this when Nahui woke to find Ángel dead? As for the station wagon—paint it black, throw some velvet curtains on the back windows, and you've got a hearse. Goddamn, what had Nathalie done this time? And had she used my credit card to rent the car? Since when did she have a driver's license? How could she pull off renting a car without a license on the day before a massive organized political protest? Did the rental place have any fucking idea just how many pounds of explosives could fit in the flatbed of a station wagon?

Nearly overwhelmed by these knee-jerk reflex concerns, I wished I could be a kid again, or at least irresponsible and uncaring. If I'd had a magic wand to wave, I would have made a clean chalkboard materialize out of thin air so Nathalie and I could spend the day blissfully scratching our nails down a blank slate. But I had no wand. Perplexed, I just wanted to understand what the hell was going on. I ran toward the station wagon.

Shivering in the freezing air, I noticed the tulle of my girl's dress peeking out from under the back tire. More of Nathalie's screams. People crossed Avenue A from the park to see what all the excitement was about. There was so much movement and response, and all I could manage was to stand there frozen in my body and wonder how the fuck Nathalie had driven over herself. It was like the scene when Dorothy's tornado lands the house on Her Wickedness—I saw only Nathalie's pettiskirt and thick heavy boots.

Have I mentioned that I've always hated swimming? As a kid, water inevitably got stuck in my ears, and no amount of hydrogen peroxide dripped in with an eyedropper would loosen it out. I was never a tadpole or guppy—or whatever the fuck it is they call you when you take classes at the Y. So I'd never progressed to the swimming-lesson level where they teach you first aid and CPR. I saw Nathalie's scrawny legs and big boots peeking out from under the back corner of the station wagon, and I knew she might die while the paramedics were on their way. She might drown, water in her lungs, and I wouldn't know how to revive her. A gust of wind from Avenue A blew my way and carried the nauseating scent of pizza to my overloaded senses. Pepperoni pizza. Nathalie might be paralyzed or near death, she seemed to be stuck under a multi-ton vehicle, and there I stood, helpless, almost heaving from the stench of greasy pepperoni pizza.

★

"Sniffle," he said. "You stayed home from school sick, remember?"

I was in kindergarten the year my father had to take an eye test at the DMV to get his driver's license renewed. He made his appointment for a Wednesday, one of his custody days. He still had visitation rights at that point, but usually, if I was sick, I'd stay at my mother's. I hadn't actually been sick that day, and my father wasn't supposed to pick me from kindergarten until *after* school. The morning we went to the DMV, my father had lied to pull me out of class early.

"I'm so sorry for the inconvenience," he told the lady at the front office to explain why he was collecting me barely half an hour into the school day. "Francisca's mother forgot she has a doctor's visit."

The secretary shook her head—those darned new-fangled two-household families, they could never keep things straight—walked over to the intercom, buzzed my classroom, and requested that I report to the office with my backpack and lunch. I did as told, and arrived at the front office to find my father, particularly frazzled but impeccably attired as usual, waiting for me.

Have you ever seen how suburban geriatrics freak when they have to give up their driver's licenses? It's like their final phase of independence has come to an end. They've run the race and their brittle bones done broke. Might as well get the rifle and send them to the glue factory. Well, even though my father was only in his late thirties when his license was almost revoked, he had that panicked air about him. He knew what the DMV would think about the fact that even with his layers of prescriptive lenses, he could barely see things that were fifteen feet or closer. He had no right to drive anymore, but he wasn't going to give up without a fight.

His kid retrieved from class, big hug given, kid strapped in passenger seat, the nearly blind man drove to get his license renewed. During our drive, he explained the plan to me. I listened carefully and, devoted kid love, took it all very seriously and planned to make him proud.

There was a large paper bag in the backseat, and when we got to the DMV he handed it to me and told me to change into the extra clothes he'd brought. A pair of pajamas. My Snoopy slippers. Also inside the bag was a coloring book and a new box of crayons—the way-cool double-decker kind with a flap lid, four compartments, sixty-four colors, and a built-in sharpener.

"When we go in," he said, "pretend you have a cold."

He was banking on the fact that people couldn't stand being mean to a nicely dressed father with a pajama-clad sick kid in tow.

"Can I really use the crayons?"

"Of course, Paca. That's why I brought them for you."

"Thank you."

Easily bribed, I did as told.

8:20 A.M., exactly twenty minutes after the DMV opened, we walked in. By that time, my father figured, the employees' cheap, bitter office caffeine diluted with powdered creamer would have kicked in. And, he calculated, only twenty minutes into a shift of municipal hell, the employees wouldn't impenetrably hate the world quite yet. My dad knew what he was doing. And so did I. I dragged my Snoopy-slipper feet for dramatic effect. My Pink Panther coloring book and box of crayons in hand, we took a number and sat in orange plastic chairs with the four license-renewal stations in full view.

"Okay," he asked, "what do you see?"

I was supposed to act nonchalant. *Nonchalant.* My father had taught me that word on the drive over.

"Pretend you're not reading the eye charts to me. Pretend you don't even know what they are. Pick your nose or something. Sniffle. You'll do great, you will," he'd said. What he hadn't said but had communicated loud and clear was: *You'll do great. You have to.*

My father didn't really have anything to worry about. I wouldn't have let a single detail go wrong. I was a perfection- ist. Any chance to impress him and I turned out in full show- off kid regalia. I would be great. I knew I would. Besides, he'd promised me an entire pack of pizza scratch-'n'-sniff stickers if he got his license renewed. He knew pizza was the king of scratch-'n'-sniffs. Root beer and Dr. Pepper were pretty good, and gasoline scratch-'n'-sniff was cool if you were into that sort of thing, but pizza scratch-'n'-sniff was kiddy catnip. The stickers were hardly proper compensation for making me an accomplice to a crime, but I appreciated the promise of reward nonetheless. Sitting in the DMV, I could practically smell my synthetic pepperoni stickers already. That reminded me. I sniffled and picked my nose slightly. I whispered the first two lines of each posted eye chart to my father.

"Station one, line one: E. Line two: F, P. Station two, line one: E. Line two: K, R. Station three, line one: E. Line two: N, Z. Station four, line one: F. Line two: B, C."

"Wait, station four, line one is F? Are you sure?"

The anxiety in his voice frightened me. I suddenly questioned whether or not I really knew the alphabet. Of course I knew the alphabet. I'd gotten tons of gold stars from my teacher for learning it before all the other kids. I answered with absolute certainty.

"Yes. Line one: F. Line two: B, C."

Cheating on the eye charts at the DMV was a piece of pie. Nowadays the whole operation is computerized to create fairly unpredictable eye chart variations, but back in the late 1970s, a finite and very negotiable number of variables was involved. There were four or five possible stations. Each station had one chart. And there were only about ten eye charts in the entire nation. Years later, my father told me that in preparation for that day he'd memorized the most common eye charts, or so he'd thought. For weeks beforehand, he'd sat on his couch working on the charts like flashcards. I doubt Dr. Hermann Snellen had meant to allow for such trickery when he invented his now familiar eleven-line charts. But then again, nobody drove back in 1862 when he printed up the prototype. Snellen had just been a nerdy ophthalmologist who wanted more accuracy in optical exams. My father was grateful for such simple aspirations. But then he found himself thrown by the *Line one: F* chart.

"Line one: F? Damnit," he said, his face turning red. "I don't know that one. Read the whole thing. Slowly."

So I did.

He concentrated. To look at him, he was just humming and drinking his little Styrofoam cup of coffee. But his shoulders were tense. His ears twitched slightly. His feet tapped out a rhythm to my alphabet incantation. His focused expression reminded me of when we'd play *Simon*, the electronic Simon says game, at home. He'd sit with his nose practically touching the small circular computerized machine to memorize the game's random patterns of pulsing lights. *Blue, blue, yellow, green, red, blue, green, red, yellow, blue*—cheap and tiny lightbulbs flashed through thick colored opaque plastic. Specific tinny sounds corresponding to each color were emitted through the unit's crappy speaker as the light pulsed. I sucked at *Simon*, but my dad cruised his way through even the most complicated sequences. We always had extra AA batteries in the fridge. My dad was obsessed. His shoulders tight and ears alert, he could memorize anything first time around.

"Station four, line one: F. Line two: B, C. Line three: P, T, E, O . . ." he repeated the eleven lines aloud.

"Correct," I said.

He took another sip of coffee.

"Thanks, kid." He pretended to check the time on his wristwatch for show, to seal the deal. Anyone looking our way wouldn't doubt for a second that his sight was fine. Truth was, he'd needed me to read the numbers on his watch to him since I was in preschool. Years and years later, when he was diagnosed with cancer, I would buy him a talking watch to help him stick to his medicine schedule. But even then, we would revert to our old habit of my telling him the time. I don't know if the robot-voiced watch became emblematic of his illness, of being alone sometimes as he lay dying, but he wore it only a week or two before he finally left it in the top drawer of his dresser, tucked under carefully folded pairs of boxer shorts and rolled bundles of brown, dark blue, and black cashmere dress socks.

The woman at station two called out my father's name. He handed her his paperwork and flubbed line ten of the eye chart—on purpose, for authenticity's sake. I sniffled. And rubbed my nose a lot. I didn't pick it. I could tell Lady Station Two would think nose-picking was gross. I sneezed once. It was a real sneeze, but I was still proud of myself for such good timing. Masters of our game, my father and I walked out with his license renewed.

Shortly thereafter, his driver's license arrived in the mail. My father looked so handsome with his shiny hair and pinstriped suit. His smile radiated. Look closely enough and you'd notice his eyes were aimed slightly off to the right of where he was supposed to look—both in the photo and in person the day he slid the renewed license into his wallet.

My dad delivered on the pack of pizza scratch-'n'-sniffs. The kids at school freaked when I told them I had three sheets of pizza. No matter what they had in their sticker albums— glitter race cars, velvet fuzzy puppies, even cotton candy scratch-'n'-sniffs—it didn't matter, my three sheets were not up for trade. I coveted them, sealed in their thin shrink-wrap plastic to keep the stink fresh, until I couldn't resist any longer. And even once I finally did peel open the pack, I didn't actually scratch the stickers with my haggard bitten nails. I only rubbed them to get their chemical funk on my fingertips.

A few days later, I was doing exactly this, rubbing the pizza stickers with my thumb, when my father and I heard the thud against the hood of his car. It was my father's weekend, and we were off for a day trip to I can't remember where. We had just stopped at 7-Eleven and I wanted a Coke from the six-pack my father had bought and placed on the floorboard at my feet. I tried a zillion times to wrangle one of the cans of soda, but my seatbelt kept locking.

"Jeez, kid, hold on a minute." My dad reached down toward the passenger floorboard, left hand on the wheel, head tilted up to see over the dash, his right hand rummaging around in the bag to wrangle me a soda. I don't know, maybe he looked down for a second too long. Maybe he couldn't have seen a damned thing in front of us even if he had been sitting upright with both hands on the wheel. Whatever happened, I was rubbing my stickers, he handed me a Coke, and we heard the thud.

My senses alert but jumbled, I looked up and saw an old man slide down the hood and slump onto the road—and all I could think of was pizza.

★

Eyes watering from the vomit I struggled to keep down, I ran to the back of the station wagon. I saw a blue uniform hat in the trash-cluttered gutter. Zoom in focus, I noticed the hat's embroidered white eagle patch. And then there was the distinctive cart with two blue canvas saddlebags knocked over in the middle of the street. Letters and throwaway advertisement newsprint fanned out almost too prettily on the asphalt like paper napkins at a fussy cocktail party. George, our neighborhood mailman, was knocked out cold on the pavement under the car's back fender.

"I thought it was a trashcan, I thought I'd hit a trashcan, I kept going. Fuck, Frank, help me," Nathalie yelped.

Crying and hyperventilating but unscratched, Nathalie crouched over George all frantic gesticulations and giant eyes. My father's blind man dark glasses kept sliding down her nose, her face a mess of blotches, dripped snot, and smeared makeup. The glasses. Shit, had she been wearing the glasses when she crashed into George? And what the hell did she mean, she thought she'd hit a trashcan? Nobody in Manhattan actually hauled trashcans into the street anymore. What did she think this was, fucking *Sesame Street*? Damnit, how could she see anything with those glasses on? As it was, she was still sort of sick. What was she doing trying to park a vehicle outside the shop when she should have been home resting?

She had no right to be out and about and driving and wearing my dad's glasses and crashing into innocent people. Again with the useless thoughts. Shit.

"Nat, I'm calling 911. I'll be right back."

"No, no, don't," she said, still on her knees, arms reaching out to grab me, the sour scent of fear detectable on her sweat-slicked hands. "No, Frank, please, no," she begged.

George hadn't moved or opened his eyes the entire time I'd been standing there. I thought I could see him breathing, but his lips were starting to turn purple and his face was as pale and green as a dark brown complexion can get. Maybe the sickly hue was just from the cold, but I didn't want to assume anything. I wouldn't listen to Nathalie's pleas. She'd clearly lost her mind.

I sprinted back to the shop and, more nerves than physical exertion, was totally winded once I reached the phone.

"*911. What is the emergency?*"

How could the operator sound so bored? Other people's tragedies were a dime a dozen to her; she answered the call like she wanted a coffee break.

I struggled to catch my breath.

"*Hello? Caller? This is 911. What is your emergency?*"

"Frank!" Nathalie wailed from the street. "Come back. Don't call. Omigod, Frank!"

Her voice seemed so far away. I could almost tune her out. Almost, but not quite.

CHAPTER TWENTY

"H ere." I handed Nathalie my father's dark glasses. Like some sort of weeping statue, silent tears trickled down Nathalie's stone face. She slid on the glasses and slumped against the shop counter as I wrapped up early and made a sign to hang in the window—*Gone Saturday for Protest. Open Sunday.* Register closed out and door locked behind us, Nathalie hooked her arm in mine and leaned on me as we walked home. When we passed the station wagon I'd parked on Avenue A, she sighed deeply. And when we reached our building's second-floor landing, she stopped. I pulled on her arm slightly to continue up the stairs, but she wouldn't budge.

"Where's Johnny? Have you seen him lately?" she asked, tears streaming from eyes still hidden under oversized glasses.

We were standing directly in front of Johnny's door. I didn't like the possibility he might hear us talking about him.

"No, I haven't seen him recently," I whispered, and tugged on her arm again.

"Well, where is he?" she asked, too loudly, and held her ground.

"Maybe he's visiting family," I replied quietly.

"No, he isn't. He doesn't have family. Where is he, Frank? *Where?!*"

I had no idea where Johnny was, but as far as I could remember in that quick moment, the last time I'd crossed paths with him had been when I'd helped him up the stairs on

Chinese New Year. He'd come stumbling home just as I was getting back from the shop. It seemed he'd had a particularly long shift on a barstool. *It's our year, kid, Year of the Black Sheep*, he'd said with a wink, his whiskey-and-beer breath hot on my face, his laugh echoing in the stairwell. Chinese New Year. February 1. Almost two weeks had passed since I'd seen him. Nathalie had a point. Going two weeks without seeing Johnny—at the mailboxes, walking around the neighborhood, whatever—*was* strange. I felt like a shit for not having noticed sooner, but I wasn't his keeper. Hell, I was having a hard enough time tending to my own life, let alone making sure my neighbors were accounted for. Besides, Nathalie didn't know if Johnny had family or not. But I wasn't going to push it. She could just win this one: We hadn't seen Johnny for a while; I was a jerk for not having noticed earlier. Agreed. Done.

I hated seeing Nathalie cry. I really fucking hated it. I knew she was totally torturing herself about crashing into the mailman. And, sure, she needed to take responsibility for what she'd done, but she didn't need to beat herself up over it. Her guilt hadn't subsided in the least after the paramedics told her George was fine. Nathalie had seemed almost more horrified when George came to and said the same himself. He'd even told Nathalie she shouldn't worry, it was an accident, everyone had accidents.

To be honest, I wondered if maybe George had killed someone. It blew me away that he hadn't wanted Nathalie at least cited for what she'd done to him. But he'd just smiled and waved away her desperate apologies. Maybe he was scared of her. I mean, Nathalie did look pretty fucking wild by the time he'd regained consciousness. If I saw a creature as frantic as Nathalie had been, I think I too would have backed away with my hands up, doing my best to remain even-tempered so as not to agitate the situation further.

I finally persuaded Nathalie to walk up the remaining

flight of stairs to our apartment—and so began a restorative day of herbal tea and hot baths and dual comatose naps, all of which seemed to have the added benefit of curing Nathalie of her flu. Her eyes brightened and her sneezes stopped.

I was making us yet another cup of tea when I tried to ask casually, "Nat, why'd you rent the station wagon?"

"It's Valentine's Day," she said.

Her answer clarified nothing. True, we were both sentimental idiots, but from day one Nathalie had threatened that if I ever came home on Valentine's Day with chalky cheap chocolates and a bunch of genetically modified and scentless red roses, she might just throw them at me. Of course, the idea had been all the more tempting as a result. And there was one year I brought home the forbidden items, along with a crappy little bodega teddy bear, just to make her laugh. But, seeing as we'd never been "do something special on Valentine's Day" sorts, I couldn't tell if her explanation for renting the car was sincere or a failed attempt at irony.

Later that night, when we were leaving the apartment to return the station wagon, Nathalie handed me my father's glasses.

"I don't want them anymore," she said, folding the glasses shut and sliding them into my coat pocket.

I pulled the apartment door shut and Nathalie stopped me. She hugged me, harder than maybe ever before. And then she pulled me to her even tighter. The plastic bulk of the glasses dug through my coat and sweater and T-shirt to thin skin and then to bones and bruised us both. Her embrace was a death grip. It was every ounce of her adoration.

"I wanted to get another tree," she said. "I know, I totally fucked up, but I wanted to surprise you so we could drive to the forest and get another sapling. And when we planted the tree, I thought maybe instead of a glittery bird like you used last time, maybe this time we could put a little plastic dove on the top branch or something. I don't know, I thought it could be like some sort of eco-anarchist protest and a Valentine all in one. Frank, I'm sorry. I'm so totally lame, right?"

So *not* lame. In fact, Nathalie had just given me thirty seconds of perfection.

CHAPTER TWENTY-ONE

We were walking home after dropping off the rental car when, practically right outside our building, Nathalie pulled me into Tompkins Square Park. My hand in hers, she led me down one of the park's circuitous paved paths, past the central bricked area with the two giant elm trees whose trunks were perpetually wrapped in remnants of strung Hare Krishna flowers, and over to the cramped and fenced-in patches of landscaping on the east side of the park.

Nathalie stopped and stood on tiptoe to lean over one of the wrought-iron fences, squinting her eyes to peer into a winter-dead strip of city flower garden.

"Razzle-dazzle," she said.

"Pardon?"

"Razzle-dazzle," she said again. "That's what this one's tag says."

She pointed to a cluster of tiny rusted botanical identification plates staked in the ground among tragically pruned and barren rosebushes. In all the years I'd walked through the park, I'd never noticed there were rosebushes, let alone that each one was tagged with an official miniature plaque.

"Look at that rose, Frank. I've never seen such a luminescent purple," she continued. "It's almost electric. Like a Lite-Brite or something."

"The roses are hibernating, Nathalie."

Sleeping flowers. Rest in peace. I pictured a funeral wreath made of white roses and baby's breath propped beside a small open grave, a banner across its middle with *Ángel* embroidered in silk thread.

"These are the most gorgeous roses I've ever seen," Nathalie said, thankfully snapping me out of my unpleasant distraction. She smiled calmly. "They have magnificent noses. Don't you think?"

Ah, I got it. Invitation accepted, I joined her game and leaned forward to where, come spring, roses would flourish. I inhaled deeply. The air was chilled damp oxygen. A blue scent. Icy crisp.

"Exquisite," I said.

"My sentiments precisely," she said, and took my hand.

We continued on our detour trip through the park, stopping at each fenced-in patch of dead plants. Nathalie described in elaborate detail the nonexistent blooms on every sleeping rosebush. I wanted to live there in that moment with Nathalie. Forever.

"I love you," she said before we headed home.

"Thank you."

"For saying I love you?"

"That too."

Dinner that night consisted of ridiculously huge slices of frosted instant pink cake. Nathalie served it on her ornate Wedgwood Valentine "collectibles"—*Ladies Home Journal* gaudy pink dishware circa 1983. Each plate featured a faux-china relief of a bewigged dude dressed in knickers and holding a rose up to a bodice-and-wig-wearing chick who sat on a swing that hung from a flowered bough. I hated those plates. But Nathalie adored her tacky collection, and she swore the plates were safe even though *For decorative purposes only, not for use with food* was written clearly on the back of each one. Whatever, the plates made her happy. Nathalie turned on the radio and brought us cake to eat in bed.

"Almonds?" I sniffed the air as she sat beside me.

"Yes, dear," she said.

The girl must have palmed a small puddle of almond extract into her hair when she was in the kitchen. She smelled like old-fashioned marzipan candy, like some hand-painted little pear. I wanted to consume her. But, marzipan being named for the god of war, I knew damn well the prospect wouldn't be without complications. Pink plates of pink cake balanced on our laps, we sat in bed and listened to the news crackling from our stereo's ancient and disintegrating black-foam speakers.

An international research team of astrophysicists took the mic. One two, one two, this was not a test. The scientists made their announcement:

The speed of light had evolved. A nasal-voiced nerdy scientist explained:

Given that the speed of light can no longer be considered a definite fixed constant, nothing, not even the equations used to calculate the characteristics of nothing itself, nothing, absolutely nothing remains as we had previously understood.

Tell me, who wants news like that?

Another astrophysicist, not of the aforementioned team, was interviewed. When asked for his professional two cents, he responded: *Exceptional results deserve extraordinary evidence.*

The evening music program began. Nathalie disappeared into the closet for a few minutes, then reappeared with the scarf she'd knitted for me and began searching through the kitchen junk drawer. She came back to bed with a huge pair of scissors and cut off several inches of that totally gorgeous soft handmade scarf—she just fucking lopped off a good chunk like it was nobody's business. Horrified, I watched her pull back row after row of the knitting until barely a few inches were left. She took a knitting needle and tried to slide the scarf back onto it, one stitch at a time. I knew nothing about knitting, but it was clear the corrective surgery had gone awry.

"Can I help?"

"Thank you, but you don't know how," she said.

Hunched over, focused stare, tense jaw, strands of yarn covering her lap and an unraveling scarf tangled on her knitting needles, Nathalie started to cry.

"I thought I knew how to fix it."

"Maybe it'd be better to start over . . ."

"No," she snapped. And I mean *snapped*.

Fuck.

I didn't know what to do. There was so much we weren't saying. I wanted to tell Nathalie I understood, that I didn't want to start over either, that I had endless love for her, and that even with the horrible story about Nahui's baby still in my thoughts, I could actually foresee planning for a baby someday—but I wanted to remind Nathalie, it wasn't me who'd bailed, who'd wanted to play blind, who'd mowed down the mailman, who needed everything to be a big grand production all the time. So could she please try to quit being so easily pissed off at me already? If either of us had any right to scream for sweets, it was me. Fuck slices of pink cake or even marzipan for that matter, I wanted Nathalie to tell me under no uncertain terms that she loved me, that she was happy with our life, that she wanted to be my girl forever and ever. Instead, I just sat there as she, frustrated and unapproachable, ate what was left of her slice of pink cake. The sound of her chewing nearly set me to tears— disgusted, revolted, scared-shitless tears.

The speed of light had evolved. Fucking ridiculous. Who could live in that reality? I imagined walking on cracked downtown sidewalks and spying with my smart eye endless concrete fluctuations squirming as quickly or as slowly as need be to avoid the extinguishing tug of shifting universal truths. It was a most unsteady stroll. And I didn't like it one fucking bit.

Acid jazz played on the radio. The music was loud. I stacked Nathalie's scraped-clean plate and pink-frosting-coated fork under my own, turned off the radio, and retreated to the kitchen sink. By the time I'd finished washing the dishes, the palpable tension in the room was just about to kill me.

"Nat, let's talk, okay?"

"Please drop it, Frank."

I sat at the kitchen table, head cradled in my hands, and I stared at the thick solid dirt permanently stuck deep between our floor's hardwood planks. Hour upon hour, I'd watched that same unchanging dirt when Nathalie had disappeared right before our anniversary. And now, as I looked at the dirt yet again, a deep well of anger I hadn't even realized I had in me boiled over. My voice, booming and determined, ricocheted off the floor and to Nathalie: "Nat, why do *you* always get to decide when *we're* done?"

She looked up from her mess of knitting, stunned. Clearly, she hadn't been expecting the attack. Truth was, neither had I, but I continued anyway, venting the hurt and frustration I'd tucked away in some shadowed part of my psyche for months.

"I mean, really, how was it okay for you to leave *our* home, *our* life, without ever talking to me about it? You just up and bailed on everything for fucking three weeks like I never needed anything while you were gone and then, oh, get the baskets of rose petals to sprinkle in her path, here she is, Nathalie's home, who knows why she left exactly or if she's even planning to stay, but it doesn't matter, I should be so honored to be in her presence, so let me just bow down and kiss her darling little feet, and if she wants a baby, damnit, give her a baby, if she snaps at you, let it roll off your back like water, it's all about her, everything is about her—"

"Fuck you," she said, her voice faint and strained.

I was shaking. Hard. My head throbbed.

We sat in silence for minutes, neither of us willing to budge.

"I'm sorry," I eventually gave in. "It's just, I don't get it—no matter what I do, everything turns so fucking impossible lately."

"Yeah, well, likewise."

"I just want us to have a happy, normal life, you know?"

"Oh, come on," she said, annoyed, "we don't want to be *normal*."

"Honestly, Nat, yeah, I think we do," I answered with complete sincerity.

A strange smile settled on her face. She got up from the bed, sat across from me at the kitchen table, and dug through the mess of our things coating the tabletop. She found my wallet, opened it, and removed the photo of the flapper girl. Nathalie's smile faded as she stared at the image. I watched as she slid the photo into the wallet's dollar-bill compartment, not the plastic picture pocket. I took the wallet from her and returned the photograph to its proper place.

"Was it like that before?" Nathalie asked.

"What?" I wasn't certain if she was referring to the way I'd repositioned the photograph or our mutual angst.

"Was it like that before?"

"Yes."

And then:

How could this be healthy, she asked, this human need for love? Was it right to want so intensely, to feel so much? She damned me for affecting her, for her wish to have a baby. A person should be comfortable all on their own, she said, without needing anyone else to make them feel whole.

I sat and listened to Nathalie. And my neck grew stiff.

If there aren't at least five people you can depend on and who can depend on you, you are in deep murky waters.

My father once threw this advice my direction. It was a strange ethos coming from a man who could have easily died alone, but I caught his words and clutched them tightly to my chest. In fact, I had come to imagine those words as beribboned medals—the sort awarded to Olympians for their exemplary efforts—and I wore them proudly. After my father's death, when I tried to run far away from home and everything and everyone I knew, those medals clanged heavily around my neck.

Then I met Nathalie. For lack of other resources, I melted the medals down to sculpt a statue in her honor. I carried that statue with me wherever I went with intentions of making each moment a monument of devotion to her. So long as I had her love, I thought, I'd have everything I'd ever need. But somehow we'd fucked up. The statue slid and cracked. I feared that all that gold, all that shimmering glory we'd once been, had transformed into a shattered mess of dead weight.

My hand massaged the knot forming at the base of my skull as Nathalie spoke. I didn't interrupt her to say that maybe I had all the same questions and fears as she did. And I refused to beg her to see it my way, because maybe if I had to beg, really beg, not just beg for play, but really beg, then maybe her love wasn't truly meant to be mine.

Nathalie sat on my lap. Slender fingers grazing my skin, she played with the fine hairs on the back of my neck.

"I love you," she said, and kissed my brow.

"I love you too, Nat."

Uncertain of what I could count on for the future, I breathed in the warmth of her body.

Razzle-dazzle. Purple buttons, peachy, sexy rexy, prima ballerina, secret love, dusky maiden, show girl, Penelope, sweet vixen, Madame Bravery, whiskey mac, impatient, tiara, angel face, plum crazy, touch of class, double talk, pretty doll.

These were not the names of all the roses Nathalie had

shown me earlier that night, just the ones I remembered the most. Our walk through the park had been so intensely lovely, and yet the sentiment of that moment already felt unreachably distant. If I had believed in the notion of appealing to temperamental ancient gods for favors, I would have gladly tattooed the roses' names on my imperfect human form as a humble plea for returned happiness. I could picture the names inked in blue gothic script up my arm like a sailor's laundry list of ports claimed. Hell, if it would have helped seal the deal any, I would have trekked to high desert mountains and plucked coccus insects off cacti blossoms to whip up a batch of holy red dye like the stuff made back in olden Aztec times. As I was thinking these thoughts, it occurred to me that, although not necessarily to please the gods but rather for my own selfish reasons, an act of devotion might not be such a bad idea. I suddenly wanted a needle tapping into my skin, searing me alive like the blood Nathalie sent flowing hot through my veins. I wanted a tattoo as reverence for love itself, for the pain of its imprint, for my healing, for the continuum of it all.

"Nat?"

"Yeah?"

"I'm going to get a tattoo."

She leaned back and squinted at me.

"A ventricular heart," I said. "On my chest. Huge . . ." I took a deep breath before continuing and hoped the gods were listening after all. ". . . with your name in a banner across the middle."

And if the gods *were* listening, I seriously hoped they'd not confuse my optimistic banner with a banner of mourning like the embroidered funeral wreath I'd imagined in the park earlier that night.

"You're crazy," Nathalie said, laughed slightly, and snuggled into my shoulder.

The suddenness of my promising something so permanent

for her—something that couldn't be erased or taken back, a declaration of love so literally carved into my body—freaked her out.

The roses from the park imprinted themselves all the more vividly in my thoughts. Razzle-dazzle. What a name for a rose. I imagined vibrant violet petals and green, green, such very green leaves, silver shimmering thorns that were as much ornamentation as they were weapon. Razzle-dazzle. Nathalie. Nahui. Razzle-dazzle girls. Somehow I was certain Nahui would have loved it if someone got a tattoo for her. Hell, she'd have given her admirer the tattoo herself. And afterward she would have reveled in licking off the blood pilled on the surface of her love's inflamed hot flesh. Tongue stained inky blue, she would have been a beautifully grotesque realization of the saying, *I'll eat you alive*.

Nathalie had whispered those words in my ear on countless occasions. Often when I fucked her. Sometimes as we fell asleep. Other times as we walked through the city. And then, always, cannibalistic little monster, she'd specify her love threat. *With mint jelly*, she'd say and lick her chops.

"Nat?"

"Hmm?"

"Are you coming with me?"

"Where?"

"I want the tattoo," I said.

She leaned back and stared at me.

"You mean like right now?"

"Yes."

"Well, alright then," she said and stood. "Let's go."

Something shifted. I saw it happen. Nathalie smiled the most toothy and quivering sexy smile I'd ever seen. *With mint jelly*. Indeed.

CHAPTER TWENTY-TWO

I don't mean to complain, but Nathalie took nearly an hour to get ready. As always, I appreciated the end result, but really, making me wait like that was all power trip. Wasn't I already submitting plenty in that I was about to get a huge tat with her name on it? Regardless, it was well past ten by the time we'd walked south of Houston to the tattoo parlor on Ludlow that every downtown hipster with ink swore by. The sign on the door said the shop was open until eleven.

When I explained exactly what I wanted to the only tattoo artist not already busy with a client, she said, "Sorry, dude, we close soon. You'll have to come back tomorrow."

"I totally understand," I said as respectfully as possible, "but we're going to the protest tomorrow."

She so wasn't impressed.

"We're open Sunday," she offered with a tired but polite smile.

"It's just, I'm out of town Sunday and—"

"You are?" Nathalie interrupted.

"Estate auction. D.C. I booked the trip a month ago . . . ?"

"Right," she said and shook her head, embarrassed to have forgotten.

"You can still cover the store Sunday, right?" I asked Nathalie.

"Of course, sweetie."

Ms. Tattoo looked at Nathalie and me as if listening to us sort out our schedule was causing her physical discomfort.

"Look," she said, probably just to shut us up, "I can outline and shade tonight, but you'll have to come back for color."

"I'd really love if I could get it now? All of it?"

Why the fuck was everything coming out of my mouth a question?

"Ribs hurt. You need two sessions."

"Please?"

"Sit," she said, clearly exasperated, and pointed to a bench near the door.

I wasn't sure if she had just agreed to do the tattoo or not, but I could practically hear her mentally adding an extra hundred to my bill for her inconvenience. And still, I was willing to pay. The shop was the best in the city. I was lucky for any abuse she wanted to dish out. So when she said to sit, I sat. She disappeared into a back room, and when she returned nearly half an hour later she held two pieces of tracing paper.

"My name's Kim, by the way," she said.

"Oh, yeah, sorry—Frank," I said by way of introduction. "And this is Nathalie."

"Figured as much," Kim barely smiled. "Okay, so here's what we've got."

She spread out the two pieces of paper on the counter between us. One was a black-and-white outline of the tattoo. The other was the stencil colored into a medical-textbook-worthy life-size human heart with a banner wrapped around its middle, *Nathalie* emblazoned in old sailor lettering on the banner.

"It's perfect," I said, beaming like the tattoo was already part of me, like I had a right to feel proud.

Nathalie stood beside me, her arm wrapped around mine. She dug her fingernails into my hand as she stared at the sketch. I thought she had something to tell me, but she didn't look up.

"So, good to go?" Kim asked.

I nodded and she led us past three barber chairs—each occupied by clients in various stages of pain and bravado—and to the back room, which consisted of a few locked supply cabinets, a drafting table, something that looked like a Xerox machine but that I didn't think was, a rolling office chair, and a doctor's examining table covered in white paper. All the walls in the shop were painted black and the back room's overall effect wasn't too unlike a dungeon, which I'm sure was meant to be part of the appeal, but considering the way the barber chairs in the front room sort of looked like dentist chairs, I kept flashing on that one scene in *Marathon Man* where the Nazi dentist tortures Dustin Hoffman by alternately drilling into healthy teeth without anesthetic and then rubbing on clove oil to kill the pain—I was a total wuss about going to the dentist. I was so fucking grateful I didn't have to sit in a chair out in the front room with everyone else watching me squirm.

Kim taped the color sketch up on the wall, fed the black-and-white sketch into the faker Xerox machine, and made a transfer.

"Take off your shirt," she said.

She said it bluntly, just like that—like it wasn't one of the scariest things she could tell me to do. I had to remind myself it was just matter-of-fact business . . . for her, anyway. Still, reflex reaction, I must have turned forty million shades of red. Stripping down to my bare chest in front of a stranger was not a pleasant prospect, but I took a deep breath and braced myself.

"Sure," I said, trying to play it cool.

Nathalie looked at me, her brow furrowed with protective concern.

"Really, it's okay," I said, and leaned over to give Nathalie the gentlest kiss ever.

Kim waited impatiently as I then removed layers of winter clothes and hunched my shoulders to peel the extra-tight white binder up off my chest, to my shoulders, and over my head. Technically, all anyone would have seen if they'd looked was slightly padded skin marked with red lines from where elasticized material had compressed just a few seconds before.

Entirely unfazed by the sight, Kim simply told me to lie down on the examining table. White butcher paper crinkling under my weight as I futilely attempted to get comfortable, I watched Kim cover a small rolling metal table in saran wrap, smear streaks of various ointments on it, fill little cups with ink, pull on a pair of latex gloves, and get her gun ready. I tried to push that Johnny Cash lyric, *Don't take your gun to town, son*, out of my brain. I wasn't going to end up dead on a saloon floor. Oh fuck, what was I doing?

Kim wiped my chest with a thick wad of surgical cotton soaked in cold rubbing alcohol and shaved what little chest hair I had with a white and orange plastic disposable razor. The razor reminded me of those vanilla and orange half-and-half popsicles that were so popular when I was a kid. I used to love them. And I'd chew on the popsicle sticks for hours after the ice cream was gone. Every now and then, the stick would splinter and there was something very particular about the taste of the wood when it did—it was like sucking on cotton, and the resulting sensation was always slightly nauseating to me. Kim threw the used razor in the trash, and I felt that weird popsicle-stick feeling on my tongue. She mistook my sour face for pure nerves.

"Breathe," she said as she cleaned my skin again.

I breathed in the strong scent of rubbing alcohol. She pressed the transfer of the sketch on my chest, slightly left of center, and handed me a mirror.

"Check if it's how you want it. Last chance."

I sat up. Nathalie was holding my hand. There was a wild spark in her eyes. She mouthed, I *love you.*

"It is exactly how I want it," I said and lay back down.

Kim rubbed one of the two ointments from the tray onto my chest over the tattoo outline. My skin tingling already, she came at me with a buzzing needle dipped in black ink.

Okay, look, I'm not going to bullshit you. Getting the tattoo hurt. It really fucking goddamned hurt. I must have drained Nathalie's hand of all its blood for how hard I clenched it with my own. For over three hours, that evil little tattoo gun's needles dug deep into me, first outlining in black, then shading with what felt like tiny slicing X-Acto blades, finally adding color. Gripping Nathalie's hand, I closed my eyes and focused on breathing, almost nodding off from the constant endorphin overload. The pain eventually became meditative, almost pleasurable in some fucked-up wonderful way.

At some point, I felt Kim wipe my chest and rub on more thick ointment. "Done," she said, and patted my shoulder.

I opened my eyes and saw the shining raised brilliance of my tattoo. I swore the heart pulsed, and the banner with Nathalie's name flapped in the breeze. Incredible. Absolutely incredible. Nathalie kissed my sweat-slicked forehead. A tear rolled down her cheek. The expression on her face confused me. Was she sad? Happy? Overwhelmed?

"Sweets?"

"Love you," was all she said.

Meanwhile, a sadistic glow warmed Kim's face. Smiling for real this time, she bandaged the tattoo and instructed me on follow-up care. Gauze and surgical tape for a binder (I folded up and stashed my usual binder in my coat pocket), I got dressed, thanked Kim, and paid. Damn, how I paid. A hefty fee and tip—totally earned and deserved, but shocking nonetheless—having made a sizable dent in my credit card, Nathalie and I walked home.

By the time we got in bed it was almost 4 A.M., and I was totally wiped out, but in the most pleasant way, like after an awesome day of work and a long night of excellent fucking. Still, I felt like I could sleep for days. I just about wanted to die when Nathalie asked me to set the alarm for 7:00 so we could get to the protest meeting place on time, but whatever, I set the alarm. Lights turned out, the clock glowed on the nightstand next to the retablo of Nahui. The tattoo making it too painful to hold my girl, I fell asleep with Nat's hand in mine.

CHAPTER TWENTY-THREE

Alarm blasting, I woke still holding Nathalie's hand. "Morning," she mumbled as I turned off the alarm. "Don't get up. I'll go get you a coffee, okay?"

"Love you," she said, stretching and taking over my half of the bed.

In the bathroom, I washed my hands super carefully and removed the bandage from my chest. I slathered A&D ointment over the tattoo exactly as Kim had instructed. The petroleum and weeping ink and forming scabs promised to be an oozing nightmare. My softest undershirt was transformed into a greasy, smeared mess as soon as I put it on. Resolved not to let such minor inconveniences ruin my good mood, I finished getting dressed and pulled the front door closed gently behind me. As I walked down the stairs, a revolting stench hit me at the second-floor landing. Overly tired, my mouth filled with sour spit, I pinched my nose and kept walking.

At the corner bodega I got Nat her coffee, sweet and light with soy milk, along with a dozen purple dahlias wrapped in a brown paper cone. I looked forward to a hug that would make my tattooed chest ache. As tired as I was, life wasn't going to get any better than it felt at that very moment.

I entered the apartment and saw a shimmer. Large and gold, a wrapped box sat on the bed where Nathalie should have been.

"Nat?" I called out and closed the door behind me.

There was no answer. The bathroom door was open. No

Nathalie. Where was she? Gruesome Hansel and Gretel flash, I wondered if Nathalie might be tucked in the oven. I skipped checking that space, but did pull back the shower curtain and look on the top shelves in the closet for kicks. No luck. Instead, I found a note on my pillow next to the gold box:

Frank,

  I'll call very soon. I promise. Love you,

  Nathalie

I was convinced it had to be a joke. I mean, I'd been gone for all of fifteen minutes and she'd still been in bed when I left. She sure hadn't had much time to dress, pack, and bail again for real. Yes, it had to be a joke. A really lame and twisted one, but a joke nonetheless. I figured she had to be hiding somewhere; she just wanted to see a look of surprise on my face when I found the gift, right? Maybe she was on the stoop . . . ? I checked. Empty. Fuck. If she'd gone to the basement, she better come back soon because we really did have to get going if we were going to make it to the protest on time.

I slammed the bodega cup down on the nightstand, and a little coffee splashed on the framed retablo of Nahui. I dropped the bodega flowers and keys to the floor. Coat shrugged off, feet wiggled out of shoes, scarf and hat peeled and left where they landed, I slumped down on the bed and waited. Five minutes. Fifteen minutes. An hour. Nothing. God-fucking-damnit. My tattoo itched like all hell. The tattoo. So not cool, Nat. I couldn't understand it—how had she let me get the tattoo? What about the baby she'd said she wanted barely two days ago? It made no sense, but there was no doubting it. She was gone, really gone. Again.

I read Nathalie's note over and over. *I'll call very soon. I*

*promise. Love you. I'll call very soon, I promise. Love you. I'll call very.
Soon, I promise, love you.* I couldn't wait any longer; I needed to
know what Nathalie had left me.

The gift box's wrapping paper was textured like gold leaf,
and the bow was starched raw silk. You had to give it to her—
for all of Nat's internal conflict, the girl knew how to make
surfaces look good. I fucking hated Nathalie's wrapping
precisely because it was so elegant and classy. To make things
even worse, the paper and bow somehow reminded me of the
stuff my father had used to wrap Nahui's book and retablo
when he gave them to me. But more to the point, it made me
insane to think that Nathalie had folded and tucked and
taped so perfectly when she must have known she was leaving
again. Didn't her hands tremble? Where were the watermark
stains from her tears? I mean, sure, maybe she'd been planning
to give me the gift for days, since long before she'd known she
was going to take off, and then, totally unrelated, she decided
to leave last minute. But, no matter, by the time I found the
gift, it was both a bribe and a reminder that I didn't know
where Nathalie had gone, when she'd be back, if she'd return
at all. Wanting to hurt the gift just a little, I ripped off its silk
bow, dropped the shimmering length of fabric to the ground,
and tore through the remaining wrapping.

Bulky plastic casing with dark wood laminate accents and
a flimsy extending silver antenna, the gizmo I held was a
distant cousin of the first radio alarm clock I'd had as a kid.
A weather radio. What the hell? A goddamned stupid weather
radio? Nathalie had left me a weather radio and all I could
wonder was *why*. Would it forecast her return? Would it warn
of apocalyptic earthquake suns? I plugged it into an electrical
socket at the far side of the bed and rolled a control knob on
the side until the unit clicked on.

*A blizzard is expected. Central Park: fifteen to twenty inches of snow
by nightfall tomorrow. It is advised to not travel if possible . . .*

Excellent. Just peachy.

. . . If you must travel during this storm, avoid traveling alone. Let a family member or friend know your plans or route. Those venturing outdoors may become lost or disoriented . . .

The radio weatherman cared. His robotic, digitally synthesized voice providing plain-speak wisdom, he was part Stephen Hawking, part Johnny Appleseed. The longer I listened, the clearer I saw his mustached face, his tin pot hat, thick flannel shirt, and heavy work jeans. His feet were bare. Big generous heart, he'd taken off his boots and given them to a poor shoeless young pioneer he'd met on the trail. And he always had a bunch of new ribbons in his pockets for the admiring little girls who ran out from lonely log cabins in the woods to meet him. The computer-voiced weatherman sat in a rustic office situated on top of Manhattan's highest hill, mugs of cowboy gritty black coffee keeping him alert as he carefully monitored barometric and temperature gauges. He scoped the horizon for storms with a handheld telescope. He kept his listeners safe. His job was hard and thankless.

Hypnotized by the steady cadence of his voice, I lay sprawled across the bed on my back and listened to the radio until sweat started dripping off my forehead and down onto the mattress. The super had turned the radiator up so high that I felt like I might faint. Prone, I stared at the ceiling. There, directly above the bed, two faint fissures in the plaster intersected. That pair of barely discernable lines quartered the room into lopsided parts. Had the cracks been there before? I didn't remember them. I was fairly certain they were new, but I couldn't say for sure. I'd never spent much time staring at the ceiling above the bed. My vision blurred.

. . . conditions will be downright dangerous . . .

Downright dangerous? Had the robot weatherman actually said that? *Downright dangerous?* The guy was charming if you gave him half a chance.

Under such intense observation, the ceiling seemed to vibrate. I planned to call the super.

There are lines on the ceiling? he'd ask.

Yes, I'd say.

And?

Yes, *and?* And what? What would I expect him to do? Fix it, of course. Patch up the fissures before they expanded and the universe collapsed. Paint them over so no trace of past damage would show. That's what I wanted.

Like clouds turning into faces and unicorns and hearts, the lines on the ceiling shifted and, strange magic, I remembered Nathalie knew I was taking a train to D.C. the next morning for the estate auction. What if I'd gotten worked up over nothing? Given all that Nathalie was capable of, it *was* possible that the note she left with the radio was just to throw me off her trail so I'd be totally surprised when she met me at Union Station as I disembarked. Maybe she was planning a little round of traveling-businessman-meets-pretty-single-girl-at-the-train-station. That could be nice. Especially if she wore her Burberry trench with a nice pair of two-tone vintage pumps . . . and nothing else. Okay, maybe some stockings. With a garter. It was freezing out, after all. A little square wicker suitcase at her side would be a nice touch. And if the fates were feeling particularly generous, snow would be melting in her hair when she met me. Nathalie's skin glowed so pretty when drizzled with dewdrops.

. . . stock emergency kits with high energy foods . . .

I would pack two sandwiches, one for Nathalie and one for me. Two peanut butter and thinly sliced banana on wheat bread sandwiches, halved with the crusts cut off. I would even pack a Thermos of tomato soup for us to share.

I continued to lay on the bed, staring at the ceiling, motionless, even as the weather radio fell in and out of tune and took to alternately transmitting static. The repetitive

high-pitched electronic wails soothing me in a misery-loves-
misery sort of way, I thought of a story my father told me once
when I accompanied him to a chemo appointment. Back
during Vietnam, he told me, a man beat the draft.

"Lots of guys did, Dad," I'd said.

"Not like him," my father replied.

And, as happened on more occasions than I liked to
admit, my father was correct.

The story went like this:

At the draft physical exams, each draftee was instructed
to put on a pair of headphones. They were then told to raise
their hand, either the right or left, to indicate when they
heard a sound in the corresponding headphone. One young
man, tested the same day as my father, put the headphones on
and consistently failed to acknowledge hearing anything each
time one of three particular tones were transmitted. The
military examiner concluded that he suffered from loss of
hearing in both ears. He was set free and didn't have to go to
war. Later, through the grapevine at basic training, my father
learned that the dismissed draftee was a classical cellist of
particular talent. As it turned out, his trained ear had been
able to identify and distinguish each of the tones transmitted
through the headphones during his physical. Pretending not
to hear three of those tones each time they were presented
was a cakewalk for him. Once a child prodigy, he'd beaten the
draft by means of perfect pitch.

"Inspiring, isn't it?" my dad had said when he finished
telling me the story.

The weather radio screeched a particularly painful jolt of
static. I jumped. I so lacked perfect pitch, but as for dodging
war duties, I was as guilty as anyone could be. I should have
been heading off to 49th Street to hold a sign or something, to
shout with a crowd in an attempt to make our voices heard all

the way to the National Security Advisor. *Dr. Rice, please place the headphones on. Now, raise your right hand if you hear the thousands of Americans protesting your plans for war. And please raise your left hand if you hear the screams of the thousands of troops who will die in your war.* Her hands would remain in her lap the entire time. The protest chants would fall on deaf ears, because sometimes even a politician who was classically trained as a pianist—and who herself had performed at benefits with the very cellist of exceptional talent who had dodged the Vietnam draft with his perfect pitch—could be tone-deaf. Truly. Entirely. And sick as it was, I envied her. There must have been such a bliss in living with absolute certainty about what was right and what was wrong. She didn't feel the need to acknowledge, empathize with, or take responsibility for any misery her actions caused. I had no such privilege. Instead, I simmered in the juices of knowing exactly what kind of selfish fuck I was. Telling myself I was too tired, confused, and sad to get my ass out of the apartment and to the protest, I knew I really just wanted to stay home in case Nathalie called.

Really, since I wasn't going to the protest after all, I should have opened the shop for the day. But with Nat suddenly gone, I just didn't have it in me. Unfortunately—since I was still planning to go to the auction the next day, and I rather doubted Nat would be back to watch the shop—that would mean it would be closed three days straight. Clearly, this wouldn't exactly be a boon for my already floundering enterprise, but it wouldn't be my ruin either, would it? At very least, I should have gone to update the sign. I momentarily considered doing that first thing in the morning, but I was already going to have to leave at the fucking crack of dawn in order to arrive at the 9 A.M. start time, so . . . Sigh.

I figured I might as well get things ready for D.C. Hoping for the off chance Nathalie might actually meet me at the train station, I wanted to look smooth. And if there's anything that says smooth, it's a sleek briefcase. Or maybe that just says "uptight," but whatever, I decided I would take the briefcase with me the next day. I reached up to the closet's top shelf and felt a forming scab on my chest rip apart and bleed. Fuck. And double-fuck. God-fucking-fuck. I pulled my father's briefcase down and brought it to the kitchen table. Gold clasps unlocked, I carefully unpacked its stored items, one object at a time, onto the kitchen table.

Briefcase emptied and Nahui's book sitting on the kitchen table, I remembered the Ash Wednesday when Nathalie had been Nahui. She'd told me I was a handsome devil in a suit. And so, although I hadn't touched my father's clothes since that night, I carefully assembled one of his suits and even pressed each item with the iron I found hibernating at the back of the closet. Can you blame me for stressing the details?

When I was done with all my pathetic preparations, I walked over to the nightstand and picked up the cup of bodega coffee I'd bought for Nathalie. I peeled off the plastic lid. A thin layer of congealed soy milk separated from the inside edges of the cup and floated in the center, an island surrounded by a perimeter of tan coffee. I took a sip. Room temperature was a highly unpleasant state of existence for a cup of coffee, and the amount of sugar Nathalie took made my teeth ache. Another sip. The bitter of cheap caffeine hit my tongue from somewhere deep in the mix. It was almost pleasant by the end of the cup.

CHAPTER TWENTY-FOUR

The East Village never wakes until noon on any day, let alone a Sunday. And when that Sunday also happens to be the first day of a blizzard and part of President's Day weekend, you can pretty much be sure you won't cross paths with anyone if you're walking to the subway at 4:30 in the morning. The entire neighborhood was like some sort of post-apocalyptic landscape. Snow tore through the sky in horizontal sheets and sliced at my face. The exposed length of suit from the hem of my coat to my shoes turned soggy. Wind howled through the fedora I'd chosen to wear. Even though the radio had warned that driving conditions would be dangerous and that travelers should expect airport delays, the weather sucked even worse than I'd expected it to. At least I was traveling by train, not driving or taking a plane. I was freezing, but everything would be fine. I marched on.

I reached Houston and was about to take my first step down the stairwell leading to the subway when I slipped on what I hadn't realized was a snow-dusted sheet of ice. Right there—at the exact steps I'd dragged my suitcases up on my very first day in New York over seven years before—I lost my gravity. My feet flew out sideways from under me and I hit the ground on my right thigh and elbow. I slid the entire width of sidewalk toward Houston and stopped with my feet in the gutter, which was thankfully frozen, but still. My slapstick routine would have made for the most awesome pratfall ever . . . if it hadn't been real.

Coat bunched up around my waist and pants practically

soaked through with snow, I shivered in what was arguably, even after a rough fall, the world's nattiest outfit. Tailored layer upon layer—my father's swankiest suit, matching pocket square, Windsor-knotted tie, fedora—damnit, why was it that on the day I finally decided to wear his clothes out I took a concrete dive?

I took a quick survey of the situation. My neck was pinched something fierce, and my shoulders were jammed. I could feel a considerable bruise forming on my right hip. The palms of both my hands were scraped. And hidden under all my layers of tweed and starched fabric, a soft cotton undershirt rubbed against the weeping tattoo on my chest. The raw skin burned slightly, but that was an expected source of ache. Snot dripped from my nose and instantly froze as I sat on the ground, dazed. How I hadn't broken any bones was beyond me.

Obviously, some people would have taken a fall of that magnitude as a sign to call it a day. But I didn't. Seeing as nobody was around to offer a hand, let alone to give a fuck, I forced myself to snap to, get up, and brush myself off. I figured my clothes would dry, and I could buy an aspirin at Penn Station. I gathered the miscellanea of my things scattered on the ground and continued down the subway entrance.

It wasn't until I sat on the train that I noticed the leather of my briefcase was scuffed. As if that mattered anyway, because, really, by that point there was nothing elegant about my given situation. Cramped body. Chilled flesh. And, like most winter mornings, my fingers were blue at their tips from poorly circulated blood. Thankfully, I continued on from the F to the C toward Penn Station without further incident— though my senses remained piqued. Fight-or-flight adrenaline coursed through me. My hands shook, and there was a detectable jaunty wobble in my stride.

As I exited the subway and entered Penn Station, I was

struck by how oddly calm the building seemed. Later in the morning, the station would be filled with travelers, but at that moment, like some deafening calm before the storm, the station was empty. I take that back. A janitor put a yellow cone outside the men's bathroom before entering to clean; a smattering of National Guardsmen armed with semi-automatic rifles wandered around looking mean; two beat cops drank cups of coffee and talked; four homeless dudes tried to sleep in corners and on stairs; an odd haggard college student or two waited for red-eye connections; and three German tourists wearing enormous backpacks examined a map.

I again contemplated turning back—to crawl into bed, wrap a comforter tight around myself, and sleep. But no matter how tempting the idea was, I knew going home was the exact opposite of what I needed. In fact, maybe I needed never to go home again. Maybe I should have followed Nathalie's lead. Nathalie, the coolest of the cool kids on the playground, taking dares and climbing up on the high bar to twirl with one bony knee locked on the metal monkey bar, her callused hands pumping momentum as she flipped faster and faster, doing cherry drops, flashing her panties and scrawny belly and knocking out a few teeth with her landing. Thinking of Nathalie made me ashamed of the ways I'd found comfort in being lint and my habits glue.

I want. I want.

I was overwhelmed with a sudden itch to run off and leave all adult responsibility and care behind. Fuck the accumulating debt and gray hairs of trying to run a shop and be a good boyfriend, fuck concerns over whether or not I wanted to be a parent someday, fuck haunting thoughts of Nahui's dead baby—fuck it all. I wanted to flit off and land somewhere I could drink huge mugs of cheap coffee and do nothing but calmly stare out a window undisturbed. Maybe I could be a roadie for a punk metal band. In Olympia, Seattle, or Portland, somewhere foggy and washed regularly with rain. I wanted to spend mindless days driving a van. I wanted to carry amps and guitars and lassos of tangled extension cords into dank clubs. Dead-end silent pauses in ragged frantic metal riffs would be my meditation. I would be the one who could make even a bad gig seem not so bad, because there I'd be, leaning against the dive bar's back wall, and, who knows, maybe I'd fall in love with someone who loved me even more than I loved them and together we'd share cartwheel idiot bliss love—yes, I wanted to run off and fall in love with a rocker chick who would most definitely have F-R-A-N-K tattooed on the narrow canvases of her knuckles for everyone to watch twitch flicker fire as she hammered her drums up onstage.

I want. I want. And then there was *I must.*

I headed toward Penn Station's Amtrak ticketed-passenger lounge—"lounge" being very loosely defined in this instance. Piped-in baroque classical music echoed loudly throughout the 1960s Tomorrowland modern monstrosity of a room. I sat in a rusted-chrome and teal vinyl chair. Circular glass-paneled walls surrounded me. A low partition-board ceiling caged me in from above. The clunky steps up to Madison Square Garden were visible behind me. Challenge that it was, I tried to imagine what the original Penn Station looked like at its grand opening in 1910. There must have been beautiful dark wood benches, wrought-iron staircases, glass vaulted ceilings, and handcrafted crown moldings. The air must have smelled of lemons and roasted chestnuts back then. But now, the air smelled only of dirty mop water and public bathrooms. Fluorescent overhead lights bounced cruel brightness off cracked gray linoleum. Add to this mess the occasional travelers rolling ugly suitcases behind them and the random whiff of the food court's tragic greasy stink—I died inside. I might as well have been a zombie for how numb

I was. I was tempted to go jerk off in a bathroom stall. At least that way I might be able to remind myself I was alive.

5:30 A.M. Violin and harpsichord Muzak drilling a hole in my skull, the tweed of my coat scratching my neck, I boarded a D.C.-bound train that smelled of rancid peanut oil from decades of spilled Styrofoam takeout meals gulped in transit. I wished hard for Nathalie to meet me at Union Station. The cabin lights flickered on and off as the train lurched into motion.

CHAPTER TWENTY-FIVE

I waited at Union Station for half an hour after my train arrived. And then I waited some more, eyes darting around, hoping to catch sight of Nathalie. I bought a cup of crappy commuter coffee and waited even longer. Three cups of coffee eventually consumed, my stomach was beyond raw. Acid burn. Pain. That was all it came down to. Pain. Heavy heart. Tired eyes. Stomach sour sleepless ache.

Fuck the estate auction. I wanted to call it a day and go to the Vietnam Memorial instead. To visit my dad. True, his name wasn't included on the wall, but that monument belonged to him just as much as it did to those soldiers actually listed there. In terms of death in the line of duty, the only difference between the boys acknowledged on the memorial and my father was that he hadn't been a war casualty until decades after his tour of duty was complete. He'd marinated belly-down in Agent Orange swamp mud. War soaked into him, and eventually it turned his cells malignant. A dead soldier is a dead soldier is a dead soldier.

Sorry to be so damned dramatic, but drama is clearly in my bones.

So I waited at Union Station. For my true love. For a girl plenty would have told me to kick to the curb, but for whom I still inexplicably held out hope. And by the time I finally whipped my sentimental sorry ass into shape and got myself on the Metro to the estate auction, I was nearly two hours late.

I almost missed the chance to bid on the damned 1930s

Royal typewriters, and those typewriters were the only reason I was at the stupid auction. The rest of the estate didn't interest me and was way out of my price range, but the six typewriters, listed at a starting bid of forty dollars each, were meant to be mine. Mint condition. Fully functioning. What a private estate had done with six typewriters I had no idea, but I didn't care either. It seemed everyone at the auction was hunting art deco furniture, fine jewelry, silver, and other snooty goodies. Nobody else bid on the typewriters. Simpletons. Those machines were perfection. They wouldn't take up much counter space and, if my luck turned good—damn, how I fucking hoped it would soon turn, how I needed it to—I'd be able to sell the typewriters at a crazy mark-up. The East Village aging trust-fund hipsters who I could imagine buying the typewriters from me probably wouldn't have a fucking clue how to insert paper into the inky metal things, but I was pretty sure that they'd love displaying the vintage lovelies on their loft desks as if they worked on their memoirs and typed correspondences every day. I knew they wouldn't even blink at throwing down two hundred bucks for the dose of cool factor. The typewriters were golden eggs. I secured my purchase with a credit card that was getting much too close to maxing out, completed all the shipping paperwork, and went back to Union Station.

It was getting late and I had no idea how Nathalie would know where to look for me, but I hoped I didn't have to start putting such surprises past her. I found a row of bolted-down chairs near the station's ticket windows. That seemed as good as any place to wait. So I did. I sat and ate my sandwiches and drank my soup, all the while watching the crowds, watching for Nathalie.

The longer I waited, the more clearly a vision of Nathalie on a bus filled my thoughts. I could see her as she stared at her own reflection on the inside of a tinted window. Her beautiful face drawn and tired, other passengers sitting near her would presume she was a stoic victim escaping unspeakable horrors. Really, it would be only guilt and a lack of sleep tugging at her face, drawing down the corners of her mouth. As she sat on the bus, she would play over and over in her mind how she'd tried to convince herself not to leave, how she'd argued with herself, bullied herself even. But still, no matter, there she was, on a bus. Leaving yet again. A day and a half had already passed since her bus pulled out of Port Authority and drove by unlit off-Broadway marquees. Unwilling to deal with reminders of home becoming more and more distant behind her, she'd slept until nightfall, until the bus had reached the unfamiliar and murky rural nowhere between home and wherever it was she'd end up. Whether it was based in some distant reality or was entirely a figment of my imagination, I could see it all so clearly.

I gathered my things, stood in line at the ticket window, and paid fare for the next train home.

Stupid little lidless blue cup of coffee in hand, I was walking down the narrow aisle from the food car toward my seat just as the train lurched out of Newark. This giant dude getting up from his seat lost his balance and knocked into me. Coffee splashed on my hand and, without meaning to, I yelped. It was so embarrassing, that high-pitched squeal coming out of my mouth like I'd been stabbed or something. Oak-Tree Neck apologized profusely. I cleared my throat. "No problem," I sort of grunted and nodded and continued down the aisle. I just wanted to sit down. Actually, I just wanted to be home already. Next stop was Penn Station. Give an hour or two, I planned to be in bed, blankets pulled over my face. Almost back at my seat, I heard a loud grinding noise, like a knife being sharpened at the hardware store, but a trillion times louder and more severe. Coffee splashed on my wrist again.

This time I didn't cry out. Or maybe I did. I don't remember. Everything happened so quickly. Certain small details of the wreck are lost to me.

I do remember dropping the cup of coffee on the train's dirty carpet. Next thing I knew, my entire body launched upward. My briefcase caught on a seat back and was ripped from my hand by the jerking momentum. I'm pretty sure my head slammed against the overhead luggage rack. And I must have tried to brace my fall with outstretched arms, because the distinctive noise of cracking bones announced my landing as I crashed to the floor. Some people screamed, but others, strangely, laughed. Personally, I focused all my efforts on trying to grip the bolted metal underside of a chair as the train started to tilt and roll onto its side. My left hand had no strength. A searing pain surged up my left arm and across my torn-tattoo raw chest. I slid into a crumpled ball on a horizontal windowed surface that should have been the wall next to my assigned seat. I tried to stand, but couldn't. I opened my mouth to call for help, but found I was unable to make any sound save for a rasping wheeze. The lights went out. Not "the lights went out" like I died or something; I just mean the train cabin lights no longer worked.

Okay, you know how people say catastrophic situations bring out the very worst or best in people? Bullshit. The wreck did nothing of the sort. Everyone in that derailed and toppled train remained just as messily human as they'd been before. As for me, I'd love to say I did something poetic or noble as I lay there trapped in the dark wreckage. Something like even though I didn't know if I'd live or not, I used my final reserve of strength to write *Nat love* or some similar cryptic sentiment on a seat cushion in my own blood. Or maybe: I dragged my broken body to another person and cradled their head in my lap as they died. (And, just to keep the facts straight, people did die that day—two, according to newspaper reports the next morning.) Shamefully, I would be lying if I claimed I did anything but whimper with bloody snot smeared on my face until either my head trauma or the pain or the thick black smoke filling the train finally, mercifully, caused me to black out.

So, no, I didn't offer my help or comfort to anyone around me. I didn't scream, *Over here, over here . . . no take her first, she's worse off than I am!* when firefighters tore through the train walls with jaws of life to rescue people and to put out the fire. Hell, I didn't even hear the emergency-response sirens when the teams arrived. And I most certainly didn't realize the crash had been caused by a statistically improbable engineering glitch involving one seriously dented but intact Jeep Cherokee wedged between train tracks and one severely depressed but physically uninjured man's failed suicide attempt. I didn't see the tracks littered with luggage, clothing, and a bicycle. Nor did I witness the surrounding snow-covered gravel turn a muddy pink reeking mess of diesel fuel, oil, and blood. There wasn't a single bit of my brain that pondered if maybe our wreckage resembled the derailment that had killed my father's sister in Chicago so many years before. I didn't pray for my father to watch over me like some sort of guardian angel, I didn't hope my mother would care, and I didn't wish for Nathalie to cover me in kisses.

I just lay unconscious in the demolished train.

CHAPTER TWENTY-SIX

A loud thunderclap noise sounded and echoed. Fearing lightning or gunshots, I hit the ground. Floodlights snapped on overhead. I lay sprawled on my belly at the edge of a shallow stage. Sweat dripped into my mouth and I tasted waxy pancake makeup. Slow melancholy music played from speakers hidden somewhere off to my sides. A scratchy resonant voice said:

I remember when I was a very little girl, our house caught on fire. I'll never forget the look on my father's face as he gathered me up in his arms and raced through the burning building out to the pavement . . .

The fabulous Ms. Peggy Lee crooned our song.

Once upon a time, I saw Peggy Lee get into a limo on Broadway in Midtown. The limo was chipped white and its dark window tinting was bubbled and peeling off. Peggy Lee was well past her glory days, but goddamnit, she rode around town in a limo. Tacky and in need of repair or not, it was still a limo, and she refused to go shopping without chauffeured fabulousness. Her arms weighed down by a trillion boutique shopping bags—linen bags, silk-ribbon-handled bags, fancy bags which surely held even fancier pirate loot—she was the definition of elegance itself.

Truly, Peggy Lee was totally stunning. Her famous face was painted-on radiance and her hairdo was . . . oh lord, there is no way to appropriately describe it, but her dyed-blond bird's nest was teased high and big, like an aura and a halo and all the heavens woven into a single crown for one very troubled but very gorgeous lady. Watching her step into a limousine was like seeing my fairy godmother glide by on a sparkling Pegasus. Strike me dead if I'm lying, but once she was inside the limo with the door closed, Peggy Lee rolled down her window, looked at me, winked her tired wink, and blew me a kiss.

I didn't wash the air ever again.

. . . I stood there shivering in my pajamas and watched the whole world go up in flames . . .

A trick to try:

Stand in a doorway. Any narrow doorway will do. Let your arms hang at your sides. Push. Press the backs of your hands against the doorframe with as much strength as you have, and then some. Do this for at least three minutes, five minutes if you can. Push. Hard. Focus. And when your egg-timer trills and your time is up, step out of the doorway. Move into an open space, either enclosed or outdoor will do, but be sure it's a space free of obstruction. Stand and relax. Your arms will float skyward. From memory embedded in your muscles, your arms will levitate without your consciously intending them to.

Your body has memory.

And so there I was, onstage, blinded, two safe deposit keys hanging from my neck. A headache crept to the base of my skull. I wanted to rip off the twine metal necklace, rub the stage makeup from my face with my bare hands, run out of the theater, and be done with it. But the show had to go on. There were no other options. So I hit my mark. And my arms floated upward in front of me. The weight of those damned keys around my neck was the only thing keeping me from floating away outright. But I couldn't control my inherited phantom limbs—my father's naïve heart, his mother's burning lips, Nahui's bloodshot eyes begging for blessing from an unforgiving and burning sun . . .

I sang.

And when it was all over I said to myself, "Is that all there is to a fire?"
Is that all there is?

"Francisca?" an unfamiliar voice addressed me.

A hand tapped my right shoulder and introduced me to the throbbing pain pulsing throughout my body. Centralized epicenters of ache located in my left arm and a spot directly above my left brow, I woke, startled, with only three limbs I was able to control and a crackling voice that no one would put onstage.

"Yeah?" I croaked.

I opened my eyes to find that I was lying in a bed with a nurse standing at my side. At least I thought she was a nurse. I wasn't sure. She was wearing lavender scrubs. Don't doctors wear white coats over their scrubs? And more dignified scrubs? Don't they walk around with stethoscopes hanging from their necks? But if she was a nurse, or even a doctor for that matter, why was she being so familiar? Why had she used *that* name?

"Have we met?" I asked.

I wasn't trying to be funny, I seriously thought maybe we knew each other from somewhere else and some other time. Where was I anyhow? . . . Forget where I was, if she called me "Francisca" again I was going to start wondering *who* I was.

"I'm so happy you're awake," she said, and smiled a sincere and huge smile.

Her cheeriness freaked me out.

"Now, sweetheart," she continued, "you'll be a little groggy. It's just the painkiller. It'll wear off by morning. We want to keep you here tonight to make sure you're okay."

Again, where was "here"?

My lips were thick and chapped. It was a battle to keep my eyelids open. My thoughts fuzzed in and out of focus in the most floating-cloud pleasant way. What meds had they given me? I wanted more.

"I'm okay," I said. A beat too late I realized my statement was in no way a response to anything she had said.

"Yes, of course you are," she laughed, in a friendly way, like we were pals. "But you sure gave the medics a scare when they found you. That tattoo on your chest was a mess. At first they thought you had some horrible chest wound."

If she only knew.

"Are you thirsty?" she asked. "Can I get you some ginger ale or water?"

She lay her hand kindly on my right shoulder. I sort of wished she would reach down and hug me. Or spoon-feed me applesauce. She wasn't so bad. She was really sweet, actually.

"What's your name?" I asked.

"Sally."

"That's a nice name."

Stoned as I was on pain meds, I listened with considerably strained effort as Sally put the pieces together for me. Most obviously, my upper left arm was broken and in a cast. Sally said a busted humerus was no big deal, happened all the time, it'd heal just fine. And she said not to worry about the two stitches that tugged on the skin of my forehead either. They'd dissolve away all on their own. I wasn't concerned, but I did wish the stitches were from a frontal lobotomy. That would have been so soothing. And as for the new tattoo on my chest, she'd cleaned and bandaged it while I was still passed out. The top layer of scabs, she said, had been rubbed right off, but it should be no problem.

As far as I cared, my injuries were neither here nor there.

I would heal. What sucked was that, besides Sally, I was alone. I had no one to call. No one would know something was wrong.

Sally smoothed a thin hospital blanket over my legs.

"I'll be back. Rest," she said.

I fell asleep for I'm not sure how long and woke to once again find Sally at my side, this time offering me something to drink from a plastic cup. I adored her for holding a bendy straw to my mouth and smiling proudly like my drinking ginger ale was the most impressive accomplishment the world had ever known. She wiped dribbled soda off my chin. If my heart hadn't already been taken by another, I swear I would have fallen in love. We could make a happy home here and . . . wait—

"Sally, where are we?"

At first she looked at me like she thought I might have a concussion, like she needed to call in a neurologist to check on me. And then she laughed and said, "Oh, I'm sorry, I guess I forgot to tell you. You're in Newark, New Jersey—University Hospital."

I swear the fates have some sort of giant industrial titanium filing cabinet filled with manila folders for every human who has ever existed. Like uptight little socialite dinner hostesses, inside each folder they log notes on what feasts they've cooked up for each guest. Clearly, all the Cruz files kept getting mixed up. I was so completely over having my family's traumas served to me like re-plated tepid leftovers. University Hospital. I was being schooled, no doubt about it. Question was: Had I finally learned my lesson?

CHAPTER TWENTY-SEVEN

17 February 2003. President's Day.

Eyes stung by gusts of snow, shoes soaked, coat and clothes thoroughly ruined, I stood outside Penn Station and tried to hail a ride home. Getting a cab at Penn Station is never easy—during rush hour in the middle of a blizzard and looking as thrashed as I did, it was near hopeless. By the time a cab finally stopped for me and delivered me to my building, the sun had long set. As if the past two days hadn't already provided enough drama to last a lifetime, four police officers, plastic-slicker-covered and shivering, blocked me at the sidewalk.

"I live here," I said, pointing up toward my apartment.

In response they eyeballed me suspiciously, and one asked to see my identification. Too exhausted to ask why or what was going on, I simply obliged. Driver's license shown and returned to my wallet, they let me continue to the door. Someone had shoved soggy rolled-up newspaper as a makeshift doorstop under the vestibule door. I started to push the newspaper aside with my foot so the door would shut and lock behind me. The cops shot me a look that wasn't a reprimand exactly; it was more equal parts caution and horror. Downtown cops who'd seen it all—finding that look on their faces was unsettling. I left the doorstop in place and stepped inside past the door. The same expression the cops wore instantly plastered itself across my face.

Holy mother of all things miserable, the stink that infil-trated my nose was beyond description. Truly. Humans should not know such odors and are therefore incapable of explaining them accurately. I pinched my nose between my fingertips and breathed through my mouth as I walked up the stairs. Another sour-faced officer stood guard at the second landing. Johnny's door was wide open; I learned the smell of death.

I remembered Nathalie's freakout about Johnny a few days earlier. I should have trusted her intuition. Something *had* been wrong. Terribly wrong. Sorry to be crude, but from the smell of things, Johnny had probably been dead the entire two weeks we hadn't seen him. And the building's radiator had been on full blast for at least as long. His dead body rotted the entire time. He'd been alone. All alone. No one had known he was dead. *If there aren't at least five people you can depend on, you are in deep murky waters* and *I don't want to die alone,* I heard my father say. Standing in front of Johnny's door, I understood.

"I'm so sorry," I thought.

Aloud, apparently, because the officer turned her pinch-faced stare toward me. Clearly, she was annoyed with each and every aspect of her President's Day assignment. Fuck her. Wasn't this her job? And didn't she get holiday overtime or something anyway?

"He's dead?" I asked.

"Oh yeah, he's dead," she said, with a callousness and disgust that made me hate her.

I tried not to let her see me hold my breath as I continued up the stairs.

Unlocking the multiple locks of my apartment door, opening said door, and then closing and locking it again, was no simple feat for a person unaccustomed to having use of only one hand. But who was I to complain? Poor Johnny. I couldn't believe he'd been downstairs, right under me, dead for all that time. I felt horrible for not knowing, for not helping somehow. The death smell seeped in from the stairwell outside my door. I opened all the windows to regulate the apartment's unbearable radiator swelter and to let some fresh air in. Beaded in sweat, my forehead pressed against the middle window's screen, I sucked in crisp night air from outside and stared at the blizzard snowfall already turning into dirty slush. I looked out at the quiet sky, and I thought how perfect it would be to smoke one of Nathalie's cigarettes on the fire escape, just to force myself into the cold for ten minutes and watch and listen to nothing in particular.

And then I saw the blinking red light.

A new message. It was either the Newark Fire Department—Sally the nurse had said someone would call if my briefcase was found at the crash site—or it was Nathalie. My pulse stopped for the moment it took to cross the room to the answering machine. I pressed Play.

"*It's me. Please pick up, handsome.*"

A beat of silence.

"*Frank?*"

Another beat.

"*Okay, I'll call back later. Love you.*"

Beep.

The end.

Fuck.

I pressed Play again. And again. And a fourth time for good measure. I sat on the floor and realized that although I knew exactly what day and time Nathalie had called—Sunday, 10:05 P.M.—I had no idea when she planned to call back, let alone come home. As I sat on the floor, I noticed the bundle of flowers I'd dropped next to the bed two nights before. Twelve sets of paper-thin petals had transformed into a shriveled and formless sticky smear of dark purple. The flowers were dead. Or dying, perhaps.

Awkward and bruised movements, I stood and reached up

around my neck to take off the sling the hospital had given me. Even the simplest movements made me flinch. After several minutes of determined effort, I'd left my tattered and bloodied clothes in a crumpled pile on the floor next to the front door, ready to be taken to the trash chute in the hall— what a fucking waste of a nice suit. I shuffled to the bathroom, sat in the tub, and turned on the faucets. Hunched over and glassy-eyed, I watched the water splash and slowly rise as I peeled off the large bandage Sally had placed over my tattoo. I sat in my sad bath of pipe-rusted yellowish water, careful not to soak my healing tattoo, failing in my efforts to keep my left arm's cast dry, and I washed myself with Nathalie's fancy honey oatmeal soap.

For too long I sat there, shivering in tepid water that had turned a revolting shade of gray. Eventually, after I drained the tub and splashed handfuls of water on myself in an attempt to rinse, I toweled off and slathered my tattoo with A&D ointment. There was something fundamentally disconcerting about having a chest that smelled like a clean baby's diaper rash, but what was I supposed to do, let the tat get infected? Pajama pants tugged up with one arm, a tangled wife-beater struggled on and immediately adhered to my greased chest, I finally sat in bed. It was only 7:30, but I just wanted to pull the covers over my head and never get up again. Too tired even to sleep, I noticed that above the horizon of bare-branch trees in Tompkins Square Park, the Empire State Building was lit up white-on-white.

It's humbling that such bullshit altruistic symbolism moved me. But it did. And for some bizarre reason I remembered a Brecht poem Nathalie had recited for me once when we first started dating. I didn't have a brain for memorizing poetry like Nathalie, but I knew the poem went something like, *At least I'm alive . . . I'm like the man who took a brick to show how beautiful his house had once been.*

"I'm that man," I said aloud—to the Empire State Building, to no one, to the empty room.

That poem is about surviving the Holocaust, Frank. Don't be such a jerk, I could practically hear Nathalie respond.

"I'm that man."

Oh, sweetheart, hush it, my imaginary Nathalie said.

The Empire State Building sparkled. If I stared long enough without blinking, it seemed to disintegrate into a shower of glittering stars. This, of course, was only an illusion.

I'm like the man who took a brick to show how beautiful his house had once been . . .

There I was, broken body, drained soul, doing my fucking best to tend to things properly, but, sure enough, not much more than a crumbled brick of my once beautiful life remained.

No matter how exhausted I was, there was no way I was going to fall asleep. Giving in, I got up from bed and walked over to the window. Screen pushed up, I climbed out to the fire escape. Leaning against the freezing metal railing, I looked east toward Avenue B.

I wanted dirt under my nails. And splinters in my fingertips. I needed another tree to plant.

A shrill ring suddenly resonated from inside the apartment. The phone. Zoned out, I only sort of heard three more rings. And then, mobilizing burst of reality, I stumbled back in through the window and rushed to the phone. I answered just as the machine picked up.

"Hello?"

Feedback screeched in my ear. I turned off the machine.

"Nat?"

A robot voice responded, "*One minute remains. To add credit, please hang up and call the toll-free number listed on the back of your card.*" And then Nat said: "Frank? Meet me in the park on Ash Wednesday?"

"Huh?" That reply was all my suddenly stunted motor skills allowed.

"Have you been drinking?"

"No."

"Please meet me on March 5th?"

"That's more than two weeks from now."

"I can't come home before then."

"So much shit has happened, Nat . . ."

"I know, sweetheart. And I want to talk to you about it. I just need some time. I'm so sorry about all of this and—"

"No, Nat, I mean . . ."

My mouth stalled and my lungs burned. Damnit. Johnny's rotting body was probably still there downstairs. My arm was broken. The train wreck. I had so much to say, but not enough composure or oxygen to say it. But it didn't matter. Nathalie allowed only a momentary silence before she continued.

"Frank? March 5th. Please?"

"Nat, you can't just fucking leave and then call and—"

"To add credit, please hang up and call the toll-free number listed on the back of your card."

"Tompkins Square Park," she said in a rush. "On the 5th. At the fountain, I'll be—"

"Your time has expired."

The robot operator disconnected us.

CHAPTER TWENTY-EIGHT

4 March 2003.

I overdosed on pills.

I hadn't really intended for it to happen. The bottle said to take two, and so that's what I did. At first. But those two weren't working. So I took two more. And then, a few hours later, two more. At one point I opened the child-proof bottle with my teeth and shook out five, maybe six, of the capsules into my good hand. I slugged them back with a glass of water and forced myself horizontal. Half an hour later, I could smell the pills on my cold sweat. And still I wanted more. I was so goddamned hungry for a good night's sleep.

In the two weeks since Nathalie's call, I'd worked endless days at the shop, desperate to make up for lost time and money. All told, I hadn't slept more than an hour or two each night. The clock had taken to laughing at me all night long. And so there I was, eyes dry and unfocused, staring at the walls. Remembering a stupid mind-over-matter trick I'd read in a magazine once, I tried to induce guru relaxation by forcing deep breaths and imagining that I was floating in a pool of Jell-O. Still, my heart raced and every cell of my body jittered. I could have sworn spiders crawled under my skin, and I was sure *After-School Special* angel-dust-overdose jump-out-the-window tragedies were on their way.

Following a few more hours of twitching on my bed with a parched tongue and a stomach that wouldn't stop knotting and unknotting and doing really fucking clumsy summer-saults up into my rib cage, I ended up on my knees in front of the toilet. Drenched in sweat and stripped down to my boxers and undershirt, I tried not to look into the toilet bowl as the pills, now a brown and earth-stinky liquid, shot up my throat and out my mouth and nostrils in burning swells.

Valerian root. From Nathalie's post-apocalypse stash. There weren't any of my old pink pills left in the apartment, and I learned super quick that the hippie alternative did not make for peaceful sleep as advertised. Even after I'd barfed up the overload, those little brown powder bombs of poison gave me heartburn. Puff the Magic Dragon, I burped up smoke clouds of nasty fungus for hours. I thought about how Nathalie had once said she thought ass tasted like dirty cabbage. Well, valerian root tasted like dirty ass.

Four in the morning, even more tired than the night before, I finally gave up and kicked myself upright. I was uncomfortably aware of a crazy vivid dream in which a giggling baby Ángel, alive and dressed in an intricate little mariachi outfit, sat in a saddle atop a howling coyote. As I'd approached him, Ángel had tapped the coyote with his spurred boots, and the two had galloped up a fluorescent-bright silver pyramid that reached high into the skies. I never did catch Ángel, but, lucky me, I must have scraped my cast against the sides of that damned pyramid over and over as I climbed it because when I woke my arm fucking ached worse than it had in the entire two weeks it'd been in a cast. Inflammation traveled from the tips of my left fingers, up my arm, past my shoulder, and, I swear, all the way to the edge of my jaw. Additional fun: The cast felt too tight and its lining snagged the hairs on my arm. I was a total whining mess.

The heating unit pinged, and a new gust of dry and overheated air invaded the apartment. Heatwaves were visibly emanating from my skin. Lingering whiffs of the vaguely still-detectable death-and-industrial-cleaner stench from the apartment downstairs filtered in. And still, for all its complications, I wished I could stay right there forever. With one catch. I wanted Nathalie shifting and settling into picture-perfect loveliness on my side of the bed. Fuck the fresh-air world outside, I would have happily watched Nathalie sleep in our bed all day if she were there.

I reached over to the nightstand and picked up the postcard I'd left next to the framed retablo the night before. Nathalie hadn't called again, but she'd sent a card. It was a 1970s tourist postcard—all orange-tinted photograph and clunky wood-cut font—of Death Valley. God knows where she'd gotten the thing, but she'd written in her pretty cursive:

3 A.M. *Ash Wednesday. Temperance.*

xoxo,
N.

I flipped the card over and looked at the Death Valley photo. A lumpy sparkling landscape of salt. The Devil's Golf Course. My father had taken his wife there to fall apart. Had I ever told Nathalie that story? I wasn't sure. No, I must have. But if I had, why would she have sent that postcard? Wasn't it sort of fucked up? I read the back again. 3 A.M. *Ash Wednesday.* Tomorrow morning. *Temperance.* The fountain in Tompkins Square Park. Tomorrow. *Ash Wednesday.* Morning. 3 A.M. Nathalie would be back. I reread the message yet again.

Eyes sore and puffy, if I had looked in the mirror I would have seen lines etched deeply in my brow and creasing vertically at the sides of my mouth. My empty stomach churned and growled. Its acidic sloshing was identical to the sound of digested food emptying into my dad's colostomy bag.

I put the postcard back on the nightstand and picked up the retablo of Nahui. That melancholy pout. Those silver eyes. I willed her to reach out and hold me like she'd done when my father died. Nothing. Looking at her sullen expression just made me feel worse. Things clearly weren't working the way they should have been. Something major had to change, but what? Retablo still in hand, it occurred to me I might have a solution.

I looked at the alarm clock on the nightstand. 4:15 A.M. I calculated a tentative timeline for my plan as quickly as my sluggish brain could, and I determined that, yes, if Nathalie really would be at the park at three in the morning, just under twenty-four hours away, I did have time to do what I needed to do. Not with any to spare, but with just enough—if I got my ass in gear, quick.

So I pushed myself up off the bed, brushed my teeth, took the quickest bath known to man, and got dressed in my most trusted skater rags. Gathering what I needed from the apartment, I packed the following into a brown paper grocery bag:

1. wallet and apartment keys
2. toothpaste and toothbrush
3. blind man dark glasses and walking stick
4. two safe deposit keys
5. honey-hued worry stone
6. Nahui's book and the framed retablo

5 A.M., I locked the apartment door behind me. On the way down the stairs, I stopped at the second-floor landing. A week before, someone had covered Johnny's entire front door with a thick black tarp which was attached to the surrounding wall with heavy-duty duct tape. They'd also put a small bucket of coal at the base of the door. To absorb odors, I think. The coal wasn't working.

I continued toward the F train at First and Houston.

CHAPTER TWENTY-NINE

I thought for sure I must have acquired a special glow. Seriously, deep down I was certain people around me would know I was on the brink of radical transformation. I wouldn't have been surprised if someone had come up to me, patted me on the shoulder, and said, *Go get 'em, tiger*. And why shouldn't they have? My story was precisely the redemption song people adored most. Like ancient myths and DC Comics combined, the fates had dumped me in a vat of toxic waste and I'd clawed my way out. Best part was, the poison hadn't turned me evil—instead, it'd given me the superhuman powers I needed to set my world right.

Thing was, I didn't actually glow. I was just some random dude standing at a JFK airline counter too early in the morning, trying to buy a ticket for the next flight to Los Angeles. Nobody cheered me on.

"We have a flight departing at twelve noon and arriving at LAX at 2 P.M. local time," the flight attendant in her blue polyester uniform said.

"Is that the first flight?"

"There's one at 6:45 A.M., but it goes to Long Beach."

"Perfect."

"And for your return?"

"I need to be back in New York by two."

"Today?"

"No, tomorrow morning."

I could tell the flight attendant wanted to give me the Annoying Customer of the Month Award. For whatever reason, she seemed entirely convinced I was a worthy recipient of such an honor. Attitude plus some, she tapped her long nails against the keyboard and came up with this compromise: "We have a flight leaving at 5 P.M. local time. Out of Los Angeles International."

"Arrive in Long Beach and leave from LAX?"

"You would get back in New York at 1:45 A.M."

"Nothing earlier?"

"No."

Couldn't she see I had no time for such delightful flirtation? Bitch.

"I'll take it."

"How would you like to pay?"

I took my wallet from my pocket to get my trusty plastic. And that was when I noticed that the photograph of the flapper girl, the one I'd found at the estate sale in Bushwick, was missing. If this disappearance strikes you as rather unremarkable, allow me to clarify that my wallet was designed in a way that would have absolutely disallowed the possibility of that photo sliding out accidentally. And neither the sturdy canvas of the wallet nor the plastic photo-display-pocket were torn. It just didn't make sense for the flapper to be missing unless someone had intentionally opened my wallet and taken the photo out. Evening television news exposés of thieving hospital orderlies came to mind. Was that why Sally the nurse had been so friendly? Was it a front? But why would anyone go through my wallet, take the photo, and then leave all the cash and credit cards? Besides, I'd seen the photo plenty of times in the two weeks since I'd gotten back from D.C. Or at least I thought I had. Regardless, the photo was no longer there.

And then I understood: The flapper Nahui-wannabe going missing from the sweetheart display in my wallet was just the beginning of everything coming together perfectly.

I handed the flight attendant my credit card.

I was on my way.

CHAPTER THIRTY

One quick look out the airplane window as we descended into Long Beach and I remembered how much I hated Southern California. Concrete glittered under the sun for miles and miles where desert tumbleweeds should have been, buildings sprawled squat and too scared to reach high into the sky, pickled people ran around in tank tops and shorts with sunglasses and cell phones as permanent appendages. Gag me with a spoon. Like, totally.

The only thing that kept me from lashing out and hitting people over the head with my cast was the fact that traveling light was one of the most pure intoxications the world has to offer. Carrying only a single grocery-store paper bag, I pitied everyone else as they schlepped their overstuffed carry-on luggage down the cramped aisle and to the airport's one baggage claim area—to the jammed conveyor belt where they then huddled around and retrieved even heavier bags. If they'd known what was good for them, they would have insisted their suitcases be lost.

All other arriving passengers busy jockeying for prime positions at the luggage conveyor belt, I walked right up to the airport's car rental kiosk. Standing there, I thought of my Thanksgiving Day drive in the woods with Nathalie and the pretty little tree I'd hauled to our rented station wagon; I thought of how I'd planted the tree for her and hung a love letter from its scraggly branch. I'd been so stupid to think I could ground her with the roots of that clunky romantic gesture.

My self-annoyed reminiscing was interrupted when the car rental employee sang out cheerily, "Reservation number, please?"

Reservation number? Wasn't Southern California the land of endless cars?

"Sorry, I didn't know I needed a reservation."

"It's your lucky day," the car rental guy said with studied customer-service enthusiasm as he typed something into his computer. "We have a Cadillac Escalade available. Fully loaded."

Like I needed a vehicle that could seat seven and suck the planet dry of all its oil? There was no reason the guy should have known, but my solo drive would total a quick hundred miles, tops. There were no foreseeable dirt roads en route, and therefore I most definitely didn't need four-wheel drive, let alone a carriage and tires so tall that driver-side stepladders were common accessories. Added displeasure, I was certain an Escalade could jam up a train track even better than the Jeep Cherokee had back in Newark. I really, really didn't want to drive an SUV.

The rental desk kid mistook my hesitance, looked at my cast, on my *left* arm mind you, and added: "No worries, the Escalade's automatic."

Sweet but dim—it's the weather; they can't help it.

"Do you have any compacts?"

He typed more into his computer. "The only other car available today without a reservation is a Hyundai Accent."

"I'll take the Hyundai."

Maybe I didn't understand English? "I can give you a nice deal on the Escalade," he said, very slowly.

"The Hyundai is perfect."

Shaking his head slightly, he clicked the request into his computer. "I'm sorry, it seems the air conditioner is broken."

It was early March in Southern California.

"That's all right, thank you."

It seemed to occur to the guy that I might be a terrorist. I mean, who else would want a Hyundai compact with broken air over a fully loaded Escalade on discount? Our transaction was nonetheless completed with deft efficiency, and next thing I knew, I was driving on the 405 southbound. It's truly bizarre how you can so completely leave a place for over seven years and then seamlessly reenter its veins. The freeways and roads knew me. I arrived at my destination in no time at all. Car parked and paper grocery bag in hand, I walked to the front door, took a deep breath, and made my entrance.

CHAPTER THIRTY-ONE

You could have kidnapped and blindfolded me, dropped me in that lobby, and I would have known exactly where I was. From olfactory clues alone. The City of Orange's Old Towne Wells Fargo Bank had a subtle but very specific wax floor polish and dirty money smell to it. That stink of manual labor and market economy collided into an unpleasant bouquet and greeted me as I walked across a long expanse of tiled floors to a carpeted area. The bank manager continued talking on the telephone as I stood at her desk. She put her hand over the receiver. Personal call.

"Yes?" she asked me.

"I need to access my safe deposit box, please." I held out my driver's license and keys.

A finger pointed skyward to indicate I should give her a minute, she shot me an insincere smile and slowly wrapped up her conversation with the "sugar" on the line. Eventually, she took my keys and driver's license. She was clearly thrown by the name on my license, which was still the one I was born with.

"It's me in the photo, right?" I said impatiently.

Fake smile now gone, she nodded but studied the cast on my arm as if it might correspond with identifying characteristics listed on an FBI criminal profile.

"I'll need your Social Security number," she said.

I hated Orange County.

I gave her my Social Security number, and she punched it into her computer along with information from my driver's license. Eyebrows raised and lips pursed, she stood, made a failed attempt to tug the wrinkled jacket of her ill-fitting suit down over her ample ass, and then led me to a safe deposit cubicle. Keys and driver's license in her possession, she walked away. What felt like at least ten minutes later, she returned with the small rectangular box, my ID, and keys. She placed these items on the viewing room's narrow shelf, stepped into the hall, and closed the door behind her. Once I could no longer hear her high heels clicking down the hallway, I took Nahui's book and the framed retablo from the grocery bag I'd brought with me.

Maybe it was only a trick of refracted light in that entirely varnished-wood room, but I swear Nahui's eyes suddenly took on an extra gleam. Once upon a time that glow would have given me shivers. For years, the raw angst Weston captured in Nahui's portrait had thrilled me. Looking into her eyes had dared me onward. But, whereas before I'd found radical inspiration in Nahui's stare, I now saw the deep suffering and loneliness written upon her features. And to be honest, I worried I'd begun to let her pain be mine.

She went through me like a pavement saw.

And how.

I didn't want to inherit the bad with the good. The bad:

Both times Nathalie bailed I'd reacted the same as Nahui had when my father's mother wouldn't be her girl; I'd stewed in my hurt and waxed nostalgic (and, yes, this was also my father's reaction when his young wife took off in Death Valley and when my mother left him in New Haven). And then there was the train wreck coming home from D.C.—I couldn't help but imagine Nahui, little Ms. Earthquake Sun herself, gathering up all the Aztec gods to cause the crash. I mean, why not? Maybe the same unified cosmic forces had created the 1943 derailment in Chicago—the cursed train wreck that killed my father's sister and that, perhaps a coincidence but maybe not, happened so soon after my father's mother left Nahui broken-hearted. And—I know I'm going out on a limb with all of this, but whatever, I'm already hanging from a bough by my fingertips—what about little Ángel and all the unpleasant similarities between Nahui and my mother's fundamentally misguided maternal instincts? Fuck if any of this was a legacy I wanted to embrace.

Time to get a reality check, Frank—that's what you're thinking, right? Point taken, but wouldn't you freak out a little too if you suddenly realized you were necrophilic? Personally, I'd never thought that particular perversion was my cup of tea, but really, when it comes down to it, isn't retrospection, sentimental or otherwise, ultimately romancing the dead? I mean, of course it's important to learn from the past . . . but I'd spent far too much time coddling what once was and wasn't and what might have been. I'd done this in regards to my father, my mother, the life I'd been born into, Nahui, my relationship with Nathalie, everything. Hell, it was probably this very devotion to the past that led me to open my shop. I mean, really, who but a nostalgic fool wants to buy and sell dead people's things for a living? Point is, I was tired of feeling alternately depleted and sustained by the memories I kept pulsing alive with each breath I took in. I'd had enough. I wanted to get on with my life, unhindered by all the things I'd never be able to recapture or change.

First plan of action on my agenda was to put as much physical distance as possible between Nahui and me. I totally needed to let go of my one-sided adoration. Nahui was a projection, a false promise, a desert mirage, an ancient myth she herself had appropriated and that I had then dutifully continued elaborating and editing in her honor. Nahui Olin. The Earthquake Sun. All I'd ever really known about her was a construct—some parts historically substantiated, some not. The illusion of her had accompanied me through times I

258 • *like son*

hadn't wanted to experience alone, but the demands of well-being and longevity finally necessitated I untangle myself from the lovely chaos I associated with her. Out of respect, I wanted to return her to the place I'd originally found her. And so I retraced my steps, and walked backward in the very footprints I'd left when we met, with hopes that I would now be able to walk away with a renewed and uncluttered stride.

Obviously, I couldn't actually leave the retablo and book back in my father's old living room. So, as gently as possible, I locked Nahui in the safe deposit box my father had purchased—but not before I retrieved the bundle of love letters contained therein.

Ready to continue on, I returned the safe deposit box to the bank manager, certain I'd never come back again. And then, naturally, with no hope of actually finding the woman in the love letters, I drove to Laguna Hills.

CHAPTER THIRTY-TWO

Same as seven years before, when I arrived at my mother's property, I worried the shoddy little car I was driving wouldn't make it up her ski-slope fortress driveway. So I parked at the bottom of the private hill, grabbed the bundle of letters, and walked up. A fancy car—not the one my mother had owned the last time I was there, but, from a quick look at the mess of trash, junk mail, and office files cluttering the seats, clearly her new car—was parked in the carport. She was home.

I walked to the front door and rang the doorbell. I waited a couple minutes. When my mother didn't answer, I knocked.

"Mom? I know you're home," I called at the door.

No reply.

"I have something for you."

Silence.

"Mom?"

Still she didn't open the door.

I placed the letters on her doormat. And then I walked back down the driveway.

As I drove away from the hilly labyrinth neighborhood, I was sure my mother was still staring out her front door peephole. Her falsely polite *Who is it?* would eventually echo into the foyer through the intercom system several times—this, her way to determine if I was still waiting but standing beyond the peephole's scope of vision—before she'd finally, hesitantly, open the door. Scared, lonely, disquieted woman, she'd find the letters. Maybe, just maybe, she'd then remember that once, long ago, she'd led with her heart. Regardless, the letters and the history they narrated were hers to take charge of. They were no longer mine.

CHAPTER THIRTY-THREE

No emotion overwhelmed me. But it wasn't that I felt numb. Rather, and this is an important distinction, I knew I was simply where I needed to be. In fact, I felt like I was walking through a process already completed. There I was, alone on a desolate stretch of Pacific Ocean beach, presenting myself to the specter of a man I'd failed to bury properly when he died. I was ashamed that I'd left my father's ashes for his lawyer to scatter impersonally in the ocean. But that had been several lives ago. I had grown up. And I wanted my father to see me now, to really see me, to look at me more clearly than he'd ever been able to in life. I wanted to say a respectful goodbye, son to father, man to man.

When my father died, I'd chosen only a few items from his home to remember him by: blind man glasses, walking stick, worry stone, briefcase, and those damned glorious suits. Obviously, my disaster of a trip to D.C. had me reconsidering plenty of things, not least of which was that I might want to think twice about playing dress-up in my father's wardrobe. Suit bloodied and shredded, briefcase lost entirely, his threads had hardly been the protective armor I'd thought they'd be. And as for his dark glasses, walking stick, and worry stone—I liked to believe that my father's blindness and worry, both literal and figurative, were not what he would have wished for me to take as my own.

So, careful of my left arm in its cast, I dug a hole three feet deep in the moist sand near the ocean's edge. And in that hole

I placed my father's glasses and folded walking stick. Handfuls of sand patted over his things in the small grave, I buried the ill-chosen tokens. Once the hole was completely filled, I took off my shoes and socks, rolled my pants up to my knees, and walked into shallow water. I leaned down and pushed my father's worry stone into the thick wet sand.

"To ground you," I said.

I wasn't sure if I was saying it to my father or myself. But I said it. Again.

"To ground you."

The sand was cold on my toes. Small sharp shells scratched my ankles. Salt water stung my skin. Seaweed wrapped itself around my feet as if in a final embrace. Somewhere overhead, even though I couldn't see it through the heavily clouded sky, I knew a high noon sun was shining. I stood and watched the waves for a few minutes. And then I went home.

CHAPTER THIRTY-FOUR

5 March 2003. Ash Wednesday.
New York City.

I waited in shadows under the Temperance Fountain's gazebo, keeping an eye out for cops and watching the traffic pass on Avenue A. Not that many people knew it, but the Temperance Fountain was the most perfect place in the city, maybe the entire world, to revolt. The Temperance Fountain. To look at it, Tompkins Square Park's smallish neo-classical monument seemed like any other old and prissy municipal structure. Sure, the fountain was interesting in that the four directions of its stone gazebo were carved with its founding fathers' Victorian ethos: Temperance (south), Charity (west), Hope (north), and Faith (east). And yeah, the slightly smaller-than-life bronze statue of Hebe—hottie mythical water carrier, standing watch atop the gazebo all gentle smile and tunic-wearing perkiness—was a nice touch, but that hardly makes the fountain sacred ground, right?

Wrong. And here's the reason why:

Hebe—maybe not all renditions of Hebe, but Tompkins Square Park's Hebe for sure—would explode your mind if you let her. She seemed so innocent—just a peaceful girl resting a water pitcher near her right thigh and gazing into the bowl she held in her left hand—but if you watched her long enough, you'd realize she was revolution itself.

Why, you might ask, was Hebe staring into her bowl instead of out into the city? Well, Hebe preferred to bow her head intro-spectively rather than be forced to face society and abide by its stifling expectations and impositions. Furthermore, she refused to imbibe Temperance's offerings and instead prepared to drink the potion of unique delights and risks she carried in her bowl. Best part was that Hebe stood with her back to the east—toward Faith—and with her bowl at the western edge of the gazebo—toward Charity. I swear, if she'd leaned down and, faithless charitable creature that she was, offered me a drink from her bowl, I would have joined her for a nightcap. As for the actual fountain's cold drinking water, since junkies used it to clean their works and to bathe in summer, same as Hebe, fuck if I'd ever let it touch my lips.

Temperance was for fools. The flapper whose portrait had graced my wallet for a short while had taught me that much. Over three-quarters of a century earlier—a camera's bulb flashing hot bright white light—the flapper and Hebe had both signaled one truth loud and clear with those serious flirt eyes of theirs: Imposed self-restraint is the most simplistic and naïve of elixirs and should be avoided at all costs. I took the flapper girl's departure from my wallet as a sign that she refused to be confined even in spirit. A person must leave behind what no longer serves them and instead take hold of what they want and need. With no hesitation. *Demand your thrill*, the flapper girl whispered in her slurred purr.

It was no shocker that Nathalie wanted to meet at the fountain. And I was glad for it.

As though I had conjured her with that thought, I heard the clicking of high heels approaching from somewhere to my left. I turned to see Nathalie walking toward the fountain. All the park's gates locked, Nathalie must have jumped the fence to get in, same as me, but somehow she'd remained the antithesis of dishevelment. The glass-bead hem of her favorite evening gown visible under her coat, her hair pinned into a loose chignon, my favorite Cuban-heeled pumps lending a regal air to the arch of her step—I watched lady elegance approach from the north, from Hope. I wondered if Nathalie realized the symbolic message she had thus communicated or if the direction of her arrival was merely the chance result of catching a train to Union Square and walking southeast into the neighborhood from there; I preferred to think it was the former.

I stood to greet Nathalie, to embrace her, to knock her down and make sure she never got away again. As I reached for her, she noticed the cast on my arm.

"What happened?"

"Long story."

Concern knitting her brow, Nathalie leaned forward, stood on tiptoe, and gave me the softest kiss. If I could have stopped time and kept it freeze-framed, I'd have wished for that kiss to last forever.

"Nat," I took a deep breath, "don't leave again."

Her lips moved as if she was going to respond, but no words came out. A cab honked on Avenue A and an electrical surge hummed through a lamppost. Vulnerability painted my neck a hot red. Nathalie's silence was the most awful sound on planet earth.

"This really fucking terrifies me, Frank."

I wasn't sure what she was referring to exactly. Coming home? My asking her to stay? Us? Regardless, of course it terrified her. Living was an inherently frightening business. And personally, even though I'd said a final goodbye to my father hours earlier, part of me wished I could have just one more word of advice from him, a little bit of illumination, anything to show me I was heading in the right direction.

Dad? Help? Please?

Nothing.

But it was okay. I knew what to do.

"Let's go home," I said, gently tugging Nathalie's elbow.

As I walked away from the Temperance Fountain to 7th

Street with my girl on my good arm, I looked up toward our building and noticed a warm light radiating from our apartment window. I was always extra careful to turn off all the lights when I left, and I couldn't remember accidentally leaving any on.

But then again, maybe I had.

Acknowledgments

With much respect and warmest appreciation, I thank: Johnny Temple, Johanna Ingalls, all of Team Akashic, Shirley, Esteban, and Cooper/Fenberg Inc. Endless thanks to Murray for his moral support and devotion.

And thank you, Mr. T Cooper . . . for everything.

Also from **AKASHIC BOOKS**

A FICTIONAL HISTORY OF THE UNITED STATES WITH HUGE CHUNKS MISSING
EDITED BY T COOPER & ADAM MANSBACH
332 PAGES, A TRADE PAPERBACK ORIGINAL, $15.95

Original stories & artwork by: Felicia Luna Lemus, Daniel Alarcón, Amy Bloom, Kate Bornstein, T Cooper, Ron Kovic, Adam Mansbach, Paul La Farge, Alexander Chee, Keith Knight, Valerie Miner, Thomas O'Malley, Neal Pollack, David Rees, Sarah Schulman, Darin Strauss, and Benjamin Weissman.

"This is a 'people's history' with tongue in cheek: delightfully funny, imaginative, but with a subtle undertone of seriousness. I enjoyed it immensely."
—Howard Zinn, author of *A People's History of the United States*

SOME OF THE PARTS BY T COOPER
*A BARNES & NOBLE DISCOVER GREAT NEW WRITERS PROGRAM SELECTION
264 PAGES, A TRADE PAPERBACK ORIGINAL, $14.95

"A wholly original novel that's both discomforting and compelling to read."
—*San Francisco Chronicle*

"T Cooper skillfully twists, entwines, and collides generations, gender identities, and sexual orientations so deliciously that I don't think there's anyone who can read this book without ruefully identifying with at least one of the central characters—and without hopelessly falling in love with at least one of the others."
—Kate Bornstein, author of *Gender Outlaw*

THE UNCOMFORTABLE DEAD
A NOVEL BY PACO I. TAIBO II & SUBCOMANDANTE MARCOS
268 PAGES, A TRADE PAPERBACK ORIGINAL, $15.95

"Great writers by definition are outriders, raiders of a sort, sweeping down from wilderness territories to disturb the peace, overrun the status quo and throw into question everything we know to be true . . . On its face, the novel is a murder mystery, and at the book's heart, always, is a deep love of Mexico and its people."
—*Los Angeles Times Book Review*

AMERICAN VISA BY JUAN DE RECACOECHEA
*WINNER OF BOLIVIA'S NATIONAL BOOK PRIZE; TRANSLATED FROM SPANISH BY
ADRIAN ALTHOFF; WITH AN AFTERWORD BY ILAN STAVANS
260 PAGES, A TRADE PAPERBACK ORIGINAL, $14.95

"*American Visa* is beautifully written, atmospheric, and stylish in
the manner of Chandler . . . a smart, exotic crime fiction offering."
—George Pelecanos, author of *The Night Gardener*

"The streets of La Paz have never looked so alive. This is one of the
best Latin American novels of the last fifteen years."
—Edmundo Paz Soldán, author of *Turing's Delirium*

WITH OR WITHOUT YOU BY LAUREN SANDERS
318 PAGES, A TRADE PAPERBACK ORIGINAL, $14.95

"A wickedly crafted whydunit . . . Sanders shows a surprising ability
to simultaneously make you feel infuriated with and sorry for her
borderline-schizo heroine."
—*Entertainment Weekly*

"Sanders's vibrant, vigorous second novel is a sendup of America's
obsession with pop culture, B-list celebrities, and prison life . . . In
lyrical, potent prose, Sanders navigates the terrain of loneliness,
obsession and desperation with the same skillful precision as her
vulnerable, calculating protagonist."
—*Publishers Weekly* (starred review)

THE BOY DETECTIVE FAILS BY JOE MENO
*AUTHOR OF THE HIT *HAIRSTYLES OF THE DAMNED*; BEST BOOKS OF 2006: *CHICAGO
TRIBUNE, BOOKLIST, KIRKUS REVIEWS*; PUNK PLANET BOOKS
330 PAGES, A TRADE PAPERBACK ORIGINAL, $14.95

"*The Boy Detective Fails* will break your heart, and then pick up the
pieces and put you back together again."
—T Cooper, author of *Lipshitz Six, or Two Angry Blondes*

These books are available at local bookstores. They can also be purchased online
through www.akashicbooks.com. To order by mail send a check or money order to:

AKASHIC BOOKS
PO Box 1456, New York, NY 10009
www.akashicbooks.com   info@akashicbooks.com

Prices include shipping. Outside the U.S., add $8 to each book ordered.